SOLDIERS OF THE APOCALYPSE

The C.A.D.S. team came through the swirling dust clouds like an apparition from a dark nightmare, 72 men riding strange low-slung three-wheeled motorcycles across America's atomic wastelands. They were like men from another world. Astronaut-like helmets with thick tinted visors rested on immense jet black, plasti-steel bodies—their arms, waist, chest, legs bristling with radar grids, sensors and weapons.

Each C.A.D.S. suit was a seven-foot-tall servomechanized death machine.

Each C.A.D.S.-suited man could take out a tank. And more, much more.

Those who came face-to-face with these computerized commandos—those who approached with malice in their hearts—soon wished they hadn't!

CADS #2

BY JOHN SIEVERT

ZEBRA BOOKS
KENSINGTON PUBLISHING CORP.

ZEBRA BOOKS

are published by

Kensington Publishing Corp.
475 Park Avenue South
New York, NY 10016

First printing: April 1986

Printed in the United States of America

FOREWORD

Only Col. Dean Sturgis, U.S.A.F. and his C.A.D.S. Unit stand in the way of a total occupation of America by the Soviet invaders.

C.A.D.S.—a commando unit created for penetrating radioactive areas after a nuclear strike, brings immense firepower to bear on the enemy with its nearly impervious servo-mechanism driven armorsuits. C.A.D.S.—a few hundred men in the ultimate battle machine.

Living gods with their computerized attack/defense system suits, armed with hawk mini-missiles, electro-ball shells, submachine guns—all computer-targeted and fired from a set of tubes under their metal sleeves. A C.A.D.S. trooper has only to point at a target, and like Zeus throwing a lightning bolt, he will destroy it. Each suit has the firepower of an entire batallion of the 1980s, and each man can voice-command a variety of Vision-modes that give data on enemy position, strategy and armament. The 7-ft. tall suit is the most powerful combat gear ever created.

But the Russian occupiers have a similar—if cruder—unit: The *Gray Suits* of General Petrin. They had engaged the C.A.D.S. Unit in the ruins of Washington, D.C. and been defeated, but not without American losses. The one man who can still lead the ravaged U.S. out of the atomic abyss — President Williamson — has been rescued by Sturgis. Now the president has to be brought to the hidden C.A.D.S. base at White Sands, New Mexico, before he is a smoldering corpse like a hundred million other Americans . . .

CHAPTER ONE

Howard Thornton sat in his chair in the living room, staring blankly at the flowered wallpaper. He hadn't moved from the chair since he'd first sat down early that morning; now it was nearly sundown. He was not really aware of anything. Not even the dark wind howling outside of his Oklahoma farmhouse.

How did it start, he wondered for the hundredth time. How had the Reds been able to catch the U.S. with its guard down? *Them liberals*, he thought bitterly. Always criticizing, always finding fault with America, getting us so bogged down in self-criticism that we forgot the real threat out there.

We'd gone soft—cutting down on military spending, wasting money on welfare programs. Letting the damned commies take everything they could get their hands on. And they never stopped. Cuba and Afghanistan, most of Africa and South America, and Asia . . . now us. The whole East Coast blown away, blown to atomic cinders. New York, D.C., Detroit and Baltimore—all the big ones—that's what the Topeka radio station said before it too went dead.

"Howard . . . ?" called Thornton's wife.

When he didn't answer, she came in and sat in the chair next to him. Agnes Thornton worried about her husband. He had always been a good man and a good provider. She had long ago admitted to herself that she had not known what love was when they first dated and married. But over the years, through the work and the fights and the birth of three babies she had come up with a reasonable definition of love, one which worked for her. One which included Howard Thornton and his strong will and the way he cared for her and all his moods and quirks.

It was Howard who had saved them all. He read the papers — watched the news. He'd known war was coming. Their son Willy had complained when Howard had used up three weeks of precious summer vacation to enlarge, fortify and shield their basement. Their younger son, Ben, and his sister, Caroline, had done their complaining every Saturday after the weekly shopping trip when they would have to move the older cans of food upstairs out of the basement and replace them with new ones.

They were not complaining now — about anything. All three of them had been silent for days, not eating, not talking, not even really sleeping; just lying down when it got dark and getting back up when it grew light, and then finding a place to sit until it got dark again. Some time over the last week the dark silence had sucked in her three children. Today it had taken her husband.

She took his hand and called his name again. Howard Thornton's eyes moved, distracted, and then focused on his wife's face. Shaking his head, almost blushing, he answered her. "Damn. Sorry, honey. I'm getting as bad as the kids."

"You've been sitting here all day."

"Don't seem much point in doin' anything else."

"You just going to sit there tomorrow?"

"Naw, I s'pose not. Wanted to board that attic window up."

"Well, that's more like it," Agnes smiled broadly. At least he was talking about getting ready to work. Now if she could just get some food into him. "Want me to fix you something to eat?"

"I don't know. I don't want us to start runnin' short."

"Howard, there's enough food in the basement to last us two months." She called over her shoulder as she headed toward the small kitchen. "Just stop being so foolish now and get ready to eat."

Howard Thornton smiled. He'd married a good woman. Relaxing just a bit he loosened his death grip on the arms of his chair, flexing his large fingers. "Funny," he muttered, "I never gave any mind to what would happen to us *if* we survived."

Howard thought back five weeks. Back to when the bombs had fallen up and down the eastern seaboard like rain, drowning everything in a radioactive nightmare. He'd listened to the hysterical newscasters ticking off the death toll of the major cities. Then the stations fell silent. When the fallout laden rainclouds came, which he measured from a geiger counter set just outside the door, he and Agnes, and their children Willy, Ben and Caroline stayed huddled in the basement. Agnes' sister, Patricia, had been visiting from New York at the time of the attack. The Russians had extended her visit.

9

Going by the book, Howard didn't leave the basement for three days, at last heading up the ladder to see what was outside. His view from the living room window was the same as always, with one small change—all the color of the world had disappeared. As far as he could see, the barn, every post and rock and tree, their car and tractor, *everything* was covered with a fine white/gray ash.

He had stayed upstairs, ordering the rest to remain in the basement. For three more days he waited to die. He ate every day, expecting to throw up. He combed his hair twice an hour, dreading the moment when it would start to fall out in clumps. Not able to do farm work, he did other chores. He swept and scrubbed the ash which had leaked under the doors and windows, scraping every mote from inside his home.

On the fourth day of *not* dying, he told everyone to come upstairs. They took stock of their supplies. There were plenty of preserves, canned goods, meats and vegetables. He had put away hundreds of packets of dried fruit and meat. Their basement well was still pumping up pure water—all they needed. And, if it stopped, there were the many cases of bottled water Howard had maintained on a rotation basis. Just as he had everything else.

They had fared well in the war.

Compared to the rest of the country they were millionaires. They had food and water, a place to live—and each other. Howard had even stocked vitamins and medicine, had bought pellet stoves to use when the electricity was gone, installed gravity toilets to keep them from having to live in their own waste. He had thought of everything—except what they

10

would do after they survived.

There would be no more farming. He was sure of that. The constant dark cloud cover never let up, circling above them like a shroud over the entire country. Patches of sun broke through occasionally. Tiny, weak thin rays of pale yellow, but not often. Crops didn't grow well without sunlight. Even if the sun came back, which—who knows—might not occur for years, what could the ground grow now? Devil rains that lasted for days burned the ground, driving the inches of ash which had covered everything deep beneath the soil, poisoning it.

Their old lives were over. And God only knew what the new ones would be like. His work was gone. The kids' school was gone. Movies and television and the Elks Club and the stores and the libraries had all disappeared in the same flashing nightmare five weeks ago.

Praying silently for something besides the Russians, he clicked on the radio. The batteries were still functioning. It started right up. He flipped through the bands, but could only find three stations, all broadcasting the same message, all in the same clear Russian-accented English:

"It is so pleasing to announce that the continued freeing of the workers in the slave state of America has progressed even faster than originally planned. General Veloshnikov, acting as interim president only until a new truly democratic election under the auspices of the Communist Party can take place, has good news indeed for the struggling masses still left in despair in the war zone . . ."

Howard snapped the radio back off. He stared at

11

it, wondering where everyone else was, why no one else could get anything onto the airways. He wondered what the point was of the Russians playing the same messages over and over. Were they trying to brainwash those left, those not yet under their power? Did they think Americans were that stupid . . . or was it something worse?

Had they known, actually *known* how depressing, how futile everything would seem to those who survived? Suddenly he stood, picked up the radio in both hands and smashed it against the wooden planks he had boarded in place over the living room window. He cracked the casing, but wasn't satisfied. Pulling back, he swung it again, sending splinters of plastic flying about the room. He clubbed it again, and again, until it burst in half, spilling its insides onto the rug.

Throwing the cord still in his hands into the fireplace, he ignored the stares of his children. What was there to tell them? "Yes, kids, yer dad's gone nuts because the best possible life choices seem to be living as a Russian slave or putting a bullet through yer brains."

He felt helpless, unable to come up with an explanation as to what was happening to their lives. He was barely capable of explaining it to himself. Howard turned away from the doorway to the next room, not noticing his sister-in-law, Patricia, enter the living room.

"What have you done now, you asshole?" she spat out.

Howard turned with a look of disgust. He had never liked his wife's sister; he could hardly stand

12

being in the same room with her. Patricia stood for everything he had always believed was wrong. She had marched in "peace" demonstrations demanding unilateral disarmament, even been arrested for sit-ins at ABM anti-missile bases. As a lawyer she became famous for winning criminal cases on the basis of technicalities, regardless of the guilt or innocence of her client, saying that under the capitalist system no one was guilty except the swine at the top. They had virtually despised each other the first time they'd met — she thinking him a redneck, and he thinking her a pawn of Moscow.

Calming himself, he said, "The *asshole* has broken the radio and thrown the bits all over the living room. Now shut up and leave me alone, or I might not be able to stop myself from doing the same to you."

"Oh, fine. Macho man speaks, mere woman listens —" Patricia screamed circling him like a vulture. "Listen, Mr. America, we're all in this together. You don't run the show. We all . . ."

Howard closed his eyes and clenched his fists into pieces of trembling stone as he tried as hard as he could not to smash her face in.

The starving, lurching mob from the East had a tall, lean leader. His name was Carson. Just Carson. He had two pearl-handled revolvers and his pals had hunting rifles, big ones with scopes. The others, the 70 or so half-naked men who followed behind, stayed away from Carson and his men. They had nothing, just sticks, axes and knives — and their hunger.

Carson was not burned like a lot of the horde. He

13

had come from a small town in the valley. Most of the others, by the look of their tatters, he thought must be suburbanites, blown out of their ticky-tacky homes, managing to crawl away. Somehow they had all learned about the West. Learned that west of the Mississippi, due to an ABM and laser shield, the U.S. hadn't been hit nearly as hard. There had been fallout west of the Mississippi, but much of that had died down. Carson knew there would be much for the taking. He had always taken — now it would just be easier. He would use the walking dead, who followed like pack dogs hoping to get a scrap, as bait. Send them in first, getting the farm folk to run out of ammo shooting the burned starving bastards. Then *he* would get the food, the women — anything of value here in Oklahoma. Maybe, if the rad-sickness doesn't get me, he thought as he led the bedraggled force further and further west, I'll set up my own little empire . . . But the growling of his stomach made such fantasies difficult to sustain. God, he was hungry! So fucking hungry! He might even do what he had seen some of the other bands of wanderers do — kill one of their own and — *no*. Not yet. Keep walking. Keep walking. There had to be a farmhouse soon that hadn't been hit, that hadn't already been looted and burned. There had to be food ahead.

Carson almost missed it, so lost was he in his own hunger. He almost missed the rutted side road through the burned-out trees, disappearing over a hill. He turned, walked faster now, following the old tire tracks. The others saw him turn and followed, stumbling on blistered feet, faces peeling and puffy from their burns. They swung their axes and sticks as

14

they groaned in animal chorus "Food! . . . Food!"

Something from outside caught Howard's attention. He hushed his sister-in-law as she raved, straining to hear it again. But she continued to berate him until he yelled, "Shut up, goddamnit! There's something outside."

Peeking out between the wooden slats covering the window, he stared at the forest line beyond their property. Whatever was coming was in the woods. He could hear the slogging sound of many feet pushing through the piles of leaves still wet from the nuclear rains which had washed them from the trees. He heard low guttural voices reciting the same pleas over and over in a chant, "Food! . . . Food! . . . Food!"

He still couldn't see them, but by the rising cacophony could tell there were many. Too many! Howard's lips went dry. His throat constricted. They staggered out of the woods. Not two or three, but dozens. The refugees of the East, burned, crippled, blinded. Driven from their homes and families forever by the bombs, they had nowhere to go but the West, dragging their hunger and need with them like a plague. Howard turned to his son, Willy. "Go to the den, boy. Fetch the rifles."

Patricia started to push her way forward. "What do you think you're going to do?"

"Protect what's mine. Even you, you bitch." Willy returned, tossing his father the .458 Winchester magnum. Willy held onto his own Winchester, handing his father a box of shells. Little blond Caroline looked on wide-eyed with a thumb stuck in her mouth as Daddy loaded up the big gun. "Get your sister out of here, Aggie."

As Agnes herded her still protesting sister and the smaller children out of the room, Howard and Willy took separate windows, gauging the range between themselves and the advancing horde. They fell and rose, fell and rose again, howling all the time. The pus of gaping sores oozed down their bodies and onto the parched ground.

"Dad," asked Willy. "Are—we gonna kill people?"

"Yes, son," answered Howard evenly. "If we have to. If they won't pass us by."

Willy stood frozen at the window, unable to move. Howard felt sorry for his son. "Dad. What if I can't?"

"Can't *what*, son?"

"Can't shoot. What if I can't kill a person?"

Howard kept watching the advancing throng. They were stumbling through the barren fields, now only a handful of yards away. Several of them had weapons. Waiting for them to raise one, Howard said with all of his conviction, "You'll do it. You'll do it because you *have* to. You'll do it 'cause those things out there aren't even people anymore. Look at 'em, boy. They're dying flesh, comin' at us with their last strength. They're comin' with nothin' in their minds but a desire to take everything we have and leave us dead in the garbage when they're done. Your mother, your sister and brother—all of us."

Outside, one of the mob raised a rifle to his shoulder, taking aim at the house. Howard watched him, fixing the shooter in his cross hairs. "Watch now, boy. See that one out there, on the left, the one aimin' to send a bullet into this house?"

Howard squeezed the trigger of his .458, sending a round at the attacker. It did exactly what he expected a 500 gr. .458 caliber bullet of .341 sectional density to do when propelled at 2000 f.p.s. — it punched a hole in the man the size of an orange, knocking him backward in a spinning arc that toppled four others behind him.

As those approaching stopped for a second, Howard shouted. "We don't want any trouble. Just go by and that one who was tryin' to shoot at us need be the only one who dies."

"Fuck you, you bastard! *We* want what *you* got," Carson shouted back.

The horde rushed the house in a tidal wave of flesh. Howard fired again and again, blasting pathways through the throng with each salvo. Willy covered the other side of the yard with his Winchester, doing less damage with his smaller rifle, but keeping the crowd back just the same.

Bodies piled up outside as Howard and his son quickly emptied their rifles. Willy ran to the den returning with an armload of cartridge boxes just as his father used up the last of his ammo. "Get back to the kitchen, boy," Howard screamed above the din. "If they haven't started to circle the house, they will soon. We gotta keep movin'. Fire at 'em from every window. Keep 'em from figurin' how many guns we got against them."

Without another word, Howard turned his back on the boy and began firing into the crowd once more. He was sure Willy would be all right. He had been less worried about his son holding up under pressure than the boy had himself. Howard Thornton smoked

17

those clambering up onto the porch, spattering the now lifeless potted plants with blood and bits of flesh. He watched each hit, trying to line up the attackers carrying the most dangerous weapons. He passed over those with one leg, the blind, or those wandering in circles, and aimed at the whole men, the leaders. Coldly, thinking of nothing but turning the crowd, he watched one man fall as his left leg disappeared from under him. A fat man his arms covered with running purple sores spun away as his shoulder burst in a flurry of flying blood. A bald woman, aiming a revolver at the window, lost her head to a single shot, the explosion scattering her brains on those around her for yards.

Loading up again, Howard listened for the sounds of the Winchester fire from the kitchen. He heard the smaller rifle's crack repeatedly, each round accompanied by his son's curses. "Die, damn you. Die, you mother fuckers! Leave us alone!"

Good, thought Howard, shouldering his magnum once more. If cursin' can help you send 'em to hell, then curse, boy — and send 'em with my blessing. Howard fired again, blowing another man's stomach out through his back. And again, flipping two men backward into the crowd. All of his shells so far had killed at least one of the crowd; and more than a few had taken down a second.

Some in the mob began to retreat to the trees, a larger group looked as if they were heading down the front drive back to the main road. The thought that he might actually win had just begun to push into Howard's brain when screams came from the second floor. Running for the stairs, he shouted, "Keep the

downstairs clear, Willy. Something's wrong up—"
Before he could finish, he saw the problem—the
walking dead had gotten into the house.

Without a thought, Howard sent a bullet through
the closest two, splattering their jellied guts up the
stairs behind them. Running forward over their
bodies, nearly slipping in their spurting blood, he
reached the landing only to find two more. Bringing
the stock of the heavy gun upward, he connected with
the chin of the closest, jamming the invader's jaw-
bone back through his brain. The gray-skinned body
folded like a milk carton someone had stepped on.
The second one came forward, madly brandishing an
old kitchen knife. "Kill you!" he raved. "Kill and take
your food!"

Howard stepped backward, bringing his rifle deliv-
ery-end up. "Sure you will, fucker." He pulled the
trigger. The knife dropped to the floor. The body that
had been holding it flew back against the wall; the
spilled guts dripped and sagged to the floor. "Aggie!"
screamed Howard. "Aggie—where are you?"

"Howard, hurry—" Aggie's voice was coming from
the ladder to the attic. Howard ran to her side,
finding her, Ben and Patricia all holding onto the
rope that held the trap door to the house's storage
chamber. His wife, half hysterical, stammered, "They,
they *took*, oh my god, Howard—*Caroline*—"

Howard moved his wife away from the ladder. "Go
to the basement. Barricade yourself in there. Load
the guns and use them—use them!" Taking the rungs
two at a time, Howard Thornton pulled himself up
into the crowded darkness of the attic. Voices arguing
loudly toward the front sent him racing forward.

19

Several of the throng were fighting over what was left of his daughter's body. Their words were slurred over their chewing. Skin dangled from the lips of one; another tore at the soft flesh of a dripping red arm. More of the pack were on the porch roof, prying the boards to get inside, frenzied by the smell of Caroline's blood. Howard raised his magnum and fired, exploding the head of one like a water balloon. The feeders turned, staring wildly at their enemy. They backed off, raising their hands in front of their faces. Howard killed all of them and then blasted at those crawling through the window.

Their horrendous screams were nothing to him. Crazed by the sight of his daughter's body, the anguished father dragged himself up through the window to the porch roof. From this vantage point, he fired on those still coming. They seemed to have no end and no fear. He fired repeatedly as they climbed over their dead comrades and came toward him. Howard realized that he was about to die.

CHAPTER TWO

Through the swirling dust clouds they came like apparitions from some dark nightmare. Seventy-two men riding strange low-slung three-wheeled motorcycles through the atomic wastelands. Their Tri-bikes had back wheels as thick and wide as beer barrels, making the sleek but oddly shaped vehicles nearly impossible to topple. They looked like men from another world. Astronaut-like helmets, with thick tinted visors rested on immense jet black plasti-steel bodies — their arms, waists, chests, legs bristling with dials, radar grids, sensors and weapons — giving them a futuristic, threatening appearance. Each C.A.D.S. Suit was a 7-foot-tall servo-mechanized death machine. Each C.A.D.S.-suited man could take out a tank. And more, much more. He was an unstoppable war machine the likes of which mankind had never seen before. Those who came face to face with these computerized commandos, those who approached with malice in their hearts — soon wished they hadn't.

At the lead of the V-shaped column of bikers rode Col. Dean Sturgis, U.S.A.F. Omega Commando Squad leader, a look of intense concentration on his face. He had the Macro Listening Device of his suit turned all the way up. He wanted to hear any Red choppers long before they arrived to wreak destruction. Because he didn't wholly trust the radar unit which had gone out on him twice already, he had programmed the MLD to mute the sound of the Tri-bikes so that he could hear for miles. Even a bird's chirping 1000 meters away could be picked up. But the only sounds that Sturgis heard through the Assist System was *gunfire*. And *screams*.

Sturgis raised his hand. "C.A.D.S. team, halt," he ordered into his suit-mike. The Tri-bikes came to a quick stop, a curtain of parched white dust rising behind them. Sturgis listened. Many shots. Different calibers. He had the C.A.D.S. suit computer analyze the sounds of the weapons. ".303 Remington, .38 revolver, .458 Winchester Magnum, 2 unidentifieds." projected the digital readout inside his helmet.

"Let's check it out," Sturgis said reluctantly. He didn't really want to stop out here in the middle of nowhere. He looked toward the truck that stood in the center of the motorized force, guarded by the one remaining Rhino vehicle.

The president of these United States was in the truck—along with 6 survivors of the U.S. Cabinet. Sturgis knew he shouldn't delay. His mission was to get President Williamson back to the White Sands underground C.A.D.S. headquarters, and to at least relative safety.

But then Col. Dean Sturgis had never been one to follow the book. That had gotten him busted half a dozen times, gotten him thrown out of astronaut training school and even into the brig. But Sturgis was someone who ultimately let his heart rule his head. Those gunshots could be anyone out there fighting for his life. It could even be Robin, his wife.

"Fenton," Sturgis declared to the Britisher who drove the Rhino, "you're in charge. Protect the president at all costs. Billy, Roberto, Tranh, Rossiter, come with me. This won't take long if all they've got is small arms. The rest of you stay here. Don't join us unless you're called." Sturgis and his four companions roared off over the rolling hills of burnt winter wheat in the direction of the gunshots.

When they crested the hill, Sturgis saw what all the noise was about. A farmhouse besieged. Once again, Americans attacking other Americans. It was happening everywhere they'd been. As supplies of canned food dwindled, those with supplies had to defend what they had—with guns. Citizen against citizen, friends just weeks before, fighting to the death. He telesighted in on the besiegers—and gulped. They looked like they should be mouldering in their graves. One was gnawing something dripping and red. A human arm. *They were cannibals!*

"Kill them now," the C.A.D.S. leader snarled over the suit to suit radio. "They're flesh-eaters. We can't let them live." Sturgis revved his bike and tore across the rutted field heading at maximum speed toward the man with the grisly repast. The flesh-eater saw them now, clutched what had been part of Howard Thornton's daughter to his chest and pulled a revolver from his waistband. Defiantly glaring at the black demon sitting atop the Tri-wheeler, he held his arm out and pulled the trigger. The bullet ricocheted off the gleaming helmet. The man fired again as Sturgis

23

dismounted, backing off as the suited-giant bristling with antennae walked toward him with arms extended. Another bullet made target, but pinged off spinning wildly. The wild-eyed flesh-eater growled, "It's mine. You can't have it . . ."

Sturgis tilted his left arm ever so slightly, firing a stream of Liquid Plastic into the man's bare chest. The man burst into flames and ran screaming, "It's mine! It's mine!" for 20 feet before he fell. Sturgis hesitated. He looked at the morsel the man had dropped. A child's arm. He nearly retched.

Around Sturgis the C.A.D.S. men mowed down one after another of the cannibal marauders, turning them into piles of steaming guts and shattered bones. Nine mm SMG bullets ripped out of stainless steel tubes slung beneath the C.A.D.S. suit forearms — barrage after barrage of whistling death. The maimed, stumbling, food-seekers from the East fell like bowling pins beneath the combined firepower of the five C.A.D.S. men. Heads erupted into gushing red whirlpools of nothing. Backbones and chests were ripped apart as if pushed through a meat grinder.

It was a smoking dance of destruction as the marauding horde jerked like puppets on the end of bloody strings, crumbling to the ground in broken heaps. Some died with grim smiles on their emaciated faces. For the next world, whatever it held, had to be better than this one!

Out of the original 8 dozen or so, there were suddenly only a half dozen left — including a very tall one armed with 2 pearl handled revolvers. The gunner ran toward the woods as Sturgis slowly trained his right arm on the man. Suddenly Sturgis was knocked from his feet, making his shot toward the running gunner go wild, the stream of fire nearly hitting Tranh who was biking after a runner. *Grenade*—the group to the left was throwing grenades—It hadn't damaged his suit but—Sturgis rose to his feet. He pointed his left arm at the five grenade throwers who scrambled to get away.

"LPF Mode," Sturgis commanded through clenched teeth. He felt the slight click, then said "Fire." The flames leaped out for 3 seconds, just long enough to set the five men afire. They ran now, ablaze like human candles. Their screams made Sturgis shudder with revulsion.

Those *things* had been Americans. Americans who had gone mad from the cataclysmic nuclear attack, reverting to a savagery that defied the laws of civilization. And Sturgis and his men had killed them—without mercy. They'd killed Americans again and again—when they should be killing Russians. Somehow it was their own kind who kept falling under the nightmarish weaponry of the C.A.D.S. suit. How the hell could the nation hold together if the survivors abandoned the most fundamental codes of justice and morality? As long as he, Col. Dean Sturgis, was alive he would uphold the old ways. When he died, when his men died, God knew what would happen. But for now, he would do his part, however it made him feel.

Howard, crouching behind the attic window, the barrel of his rifle resting on the sill, had witnessed it all. The arrival of what he took to be robots, the slaughter of the farm's attackers. The robots, or whatever they were, had killed them all. No wonder we lost the war, he thought — if the Reds have *such* weapons.

To his horror the robots turned toward the house. Howard gasped, his mouth dry, "They're after *us* now."

A voice boomed out at tremendous amplification from the lead robot. "This is Commander Sturgis of the United States Air Force. Is anyone alive inside? We're here to help you. Hold your fire. Come out with your hands up and be identified."

"It's *our* people, *our* people," Howard's wife screamed emerging from the stairwell and running to his side. "They've come to . . ." Howard cupped his hand over her mouth.

"Hush," he hissed. "They *say* they're Americans, but how the hell do we know?" Howard leveled the rifle in the window and fired at the lead figure. He scored a hit, but saw the bullet ricochet off the armored skin.

"I said *hold* your fire. Come out with your hands on your heads or we'll destroy the house. You have two minutes." Sturgis slowly raised his right arm toward the rifleman.

Howard squeezed the trigger again. Nothing happened. He was out of ammo. "We'd best do as they say," he sighed. "Let's go — you get the kids."

With Howard in the lead the family marched into the yard. One of the robots walked toward them. Howard stood frozen, his legs quivering in fear. The creature reached for its helmet and opened it.

A human face was inside. "I'm Col. Dean Sturgis,

U.S. Air Force, Omega Squad. Looks like you had a real tough time here."

"I had to kill them. They killed my daughter Caroline. They *ate* her, ripped her apart like rabid dogs. I killed, I killed and I'd kill again." Howard started weeping, letting his arms fall to his side.

"Listen to me," Sturgis said firmly. "There will be many more coming. It's inevitable, as supplies of food run out, as word is passed that the West is in better shape. Prepare. Get together with your neighbors. Find the most defendable house, fortify it, bring all your weapons, your families there. It should have a well. You should be prepared for a long siege. Do you understand? Are there neighbors that are still alive?"

Howard wiped his eyes, "I don't know. I just don't know. The Jeffers place . . . down the road a mile. Him and his wife used to visit . . ."

"Then go *now*, quickly, before more of these pitiful subhumans show up."

Agnes came forward, as Sturgis mounted up, her country face and her calico dress like a snapshot of old America — the way it was, the way it would never be again. She was wringing her hands, long scrawny hands. She was so thin and shaky. "Mr. — Mr. Sturgis," she stuttered, "I don't know how to thank you — not for saving us — but for killing those people that — killed — my Caroline. I — I —" She looked down, then rushed forward and hugged Sturgis' suit with her long skinny freckled arms. Sturgis stood there and let her weep for a few seconds until her husband pulled her away.

"What are you men?" asked Howard, "Astronauts?"

"Just soldiers with a few tricks up our sleeves," Sturgis replied.

"Good luck!" the C.A.D.S. commander said, snapping his visor shut and revving the engine of his Tri-bike. Sturgis signalled his four companions and together they rode across the fields, disappearing from sight in a swirling dustcloud. Sturgis hoped the Thorntons would make it. But he knew their chances for survival were ten thousand to one.

CHAPTER THREE

General Anatoly Bukarov was dressed the way he hated to be dressed; itchy wool shirt, starched collar with twin red stars, formal jacket full of decorations. It was 6 A.M. Washington time, and Bukarov was dead tired and extremely uncomfortable. It was too cold, and his dress pants were way too tight. He should be wearing an Arctic parka, but today he had to be dressed like *this*! The other generals and admirals who were present were in dress-uniform also. Because the meeting about to take place in the American Senate Chamber was being telecast directly to the premier's suite back in the Kremlin by satellite — Russian technology was truly a marvel! So they must all be neat — even though the furnace was not functioning in the middle of February, even though everyone was shivering.

General Veloshnikov, the privileged pig, was present only by television. The Supreme Marshal sat 1500 miles away, cruising off Charleston, warmly ensconced in his giant Command-Center submarine *The Lenin*, where he had every amenity, every convenience. And *his* air was pure. Bukarov had been told that because Washington was only neutron bombed, all the radiation had dissipated from the area. But could he be sure? The Soviet Supreme Command had erred on practically all aspects of the nuke war! What of the radiation drifting from the five-mile wide, two-thousand foot deep crater that had been New York City? What about the residual fallout from Boston, Baltimore, Atlanta? Sure, the worst fallout had been the first week, but he doubted the scientists who said there were safe levels of radiation. What's a safe level for a poison?

Bukarov stood glumly on the platform where President Reagan had once stood, where Lyndon Johnson had once announced that he was sending massive numbers of U.S. troops to Vietnam. Here he was, in the most historic place of America.

He should be enjoying it, savoring the moment. But he was freezing. And he was *afraid*.

Chairs were brought to the platform and they were all seated in a semicircle around the lectern. General Petrin, the leader of the special unit designated the Gray Suits—a high-tech battle-armored squad that was allegedly invincible—was to be "interviewed" by the premier first.

The premier's televised face appeared on a huge screen in the front of the chamber. Veloshnikov's face appeared on the smaller TV screen next to the premier's giant color presence.

The premier questioned with a method that was sheer bullying. The premier's yes-men called it "the socratic method" or "playing the devil's advocate", but it was pure terror. The premier began each question with an accusation. He should send medals and here he is, Bukarov thought, assembling us in a frozen city to listen to his tirades, to *accuse* us for *Veloshnikov's* mistakes.

The premier on the screen lit a cigarette as they all sat stiffly at attention on cold chairs. The premier leaned forward, his elbows on the far-away table, wiped at the lock of straight black hair that fell across his high forehead.

"*Bukarov*," he snarled into the camera, "Stand up!"

Bukarov paled as he stood to attention. Why was he being called first? It was supposed to be Petrin.

"You have been unable to crush the so-called Revenger rebel forces? Explain why you should not be removed and court-martialed for your failure."

Bukarov stood stiffly, smiling a false smile. He was nervous — but he had prepared for this moment well. "Premier, it fills me with pain that I have been unable to destroy this rebel force. They melt into the mountains. They are many and well equipped and are led by men who don't care if they die or not. This rebel group has complete knowledge of the rugged terrain. I have been deprived of winter-trained troops — the Afghanis under me are used to — "

"There will be no more excuses," the premier cut him off. "The Appalachian mountains must be brought under our control."

"Yes, Your Excellency!"

The satellite image of the premier wavered a bit, then steadied. Bukarov waited a long time for the premier's next words. A trickle of cold sweat inched out of Bukarov's toupee and down his short forehead. The premier took a long drag on his cigarette. Probably to draw out the suspense. Would Bukarov be excused, or arrested and executed?

At last the premier uttered, "Oh very well, General Bukarov. Report to me in two weeks with definite progress. Sit down my fat friend."

"Veloshnikov!" shouted the premier. "You have disappointed me." The premier jabbed a finger at the screen. "Supreme Marshal Veloshnikov. Weren't most of our nuclear bombs supposed to explode in mid-air, not on the ground, to *minimize* the fallout that would reach the Soviet Union? What went wrong?"

"The fallout is greater than expected," Veloshnikov said smoothly, "because a chain reaction occurred when our missiles set off the nuclear materials of the American power generating stations. Why, the Indian Point nuclear generator in the state of New York alone added—"

"Yes, yes," the premier said, waving his hand before the camera, "but *why* wasn't that anticipated in your plan?"

"It was, Your Excellency. But our missiles were incorrectly programmed. They exploded off-target, too close to the nuclear facilities in the United States. The *plan* was perfect. The missile computers were defective. If you are looking for those who failed you, look to our technicians, our missile factories and their managers. They are the *traitors*."

The premier sat silent for a while, patting his fingers together, then said, "I accept your argument for the moment, Marshal Veloshnikov. There will be an investigation as you have indicated. The KGB will be on it. Now, what about the loss of the *Peter-the-Great*, our greatest vessel at sea?"

"Five hundred targets in the United States were

annihilated," insisted Veloshnikov. "We lost only five cities and the *Peter-the-Great*. Without my initiatives, there would have been greater losses. Our pre-emptive nuclear strike to prevent an American attack was largely a success . . ."

"*Success?*" raved the premier. "*Success?* Do you realize the levels of radioactivity in our Motherland? Millions have died here from the fallout that is encircling the world; we are having the coldest February on record all over Mother Russia because of the fallout clouds. Many babies are being born hideously deformed. And you call this a success?"

"Yes, Your Excellency. For if we had waited for the U.S. to attack us, it would have been far worse. We acted in the nick of time. We had no choice. Our losses are infinitesimal compared to the Americans. And it is we who are preparing to occupy the Eastern half of the United States. The American military might threatens us no more. All these things have been accomplished by my plan. It is the laser defense forces of Leningrad and our other nuked cities that are responsible for letting the U.S. planes through. My plan was, and *is,* excellent."

The premier seemed out-debated by his closest rival. He coughed. "Very well, that's all—for now."

Bukarov involuntarily clenched his fists. Why that bastard got away scot free!

Admiral Tvosky, who lost half of the Soviet fleet in New London harbor to a bunch of ragged American defenders—civilians with Molotov cocktails and booby traps—was next. He was berated and browbeaten into a near whimpering state by the premier's scathing denunciations. At last Tvosky was ordered arrested.

"No," the admiral screamed. "No! It was Major Krezhkov who botched New London. He has committed suicide, leaving me holding the bag!" The premier's gold-capped smile gleamed, as Tvosky was led away.

"General Petrin! Please come forward." Petrin stood up, a muscular crisp-looking officer. "It was your Gray Suits squad who allowed the U.S. president to escape. Tell us how this—*faux pas*—came about. Tell me how the American commando unit managed to take the president and his staff from under your nose?"

Petrin spoke in a steady calm voice of superior weaponry on the Americans' battle suits; of the fact that the Americans had the blueprints to get down to the bunker that held the president. Everyone listened attentively, even Bukarov, who admired Petrin for his military mind, despite the debacle at the White House.

"You'd best destroy this U.S. Commando Unit, Petrin, before they make your Gray Suits extinct!" the premier snarled. He switched off and the telescreen went dead.

One of the admirals who had been expecting to speak blurted out, "Is that it? Is that why I flew all the way from Montreal in extremely bad weather? To sit here with my speech on my lap and not be heard?"

Bukarov turned to him and said coldly, "The premier speaks to whom he wishes, and calls whom he wishes. Do you have any problem with that?"

Ashen faced, the admiral said, "N-no. Of course not. It's j-just that my speech was so good—I—I—"

"I suggest you get back to Montreal and see to your sailors," said Bukarov, "and expect a visit from the KGB," he added, too softly to be heard.

Veloshnikov breathed out a sigh of relief as he got off the tele-link with the premier. He was coiled tightly as a spring. But five minutes after the interrogation, he was in a bath, covered with bubbles, smoking a cigar and listening to a Duke Ellington cassette. The music poured down from walnut speakers mounted in the four corners of the room.

With a soapy hand he picked up his red phone and ordered that reconnaissance jets continue to systematically survey the area west of the Mississippi. Those areas that had not been surveyed: most of Texas, New Mexico, and Arizona. A lot of land. If the American super-squad was based out there, they could be well-hidden. Helicopters would be better, but they didn't have the range. As an afterthought, he also ordered fueling stations set up at the required distances from the East Coast. "If anything suspicious shows up on the aerial photos of the reconnaissance jets, notify me. Use the maps and intelligence gathered by our Cuban allies—the ones in our file marked 'Mariel Spyscan'—to select airfields with large fuel dumps that our attack helicopters can use to refuel."

Satisfied at last that all that could be, was being done, he soaked for a long time, listening to what might be the last recording that wasn't melted and radioactive of the great jazz musician. He thought of his wife and kids—how they had died in Hanoi when he was stationed there. How the U.S. B-52s had come

35

in the night and bombed Hanoi in a surprise raid. That was 1972. The so-called Christmas bombings. Christmas Eve 1997, Veloshnikov had gotten his revenge. Almost 25 years to the day, he had paid America back. Destroyed the country that had destroyed his life, that had destroyed his family before his eyes. Destroyed the country that had dropped the bombs that he still carried shrapnel from in his gut.

But as long as that black-suited American commando unit lurked out there, the Soviet victory was not fully accomplished. They had to be destroyed, soon, completely. Only then could his wife and children rest in peace.

CHAPTER FOUR

Sturgis wondered how much longer his men could hold out. They'd been on the move for 25 hours since the bit of butchery in Oklahoma. Sturgis knew he was running everyone into the ground, including himself, but he *had* to. He and his men had the president of the United States to deliver. There were just a few hundred miles remaining between their current position on Route 82 — and the C.A.D.S. home base in White Sands. Crossing the Texas border into New Mexico had raised the morale of the men. Knowing they were close to their objective, home, R&R, they joked with each other, trading affable obscenities over their suit radios — until they came to Artesia.

Something had hit the town recently with a lot of firepower. It had been blasted to bits by conventional explosives. The radio chatter among the men ceased as they surveyed its ruins. The roar of their sleek, black Tri-bikes was the only noise as they rolled down the rubble-strewn main street.

Sturgis looked around, scanning the still smoking debris with his suit sensors — Visual, Infra-red, Sonic amplifiers . . . but there was nothing. Bodies lay everywhere, splattered across storefronts, slumped over in automobiles and along the street. Many of them still clutched pistols in their cold hard hands.

The C.A.D.S. men had already seen hundreds of smoldering towns and cities in the East, destroyed by the Red nuke blasts. They'd grown accustomed to the sight of carnage, the spectre of death and chaos stalking across the face of America in *the aftermath*. But this was a town that had survived the war. Who had destroyed it? Why?

Sturgis and his men spread out, looking for clues. Billy found a wrecked chopper in a collapsed building. The bodies inside wore Russian uniforms.

He informed Sturgis, who came to take a look. "So they're out here, they've come this far west," Sturgis muttered.

Reds. It was the Russian butchers who had mercilessly shot down the population of an entire town. But why Artesia?

Fenton radioed, "Wasn't there an airport near Artesia?"

"You bet," came Billy's southern drawl. "I knew a guy who used to fly a commercial short-haul out of here."

Sturgis cut in, "Where you have an air field, you have aviation fuel. We know the commies plan some sort of move west. They might be looking for a refueling station—at this town's airstrip, maybe. Fenton, access the Artesia maps on the Rhino computer."

"I'm way ahead of you," Fenton replied. "Computer info indicates the airport is just 20 miles outside the center of town. It also indicates there's a large fuel storage tank out there."

Sturgis looked about him. "The town is still smoldering—the Red choppers can't be too far. Men, we're on chopper alert. Fenton, hide the Rhino in that garage building to your right. Get the truck in there too. Fuentes, Rossiter stay with them. The rest of us will check the airport out. If the Reds haven't taken the fuel yet we'll blow the damn thing up."

Sturgis felt a bitter bile rising up in his stomach. Everywhere they saw only death. Everywhere they went, it followed close behind them ready to claim more souls.

Sturgis' helmet com-link buzzed. "Looks like lots of Soviet effort went into turning Artesia into a slaughterhouse," a voice said. It was the drawn out Asian accent of Tranh Van Noc—Tranh and Sturgis had been a team since their covert missions together in Indo-China in the early 1990s.

"*Too much* effort," answered Sturgis. "They don't want any witnesses to what they plan to set up here! All the more reason to proceed with caution." Sturgis looked up into the clouds overhead. They were as dark as ever. Breaks of light appeared in spots, but for the most part, the sky was a near solid slab of gray and black billows, which never stopped swirling. I *know* those Red choppers are up there somewhere, he thought uneasily.

The line of attack helicopters swept forward, scanning the prairie beneath them for any signs of life. Their radar watched for ground movement; their heat sensors strained to detect the slightest life readings. Bored and sullen Russian men waited at their machine guns poking out each side of the sleek choppers.

Major Pitrochev was not a man interested in slaughter; he had taken no particular pleasure in the laying waste of Artesia. But the Americans had to be killed. Policemen with their tiny handguns, hunters with rifles, children with homemade bombs. They died bravely, hopelessly outgunned by the firepower of his helicopters, the most effective airborne attack machines in the world. The Americans died in waves, one after another, and yet they had kept fighting, kept dying, kept coming until every last one of them had thrown their lives away trying to destroy him and his men.

That the townspeople had actually brought down three of his craft was amazing in itself, but the price they had paid to do it was what truly had astonished the Russian. Will we have to kill them all? he thought. Kill every goddamned American in this country?

His thoughts snapped back as a soldier notified him of a new reading on his scope. "I have a massive heat reading, sir."

The commander moved across the bay of the helicopter. "What do you think it is?"

"A large number of high-rev engines, sir."

It's them. Those *robot-suits*. The ones the high command wants so much. I have them, thought Pitrochev.

"Give the following orders to all gunships; they are to tie-in with our master targeting computer. Each gunner is to have his own target. How many engines do you read?"

"The reading is fifty to seventy separate targets."

The commander smiled; he had a squadron of 14 choppers. Each contained four missile stations. With one strike, they could decimate the Americans—kill them in a single battle. The energy readings coming to the ship were too powerful to be anything but the armored Americans on their high-tech motorbikes. The ones who had taken the president from deep in the heart of Russian-occupied Washington, D.C. The ones the high command would give anything to see destroyed.

General Pitrochev, thought the major with a kind of joy. That has a good sound to it. I think I'll grow used to it rather quickly.

Aloud, the Russian growled, "Have all target-computers finished intercept synchronization yet?"

"Yes, sir. We're tracking the Americans now. Each launch bay is trained on a different target."

"Then on my command . . ."

"Tranh!" Sturgis directed the Vietnamese's attention to the writhing cloud masses far to their left. "What do you make of that?"

"Christ, Sturge—it's chopper turbulence! They're stirring up the whole damned cloud mass!" As he spoke the radar systems of the C.A.D.S. suits flashed out a warning within every man's helmet.

"*Attack Imminent,*" the words read out in brilliant red letters at the bottom of their visor screens. "Airborne force locking radar-sighting systems. Attack within 30 seconds."

"Mode Blue!" Sturgis yelled into his mike, as he

41

scanned the approaching turbulence. Before he stopped speaking, the visor of his helmet was alive with a slightly blurred grid map display showing the strength of the enemy. "They've got rockets. Everyone — break formation — *Now!* Off the road. Move, move!"

Like wind-blown dust, the C.A.D.S. troopers scattered across the surrounding prairie floor seconds before the sky was torn open by a raging blast of missiles. Each chopper sent out two air-to-ground Zircon-5s, which disintegrated the roadway in a blinding cloud of fire and exploded cement.

Five Tri-bikes and their riders went up in the blast, torn apart in the fury like rag dolls in a tornado. Sturgis switched his visor to Macro-View, which instantly gave him a holographic 3-D image of the battle zone.

His suit's internal computers and radar showed him where his men were, and what formation the choppers assumed behind the clouds. Blanketing the screen with the TA Mode, the Trajectory Analysis, he took in the enemy's firepower and impact capabilities at a glance.

"Damn rockets must be computer aimed — we're sitting ducks," Sturgis yelled into the suit mike. "Auto-Evasive. Run a set of circles on the bastards. Let the bikes continue on automatic and use those bloody suits the way Uncle Sam taught you."

Inside the Rhino hidden from view in the garage in Artesia, Fenton anxiously monitored this latest development on his headphones. He itched to be in the thick of it. He looked over at the president. "I've been monitoring the battle up the road. Sturgis needs the Rhino. But, I was ordered not to leave you and your aides without protection—"

"If Sturgis and his men lose that battle, there is no hope for us. I'm Commander in Chief—I countermand Sturgis' order. Let's *go*!"

The Russian choppers dropped from the clouds, spewing missiles and 9mm machine gun fire. A concentration of rockets destroyed another C.A.D.S. bike and rider. With the Tri-bikes turning sharp circles in every direction in computerized evasion maneuvers, the suited men aboard them were able to turn their firepower on the choppers.

"Hit them with machine gun fire as they come in," Sturgis commanded. "Then try for E-ball shots in their engines—fire IR Mode—Heatseek."

The helicopters swooped down like a flock of blood-seeking hawks. Slugs bounced off the C.A.D.S. armor like rain pellets. The prairie around them rose and fell in puffs as gunfire sent the sand dancing. The troopers could feel the shock of the bullets crackling against their velcron/titanium/plastic suits and several nearly fell from the impact. But they fired back with their own artillery. Two choppers took direct hits from the luminescent blue E-balls cracking with static electricity as they flew. Shrapnel and body parts showered in all directions as the splintered craft fell to earth.

More choppers passed overhead; all the C.A.D.S. troopers raised their right arms, loosing a hail of upturned lightning into the sky. A dozen E-balls climbed swiftly through the air, sparking with violent electrical energy. Many of the armor-piercing explosive balls found their targets, turning half the Russian squadron into a rain of scrap metal mixed with blood.

Suddenly, Billy Dixon's voice rang in Sturgis' head set. "Screw it, sir. This way's too slow." With a rebel yell, he threw on the jet nozzles on his back, shooting nearly 60 feet into the air in an instant. Reaching out, he pointed his suit's fingers out like darts, letting go a stream of 9mm SMG fire right into an oncoming low-flying Russian chopper. As the pilot's window shattered, Dixon jetted alongside. He reached out with his steel arms and pulled loose great chunks of the helicopter, making a hole big enough to allow even his 7 foot suit access to the craft's interior. The second his head came through the ripped side, the barking of Turgenev service revolvers cut the air. Bullets slammed against his visor, then shoulders, waist and legs—doing no harm. Ricochets screamed back and forth between the metal walls inside the cabin.

"Welcome to hell, boys," Billy said. Raising his arm and turning his wrist slightly, he brought the LPF flame thrower into service. Pointing toward the cockpit, he fired a stream, flooding the area with liquid flaming plastic. The fiery goo stuck to every surface it touched, burning with a malevolent energy. Flaming Reds leaped madly from the side bays, racing their out-of-control chopper to the ground. Billy shot backwards out of the hole he had created, lowering himself gently with his jet nozzles as the helicopter crashed nearby.

Other C.A.D.S. troopers copied his idea, getting

up into the air. One C.A.D.S. man caught the edge of a bay opening. Five Russians ran forward; it was like trying to push over Mount Everest, as Horner pulled himself up and in as if only the air was resisting him. Once inside, he didn't even bother with weapons — his gloved hands like steel vises grabbed them by the throats or skulls and squeezed them into a pulp that oozed between the suited fingers. One by one they popped like bugs under pressure, covering the suit's outer armor with blood and large, sticky chunks of muscle and bone.

Aboard his command chopper, the Russian major in near shock from the ferocity of the American attack, ordered his remaining choppers to head upward and out of the Americans' range. Only 5 ships followed him. Major Pitrochev sat in his sweaty chair in stunned silence. It had been only two and a half minutes since he'd ordered the strike. *Two and a half minutes!* What were these Americans? What were these *things* that had torn his command out from under him? Thousands of rounds of ammunition, dozens of rockets — nearly 50 men dead — 8 battle copters downed. How many Americans had died? Two or three? *Six* at best.

"Quickly, radio our position to Charleston," he commanded the radioman. "Inform them that we have discovered the American super squad — the black-suited ones."

After a minute with his equipment, the radioman responded, "I'm sorry, sir, but our transmissions are blocked by interference. I can't get through."

Damn them, Pitrochev thought. They've outfought me. But if I can't destroy the commandos, maybe I can get their president. "Tell me," he asked his radarman, "From what direction were the swine riding, when they were first spotted?"

"From the east, sir."

"Artesia! They must have the president hidden in Artesia!"

Pitrochev ordered his remaining choppers to wheel around and toward the town.

Several miles down Route 82, Fenton pushed the Rhino at its top speed — 60mph. The tough Britisher wished he could get there faster, for the battlewagon he manned had computerized, laser-targeted twin 40mm machine guns, and six Redeye ground-to-air missiles. Firepower Sturgis could doubtless use this minute! It was fully armored, and capable of going forward, backward and sideways thanks to its special design.

Fenton glanced over at the president. How could he be so calm?

"What is it?" the president asked, noticing the look.

"No disrespect, sir. I was wondering why you weren't afraid," Fenton asked, keeping an eye on the road.

"I'm frightened, of course," Williamson responded. "Everyone gets scared when bullets start flying, but in this world gone mad I'm not afraid of dying. The dead may be the lucky ones." Both men smiled but only for a moment.

Roberto Fuentes, one of the Tri-bikers escorting the truck just behind Rhino radioed Fenton, "Don't look now, but I think we got trouble."

"What's happening?" the Brit asked.

"I'm getting six bogies at one hundred eighty degrees. Do you copy?"

"Yes, I do. Say your prayers, men."

"They're coming for us," Fenton spoke evenly. "Fuentes, scan in I.R. and Blue Mode. Rossiter, scan the skies with G.I. and Apli-sound. See if you can keep a fix on them."

"Ahead of us. Already have something at five hundred feet up. Five, no six choppers," exclaimed Mickey Rossiter.

Fenton snapped, "What *bearing*, Mickey?"

"Now at two hundred fifty degrees—G.I. analysis is that they're Russian White Wolf attack choppers!"

Fenton flicked switches. The Rhino's G.I. Mode— Geometric Identification—showed him the same readout. The dashboard's sweep-n-scan screen lit up with the Soviet choppers' specs. Fenton whistled. They were fast—three hundred twenty knots—and well armed.

"I've got them on I.R.", Fuentes reported, "And they must be loaded for bear. They're running hot from overweight!"

Fenton cursed. He kept flicking the radio switch, trying all channels in an attempt to contact the main force, which should be somewhere dead ahead, near the airport. The jamming was everywhere. The choppers would be on them in less than a minute, according to the readout on the sweep-screen. No way to outrun them.

Unless—

"Turn around, man," Fenton commanded, "We're

47

going right back down their throats." With those words, Fenton twisted and pulled on the big steering wheel, and the Rhino rolled almost *sideways*, off the pavement, on its big spherical wheels. Then it pivoted on its gyro-system, and was headed back in the opposite direction.

The truck and the Tri-bikes had to wheel about, not having the unusual turning capabilities of the Rhino. But with their greater speed, they quickly caught up to it.

The president called out, "I'll steer." Fenton nodded, opened the roof hatch and manned the twin-55 cal. guns and the missile launcher. His huge frame jutting up into the wind, Fenton, laser-sighted on the first White Wolf, which was screaming at them just over the pavement ahead.

The chopper whooshed over his head. Fenton spun the rocket launcher and fired after it. Two Redeyes took to the tail of the chopper, which instantly began climbing and taking evasive maneuvers.

One Redeye made target, and the sky was filled with an orange explosion and a rain of twisted steel.

A second chopper was upon them out of nowhere. It fired a rocket that blasted Fuentes from his bike and nearly rocked the truck off the road. Fuentes survived, thanks to his suit, and tried to stand up, but his servo-mechanisms were damaged. He lay there helpless as the chopper wheeled. Fuentes got the suit functioning by manual-override just in time to avoid the next strafing attack, and rolled out of the way.

A third chopper, trying to avoid Fenton's next missile, twisted and climbed so wildly that a Russian fell from its gun bay, his arms circling wildly until he hit the ground with a thud.

Rossiter was firing as he drove; Fenton sent a howling rain of .55 cal slugs into the air, some tearing through a chopper's rotor-mechanism. It lost control and flew into the roadway behind the Rhino, spewing out its parts in an eruption of steel and flesh.

Rossiter got a laser-lock on the fourth chopper and let loose an E-ball. It rose in blazing fury and hit its target, which fell like a gnat swatted out of the air.

"Four down, two to go," Fenton shouted down the hatch opening. "I sure as hell wish Sturgis was here."

As if in response to Fenton's wish, scores of Tri-bikes came into sight, racing toward the battle across the prairie-land. The first phalanx of Tri-bikes was in position and firing at the last choppers before they even realized they were there, because low clouds drifted over the killing-field.

Tracer shells and E-balls lit the sky like it was the Fourth of July, tearing through one of the White Wolves' armor plate like rocks thrown through windowglass.

The last chopper rose up through the cloud cover and out of sight. "Hell, he's high-tailing it," Fenton cursed.

Sturgis' voice crackled now on the radio, "If that bastard gets away he'll bring his buddies. Our only chance is if he goes to the airport to refuel. Billy! Come with me. The rest of you keep on heading toward White Sands. We'll catch up."

Major Pitrochev's helicopter touched down hard on Artesia's single runway. He commanded, "Get us refueled quickly. We must get back east and report that the enemy commando unit has been found."

His men scrambled toward the fuel tanks, bending low to avoid being sliced by the swishing rotors.

Pitrochev realized with growing horror now that he would be lucky to remain *Private* Pitrochev once word of this defeat reached the ears of Marshal Veloshnikov. How could he explain that he had lost the other White Wolves to the Americans? To a *ground* force? Maybe it would be best to make up a story about a squadron of enemy fighter-jets at Artesia's airport. A surprise attack, with ground troops too, and mobile anti-missile rocket launchers. And the robot-like U.S. commandos — they were here too, of course. Maybe Veloshnikov's hatred of the U.S. enemy would sweep away reason, give credence to Pitrochev's lies.

Turning to his radioman he asked, "Are the airwaves still jammed? What the hell is that interference?"

"Still jammed, sir," the radioman responded. "Radioactive clouds to the east are causing the interference." Pitrochev saw movement through the windscreen of the chopper. Two strange low-slung vehicles — the commandos' motorcycles! Before he could even yell out, one of the black figures riding toward them released a mini-missile of some sort.

Pitrochev ducked as the missile tore out the port side of the chopper, just a few feet above him. He felt the concussion as the fuel tanks erupted into hell fire. The pilot was trying to take off. Then came another blast. Death screams. Through the smoke he saw the controls sparking and sizzling, hopelessly shorted out. The radioman and the pilot were slumped bloody messes barely recognizable as human. The chopper dropped to the ground like a wounded bird. The major realized now there was no escape—by air anyway. He decided to roll out of the burning craft and make a run for it if the firing died down.

Sturgis was back on the ground, watching the licking flames consume the chopper and ignite the bodies strewn around it. This was one round for the Americans, anyway. He walked toward Billy, and was about to congratulate the southerner when he saw a figure running, bent over, from the chopper. He let him get 10 yards, then cut him down with a burst of SMG fire.

Scratch one more Red who thought the pickings were going to be easy, Sturgis thought. America has not yet begun to fight.

CHAPTER FIVE

After Sturgis' wife, Robin Adler, and her young ward Chris left the besieged fortress-farm in Virginia, (see CADS #1), they headed south. They managed to avoid all contact with Reds or marauding gangs of survivors by keeping to the high country, away from roads, or even the sounds of vehicles. There were cars out there—cars with fuel to drive around. But she knew they meant danger—death.

Robin felt terrible about having to leave the farm—it had represented not just safety to her, but a link with the past, before the nuclear cataclysm. And now—if Dean came—she wouldn't be there. She prayed that the motorcycle gang hadn't been able to get inside the cliff-fortress, and that Sturgis would find her note. She and Chris had managed to grab some down parkas, backpacks, sleeping bags, rifles and ammo. But there had been no time to get any supplies for a long journey. They were on their own now, trekking through the snow-covered Appalachians. Somehow they had to learn quickly how to survive.

Chris, who still spoke infrequently, at least had

regained his mental and physical abilities. His eyes were clear now, but though the right side of his face was no longer infected it wasn't healing well. The injury, carried by a distant nuclear flash, perhaps never would heal. It had become a solid mass of scar tissue.

She had kept him away from the mirrors at the farm. And then one morning, she awoke to find him staring into her small pocket mirror, as if hypnotized. He had looked up at her with the most pitiful expression she had ever seen. Yet looks mattered little in the new world of infinite death and ugliness.

Now as they walked through the mountain range, Chris seemed to be growing more and more alive. He looked at everything with alert eyes, scouting ahead, rejoining Robin with a big grin. He slowly realized he was important to her, that he still mattered. Robin felt a deep tenderness toward him — almost as if he were her own son. She was thankful that Chris was with her; the journey would have been miserable otherwise.

The boy turned out to be a whiz at forest skills — climbing, building shelters, compass and map use. On the very first day out they came to a steep rocky cliff with a ravine between it and another cliff to the south. They were up a slope nearly 1500 feet, descending toward an ice-covered lake. Chris took out one of the detailed U.S. Geological Survey maps he had brought from the farm and laid it flat on the pine needled ground. He oriented the map so that the terrain ahead, as far as he could figure, matched.

"The landmark ahead — that reddish cliff — is distinctive. See? Here it is on the map 'Old Redface' they call it. Give me one of those stick matches you keep in the plastic bag."

She did, and he placed it vertically on the map. "This here's our position, Miss Adler. Now, we put another matchstick — you hold it — on 'Old Redface' there on the map."

"Now what," Robin asked.

"Now we get out the compass — we really have to get a better one first chance — and we check to see if I've found a cliff that looks like Old Redface but *isn't* it."

"How can you know for sure?" she said, raising her eyebrows.

"Simple. We put the north-south bearing of the compass parallel to the north-south line of the map. If the needle of the compass coincides with that line, then we must have the right landmark — see? It does. That's 'Old Redface' for sure." He looked disappointed. "We haven't come very far today."

"Don't know what I'd do without you, Chris," Robin said tenderly.

Chris squirmed a little and said, "Get lost, probably. C'mon let's get huffing."

The mountains grew steeper and the forest thicker until they had no idea what slopes they were crossing. There were no more landmarks, just endless rolling wilderness. They couldn't find the roaring rapids they crossed on a fallen log, on the map. But Chris suddenly had an idea. He pulled the map out with a broad smile.

"Miss Adler," he said, "we have been using a bad compass. It probably got de-magnetized by the nuke explosions."

Robin sat down on a rock, feeling defeated. "Then we're *lost*."

Chris said, "Not necessarily." He pulled out the map that adjoined the map he had been using and said, "This is the only area *without* significant landmarks in the whole region. *Except* for the Watchatonee Creek."

Gleefully, the boy found their current position, using tracing paper, making a mark for three rolling hills ahead and one behind them, and moving the diagram over the map until he was satisfied. "Throw away that compass, Miss Adler. A bad compass is worse than none at all!"

They trudged off again, Chris leading the way with a new burst of optimistic energy.

After a while, when they walked alongside each other again, Robin asked him, "Where did you learn all this woodsmanship?"

"Boy Scouts," he said, triumphantly.

"So you were a scout, what luck for me!"

Robin was pleased that he was becoming more communicative. He wasn't turning his 'ugly' side away all the time either. Maybe because Robin had stopped wincing whenever she saw it. Their relationship of mutual support was settling into a routine. To Robin, Chris made up in at least a small way for the pain in her gut every time she thought about her pupils in Baltimore, about how most had been cremated in the atomic hellfire there. The leaders who had ordered that attack were still alive somewhere — a concrete bunker, secure, well fed.

* * *

56

That night, instead of dragging his sleeping bag off a way from Robin, Chris slept right alongside her, by the smoldering fire. They had been lucky that the temperature stayed around 30° F. night and day. Even so, Robin was developing a sore throat.

She slept well, knowing her companion was alert to any danger.

She awoke in the twilight before dawn. There was thunder—or artillery fire—off in the distance. The noise seemed to drive Chris into a panic. He ran to her, and she clutched him close, soothing him, stroking his hair until he stopped quivering.

After a while the noise stopped and they set off again, south, always south, away from the big cities and the radiation, away from the nightmare world, deeper and deeper into the mountains. They walked through the amazingly silent winter woods as if in a dream, the stillness broken only occasionally by the reassuring chattering of birds—sparrows and finches—or the sudden fall of an ice-laden branch. Their relationship grew deeper in the magical stillness of the wilds. She came to depend on his ingenuity and energy, and he on the loving friendship and concern he had received little of from his parents, when they were alive.

They were out of food when Chris devised a plan to capture the now abundant game. He would circle ahead in the woods and run toward her yelling and beating two branches together.

She waited with her .30-.30 lever-Winchester, a long time. She began to think something was wrong when she heard the sticks banging. Then came a slew of hopping rabbits and something bigger—a buck. A six-point buck! She sighted it in the telescopic lens and fired. The buck jerked suddenly and fell into the snow, dead before it hit the ground. A good clean shot. She sighed in relief.

Chris knew how to skin it—thank God. Though Robin felt a little squeamish, she watched him peel back the hide with his long hunting knife and then slice out the tenderest parts into steaks. These were the skills she would have to know. The days of daintiness were gone forever. Survival meant knowing everything—and fearing nothing.

They walked on for days, and bagged an occasional rabbit, in between sinking more into the peace of the mountains. It was as if there had been nothing horrible back there. As if *it* hadn't happened at all.

Eventually they came out of the forest, somewhere near Walhalla, South Carolina. That meant that she was nearly 90% of the way to the rendezvous spot she had mentioned in her cryptic note to Dean. He would come—sooner or later—*if* he were alive. *Oh God, please let him come, let him be alive*, she thought, as they walked down a snowy slope.

Because she was thinking instead of watching where she stepped, she didn't notice the ropes disguised as thick vines hanging from two trees. She stepped between them and was yanked up so swiftly that her breath was taken away, and her rifle torn from her grip. The loop of rope hoisted her ten feet into the air and left her dangling like a yo-yo.

Chris ran toward her, but before he got a yard he too was pulled upward, his foot in a snare. They both swung back and forth. Robin tried to work the knot of the loop around her ankle loose. Chris reached for his knife, only to find it had fallen to the ground. They were captured—but by whom? No one was around. Their captors might not be back for days. Perhaps the ropes had been meant for game. In any case they could freeze to death before anyone came, Robin realized. She struggled frantically to free herself.

Suddenly there were sounds—footfalls in the snow, crunching heavy-booted men running. Several men appeared out of a copse of trees, shouting and laughing about what they had snared.

There were three of them. Two in lumberjackets, one in an ill-fitting U.S. Army field jacket. They all carried rifles slung over their shoulders.

"Well, lookee here," the tallest of the three, who had a broad red face and a bulbous nose, said. "A surprise—yessiree. We were expecting a Red jackrabbit. Now what might you two be?"

"Watch out, Jeb, they's got a powerful lot of weapons they dropped down here on the ground. Take a look see at this stuff! Best keep an eye on their hands. Keep a bead on her, Al."

The man with the army jacket raised his rifle without much enthusiasm. "Aw hell, she's an American jes like us. Ain't like she's one of those Cuban soldiers we strung up the other day."

"How the hell do you know she's American?" asked bulbous-nose. "Them Russians look jes like Americans."

The man with the army jacket spat out his chewing tobacco on the snow, staining it a deep brown. "Aw

59

hell, Jeb, I jes *know* — Aren't you American, lady?"

"*Goddamn right, I am*," Robin replied. "Now let us down. I don't like talking upside down."

"What kinda accent is that, lady? Northern?" asked the one called Jeb.

"Baltimore! I'm from goddamn Baltimore — now let us down!"

Jeb narrowed his eyes, raising his rifle a bit. "Talk some more, lady. I want to be sure of your accent. Say 'She sits by the seashore and sells seashells.'"

Exasperated, Robin blurted out, "She shits by the seashore —"

They all laughed. "A Russky would never make that mistake," Jeb chortled, handing his rifle over to Al and going over to the tree to do something with the rope holding Robin. Soon she was lowered to the snow. The minute she was down, she made a dive for her rifle. Al stepped on it.

"What's that about, lady?" he said.

"How do I know you guys aren't rapists, or —" She eyed their weapons.

"Hell," Jeb exclaimed, "our wives are tough southern mountain ladies. They wouldn't stand for none of that. Now get up — away from that there rifle." As she did, Chris was lowered to the ground too. He stood up rubbing his ankles.

Helping Robin to her feet, Jeb demanded, "What the hell is a pretty thing like you doing out here? Running from the Reds? And who's the kid? He yourn?"

"I'm trying to get to Georgia — and he's — mine — more or less . . ."

"You are *in* Georgia," Jeb said. "The proud and

60

free Peachtree state welcomes you and your kin."

Introductions were made all around, once Chris walked around a bit bringing back circulation to his leg. Bulbous nose was Jeb, Army jacket was Al, the tobacco spitter, and Hiram was the short one with the red hunting jacket. All three, Robin thought, looked very country, and very rugged. She hoped they were good people. If not—

Jeb handed her back her rifle, after wiping it off a bit. She decided that she would trust the men completely. After all they trusted her. Chris practically kissed the knife when Hiram handed that back to the boy.

They invited Robin back to their house. "Ain't much," said Jeb, "But it sure as hell beats standing around in the snow."

"Let's keep close to the tree line," Jeb explained as the group walked. "Red heli's have been by here twice. We even had a few Cuban scouts. We finished them off before they could radio back they found something. The air and water is still pretty good here. Well water and mountain air. But down in Atlanta, let me tell you—it's hell. Reds dropped something called yellow rain. Burns the skin. Kilt most folks down that way right off."

"Bacterial warfare," Robin exclaimed.

"S'pose so," Jeb continued. "But like I says, up here, they don't control shit. We're organized, armed, self-sufficient. But you'll hear more of that over some hot grits and fatback, next to our warm fireplace— s'pose you'd like that?"

"I'd like it fine," Robin smiled.

"Jeb," she said, stopping in her tracks, "We can't

61

stay long. I've got to make it to Smoky Mountain Monument Park as soon as possible — I said I'd meet my husband there. Did you hear about anybody named Colonel Dean Sturgis, U.S. Air Force? Has any of you," she pleaded.

"You jes relax, there now," Jeb said, putting his arm over her shoulder and directing her onward. "I haven't heard any name like that, but maybe someone back at the cabin has. In any case, we'll get you on your way after you have a few decent meals and a warm place to rest for a spell."

Robin sighed. Of course, he was right. She was bone weary and probably looked it. And Chris was too. But she would insist on leaving for the rendezvous point as soon as possible.

They walked onward, hugging the treeline for a long time, until they came to a secluded valley filled with green pines. Almost hidden in the thickly wooded bottom of the valley was a farmhouse, with a wisp of blue smoke rising from its chimney. As they approached, the door swung open and they were warmly greeted by womenfolk in country paisley and aprons. The smell of baking and good strong coffee wafted on the warm air from inside.

Robin felt like she was in heaven as the women took her in and tended to her needs, letting her take a hot bath behind a curtain and then, as Chris splashed in the hot water of the old tin drum, she ate to her heart's content of biscuits and grits and pork.

Over the next few days, Robin learned from Hiram's wife Babs and Jeb's wife Sally-Ann about the local resistance, while the menfolk were out deer hunting. It seemed that the freedomfighters of the

Appalachians were growing in strength and organization under the leadership of a still active unit of the Georgia Home Guard. The third day she was at the cabin, the men came back with plenty of deer meat, and at about the same time some battered jeeps and a truck pulled up. The vehicles bore U.S. markings, and were camouflaged with branches and leaves.

"Freedom lives!" was painted in brown across all the hoods of the jeeps. The soldiers that arrived weren't spit-and-polish types. They wore fatigues and they weren't clean shaven. But they had spirit and enthusiasm. They had a lot of captured Kalashnikov assault rifles and ammo, which they distributed to the mountainfolk who came by upon getting the news. The freckled children of Babs and Sally-Ann ran around, in and over the vehicles, playing war. Everyone had a venison meal with cornbread, and the latest news was reported. Every day Reds were killed by snipers, their ammunition dumps were raided, their convoys attacked and destroyed. But the Reds were landing a massive invasion force in Charleston, and once that was accomplished, the local resistance would be totally outmanned and out-gunned. And Resistance scouts had seen yellow cannisters—the deadly yellow rain shells—being unloaded at the Charleston dock.

Robin asked about Sturgis, but no one had heard of him. She decided that she would head out for the rendezvous point at dawn. She had to find him. Had to be with Dean. Even if there were only days more to live before the yellow rain fell on everyone left alive in America.

63

CHAPTER SIX

"Where the hell is it?" Sturgis grunted through clenched teeth, searching at a slow 35 mph in the cold, howling February wind blowing across the New Mexico desert.

Where was the base? The landmarks seemed gone. Everything seemed different, unlike the terrain they expected.

Sturgis had the C.A.D.S. force spread out side by side in a two-mile wave across the desert. Billy Dixon lead an advance guard of six men some ten miles ahead, while Roberto and Tranh covered the wings far to the north and south with two-man scout detachments.

"All units, report," Sturgis said into his radio. "Roberto?"

"*Nada*," he replied. "I know we're in the neighborhood. I *should* see landmarks. But the compass just spins. Magnetism's gone wild around here. And the damned sandstorm has created new dunes!"

"Same here, Colonel," drawled Dixon from his advanced position. "Too much rad interference. It's worse out here than I expected. They could be in bad shape at the base."

"No worse than us," gasped Rossiter from the rear guard. "Colonel, my air conditioning unit's going on the fritz. Can I pull up to fix it?"

"Hang on Rossiter. Give it ten minutes. Can you?"

"Yeah, Rossiter," said Billy. "You could afford to sweat off a few pounds."

"Hold it!" said Tranh from the southern flank, "I think I'm on to something, Colonel. I think I see the air strip. But . . . strange . . ."

"What?" said Sturgis.

"It just doesn't look at all like the old White Sands. Just the concrete and a bunch of big strange dunes, no buildings. I'm going in."

"Right. We'll follow you," said Sturgis, scanning in all modes but getting a crackling interference-filled screen.

One hundred feet below the surface of the artificial dunes that Tranh had spotted, General Knolls and Van Patten sat detained in a small cubicle, waiting. For nine days now, since the upstart Colonel Clearwell's *coup-d'etat*, Knolls and Van Patten, along with 100 other offices and civilian officials had been under house arrest. Things had taken a desperate turn within the secret military base.

For the first week after the C.A.D.S. Force left the base on their mission to Washington, all had run smoothly at White Sands, considering the fact that they were in the midst of the greatest calamity in history. General Knolls and a team of military and civilian leaders had maintained order, and undertaken a massive restructuring of the base. Their first order of business involved eliminating most of the above-ground operations of the base to reduce their visibility. The Russians were sending out MIG reconnaissance jets and the complex of facilities above ground was bound to attract their attention sooner or later. So everything was torn down and the materials hauled underground for use in construction projects. Only the air-strip was preserved, but it was disguised to appear as a dead-end spur off a desert road. The rows of fruit trees used to cloak the base's activities during peace time were also eliminated, although much of the plantings were saved and shifted underground. There, makeshift rooms with artificial sunlight were established to begin growing low-rad, fresh food for the base.

To meet the new space requirements, additions were started in the subterranean caverns. Two new levels were opened up utilizing the natural caves, adding nearly 30 thousand square feet of space.

Refugees began arriving at the base about one week after the nukes fell. Many people in the region knew there was some sort of government facility at White Sands—and it was to their government that these people turned. At first they arrived singly or in small groups. Then, unruly armed bands began to show up demanding accommodations.

Knolls and Van Patten were determined not to turn citizens away as they worked their men feverishly adding accommodations. Food supplies barely kept up with the growth, however, and fear gripped the base, as personnel began to resent any new arrivals as threats to their existence.

Colonel Tom Clearwell, a desk jockey who had operated the Army recruitment program in Albuquerque, took advantage of the unrest. Clearwell had by chance been at White Sands, lecturing servicemen on changes in their benefit program, when the Russians had hit. As dissension grew, he assumed the leadership of that party seeking to prevent any new refugees from entering White Sands. They called themselves the Defenders!

Through a series of secret meetings he had managed to gain the support of about 100 of the camp's 2000-plus inhabitants. One night, they had overpowered the guard, placed Knolls, Van Patten and the other officials under house arrest, and taken over operation of the base. Another 300 quickly joined the upstarts, while the loyalists were disarmed and quarantined on the fourth and fifth levels. Two-hundred men had been banished from the base as "undesirables," sent out to wander in the radioactive wasteland.

The fourth and fifth levels were the newest additions to the base. Raw and unfinished, strung with bare bulbs on extension cords, they consisted primarily of rock-walled caverns with few if any amenities. A few makeshift cells had been hastily erected on the fifth level, and it was in these that Knolls and the others now sat.

The top two levels were now occupied exclusively by Clearwell and his party members. Already they had repulsed hundreds of Americans seeking shelter at White Sands. The heavily armed "Defenders," their arsenal including 26 C.A.D.S. suits and a wealth of conventional weapons, would meet refugees as they arrived and send them packing. So far, no group had been willing to take them on. Clearwell was more than ready to use violence if necessary to keep White Sands "clear from contamination."

As Tranh and his squad sped across the sands searching for the base, Clearwell and his men scrambled to meet them. They sent up C.A.D.S. clad troops, although their men had not totally mastered the complex units, and 50 others armed with automatic weapons and grenade launchers. Tranh saw them, pulled up.

He gave the code word "Elephant," when the force appeared suddenly from the mock-dunes. As he approached to within 20 yards, one of the C.A.D.S. rebels stepped forward and addressed Tranh on amplification mode. He threatened with his weapons-arm, shouting, "Come no further. Go away!"

"Are you serious?" asked Tranh over his amp-mode. "Elephant! Hey, it's us, Sturgis and his men! I'm a member of this base."

"Stop," shouted the C.A.D.S. trooper again. "This base is off-limits. Proceed no further."

"Off limits?" said Tranh. "You're crazy. This is *our* base. Who are you men?"

"We are the Defenders. We're in charge of this base."

"Who is your leader?"

"We're under orders from Colonel Tom Clearwell, U.S. Army. He's military governor of this region."

"By whose order?" Tranh asked. "What happened to General Knolls and Van Patten?"

"Colonel Clearwell is military governor of this region and his orders are no strangers are to enter the compound. Now move on and nobody will get hurt."

Just then Billy and his squad appeared over a crest in the north while Sturgis and the main column kicked up a cloud of sand on the eastern horizon.

"What is this? An attack?" asked one of the Defenders.

"If you want it to be, it is," Tranh said. "Now why don't you get this Clearwell on the radio and let him know he's in for some pretty heavy company, like President Williamson, General Burns, Admiral Turner, Colonel Dean Sturgis, who will be most interested in this Clearwell's status as military governor."

The hum of Tri-wheelers filled the air as Billy, then Sturgis and the main force, stormed up to the scene, blazing dust behind them. Sturgis snapped his visor up, and stepped forward.

"I was monitoring your conversation. Take me to this Colonel Clearwell immediately."

One of the Defenders relayed the message.

"Bring them in," Clearwell said dryly over the intercom from his command post inside the base. He knew enough about the C.A.D.S suits to understand that he'd do best to accommodate Sturgis until his men all got out of their battle gear. Then . . .

Sturgis and his men rode down the ramp which appeared as steel doors swung apart in one of the dunes. The Rhino and the truck followed and pulled up off to the side.

The first level, much larger than any of the others, was a garage-like enclosure serving as a staging area for traffic in and out of the base. A variety of surface vehicles, including tanks, jeeps, armored cars, and extra Tri-wheelers, stood parked around the perimeter. The ceiling was especially high, a good 70 feet, giving the space a cavernous feeling. About half way up the walls an iron catwalk ran the full circuit of the 400 by 200 foot room. Colonel Clearwell, with 26 C.A.D.S. equipped men, stood on it, staring down at the returning unit. Fenton maneuvered the Rhino down the ramp and over to the side. Sturgis ordered his troopers to dismount but keep their suits on — for the moment.

"Welcome to White Sands," said Colonel Clearwell, saluting from his perch on the catwalk. Sturgis looked up with a scowl.

"Colonel Clearwell! What in the hell is going on here?" said Sturgis. "Where is General Knolls?"

The crisply dress-uniformed Clearwell replied, "It became imperative for me to take over and arrest General Knolls. There was no choice for the safety of the base."

Sturgis eyed the C.A.D.S-suited guards stationed around the catwalk. He wondered how well Clearwell's men knew how to operate the suits.

"Colonel Clearwell . . . Why do you feel it necessary to greet us with a C.A.D.S. Force?" Sturgis asked.

"I just want you to accept the fact that I am in charge now, Sturgis. You're welcome here, *if* you understand that."

Sturgis smiled. "I never liked Knolls, Clearwell. It's

71

fine by me if he's out and you're in."

Clearwell smiled, signaled his C.A.D.S. men to lower their arms. He looked relieved. "Good, now we—" He never got to finish his sentence.

Sturgis slammed down his visor and cut Clearwell in half with a burst of SMG fire. "Kill them all, men!" he yelled into his mike. His squad aimed their weapons-arms dead on the men on the ramp. All hell broke loose. Most of Sturgis's commandos, though surprised, fired. Two of Sturgis's men were ripped apart by Defender E-ball fire in the first second, but twenty of the Defenders were blown to a bloody pulp in the next few moments.

The six remaining Defenders in C.A.D.S. suits hit their jetpack power, and lurched wildly into the air, not quite able to control the weighty C.A.D.S. suits. Instantly there was so much smoke and fire, so many richocheting bullets and E-balls, that it seemed as if hell had opened up and poured forth its hot fury upon the human race. The Rhino buffeted as an E-ball hit the dirt just below it, but its heavy shielding kept it from blowing apart.

Sturgis, once Clearwell had bought it, took to the air with the others, spinning as he flew up into storm of blood and flying shells. Firing on automatic, he nearly hit one of his own men whizzing by. The ill-trained Defenders were picked off, despite their frantic efforts to fight back. But not before two more of Sturgis's brave, exhausted fighters had fallen from the burning air, their bodies blown to fragments by a last few E-balls shot from the enemy. Madly jetting past one another, the C.A.D.S. team scanned for any who might have escaped. But there were none. The *coup d'etat* of Colonel Clearwell was over. Sealed in blood.

The civilians had been helpless witnesses while the one minute war had been going on. President Williamson and the others stepped out. "My God," the president exclaimed, seeing the smoking holes in the cavern's walls, the torn and twisted balustrade, the balcony half blown to kingdom come—and the bodies—like lobsters roasted inside their shells, and exploded all over the room.

"It's over, sir," Sturgis saluted. "Had to be done—we would have never gotten another chance like this."

"More death, more tragedy . . ." the president mumbled. Then, pulling himself together he said: "Sturgis, you are to be commended. Imagine if someone had done to Hitler what you just did to Clearwell and his men. The world would have been saved much agony. It is true leadership to take initiative. Well done."

Sturgis and his men worked their way through the White Sands headquarters freeing the imprisoned officers. There were a few skirmishes here and there, but faced with the overwhelming superiority of the C.A.D.S. unit, and with their own leadership dead—the resistance crumbled.

At last Sturgis reached the lower level and came up to a cell holding General Knolls and his top brass.

"Well, what have we here?" Sturgis asked, unable to resist savoring the moment. Just weeks before when Sturgis had gone A.W.O.L. he had ended up behind bars. Now the tables were turned.

"So even you have joined the bastards?" Knolls spat out in disgust, his face up against the bars.

"No, General, I may be a bastard, but I'm a loyal

bastard. Stand back!"

Knolls and twenty of his officers headed to the back of the crude chamber. Sturgis sent a stream of 9 mm slugs into the lock. It blasted apart as if struck by lightning.

"Thanks," Knolls said gruffly. "Wait till I get my hands on Clear—"

"They're already dead," Sturgis said softly. "Every one of the suckers."

That evening President Williamson addressed the entire base over the P.A.:

"Fellow citizens, this is President Arthur Williamson. The illegal actions of Colonel Clearwell and his conspirators are now a thing of the past. You civilians who joined him, although your actions are abhorrent to me, are granted amnesty on condition that you freely admit your error. Join with the rest of us in the great struggles that confront us. You elected me to the office of vice president, but President Armstrong is dead. A fatality of the war like so many millions of our fellow countrymen. As the new president, I intend to do my utmost to preserve, defend, and restore the American way of life. But we *must* work together.

"This base now constitutes the capital of our cherished nation. Rather than turning away fellow citizens seeking refuge, we must welcome them with open arms—establish a new American Armed Force. When overcrowding becomes a problem, as it already has, we will establish colonies nearby and create a network of strength and resistance against the Russian invaders. Colonel Sturgis and his C.A.D.S. force represent our nation's will, and its hope for the future. He and his men have rescued a nucleus of military and civilian leadership. During the course of the next several days we will be meeting to plan our immediate course of action. We will all be called on to help with the work. I can tell you that there is a strong resistance mounting against the Russians. Your fellow citizens, despite their adversity, despite hardships, are up in arms against the invaders. When the time comes, we will do our part to lead the counter-attack.

"I will address the entire camp on a weekly basis, keeping you posted about any national developments. I ask all of you to do your duty as citizens. Thank you."

When he had finished, Williamson turned off the P.A. mike and turned to Knolls and Van Patten, the base's chief scientist. "Now, gentlemen," he said, "if you're not too tired, I'd like a tour of the base to see what sort of facilities we have to work with here."

"Yes, sir," said Knolls. "It would feel good to move around a bit. I've been pacing that damned cell like a centipede."

General Burns and science advisor Sidney Gridley joined President Williamson, Knolls, and Van Patten on the tour. They visited the new levels, where Knolls explained how the evacuated rubble had been transported to the surface via convoyor belt to form the mock dunes on the surface. Then they moved up level by level. They visited the extensive machine shops and mini-factories on the first level, the communications and computer center on the second level, the vast proving ground caves off the fifth level, as well as all the various laboratories throughout the base.

They could see the problems of overcrowding and the stress caused by isolation and fear. As they walked through the barracks they saw the groups of women and children crowded into the small rooms, sitting idly, listless, staring at walls.

"Increased demands on the base's two power generators causes frequent blackouts," Knolls told the president. "The diet has to be kept simple and sparse, as supplies are critical. There is plenty of water supplied from an underground spring system, but Van Patten points out that it is only a matter of time before the water table becomes tainted with radioactive seepage.

"Suicide is going to be a problem," Knolls added grimly. "And our medical services are terribly inadequate. There are almost five hundred patients with only four doctors and six nurses to care for them around the clock.

"Still," he went on, "we're making some progress, Mr. President, especially with the agricultural station.

"At least Clearwell didn't do any actual damage to the base. Everything seems to be operating fairly well, considering."

"But surface rad levels are increasing daily," Van Patten cut in with concern. "Basically we have two choices. Dig deeper and remain subterranean for a long, long time, or try to move the whole operation to a safer area."

"And what do *you* suggest?" Williamson asked.

"Well, there's no harm in sending out a few groups to establish colonies, like you suggested, Mr. Presi-

76

dent," the scientist said, "but I think we should continue to dig deeper, expand the base. If we tried to move all the equipment outside, the Russians would spot us for sure. Besides, realistically, where could we go? I doubt if there's any place on the continent that's safe. Nuclear-winter is with us now. I sincerely believe the survival of the human race depends on learning to live underground."

"And what do the rest of you think?" Williamson asked, his expression growing grim.

"Well," Gridley spoke up, "I suppose Van Patten's right. We need secure shelter. And the underground's about the only place left. But I think we ought to do a little bit more than dig in."

"Like what?"

"Attack," bellowed General Burns, chomping on a well chewed cigar.

"Attack?" interjected Van Patten. "Attack them with what?"

"Attack them with the C.A.D.S. force," Burns nearly yelled. "Our boys fight tougher and smarter. From what I've seen, Sturgis and his boys, resupplied, can dent the Russians *bad*."

"A *dent* sure, but then what?" Van Patten asked. "We would lose White Sands' only adequate defense force. We're in no position to attack!"

"I'm afraid," said Gridley, leaning heavily on his knobby cane, "it might not matter whether we attack the Russians or not. In fact it may not matter *who* wins. There is an unprecedented environmental disaster out there, gentlemen. My preliminary data suggests that it will be pure luck if the earth's soil will ever again support plant life. And without plant life—"

Burns shouted "Hogwash! Alarmist nonsense! The thing to do is—"

"Gentlemen, gentlemen," said Williamson, waving his arms to quiet them down. "That's enough for now. I want a meeting of all top personnel for 0800 hours. Gridley, you will elucidate more comprehensively what you've brought up."

The council convened at 0800, with all present. All were quiet as Gridley, a man of sixty with a head of wildly tousled hair, stood up. Gridley had bad knees aggravated by arthritis, and he limped to a mike supporting himself with his omnipresent knobbed cane. The presidential science advisor was to speak about the ecological situation of the United States and what *future*—if any—there was.

In a shaky voice, almost apologetic, he rattled off the tentative nature of his report, the fact that he wasn't really qualified to do such a study and so forth. Finally General Burns shook his head, stood up and hollered, "Will you get on with it, Doctor? There *are* other matters. Do you have a *synopsis*?"

Gridley cleared his throat and with an icy glance at General Burns began reading his report. "In *summary*, then, gentlemen, we all have an ecological apocalypse on our hands. From the reports Colonel Sturgis and his men have given us of the rad readings, cloud cover and the like to the east, plus my own observations, I believe it is unlikely that there will be a spring this year."

Those in the conference room were stunned. "No

spring? Sturgis was the first to speak up, "Doctor, what does that mean? Is there to be a continual winter? Won't it warm up?"

"Oh, I think it will warm up—perhaps too warm. If my data is accurate—ahem—to make it short, there are no bees in the hives we have here at White Sands. The queen bees died of radiation. And I don't expect many insects will have survived in the whole country—except perhaps cockroaches. Even the worms that loosen the soil for plant roots would have died under the ash, oxygen-less from the radioactive areas—the eastern cities. Nature *needs* bees and worms, flies and grubs. Pollination, fertilization can't occur without them."

"Will anything survive?" Sturgis asked, a sickly look on his face.

"Oh yes, in the various lower-rad areas I specify in my report. Though many will grow too *fast* and die with cancers, some growth will be mutated . . . The same with human children. Though there has been one healthy apparently normal child born at White Sands in the last month, there have been stillbirths and one—one—*abnormal* that had to be done away with. It's the same with the plants. Many that grow will be sterile, or uselessly mutated. All the varieties of grass—even weeds. Of course, this will hardly matter if bees haven't survived to fertilize the flora and fauna of the nation, or if the cloud cover continues to prevent most of the sun's rays necessary for photosynthesis, or if—"

"Good God," Burns cut him off shaken, "is it—the end of the world?"

The president's scientist leaned forward to the mike

and spoke in a whisper. "I don't know—I honestly don't know what will happen. The only thing I *can* say as a ray of hope is that, since eighty percent of the nation's citizens are dead, there will be fewer mouths to feed. We might—by again, extremely loose guesses based on incomplete figures—be able to feed those who remain alive on the stored canned foods that exist in the nation for a year or more. Perhaps *next* spring the elements with a shorter half-life will have dissipated enough to allow—more normal growth—"

"*Half-life?* What's that?" Burns asked.

Sturgis spoke up, "Each radioactive element kicked out by the nuke blasts has a radioactive life expectancy of differing lengths—plutonium, uranium, cesium—eventually, all the radioactive elements will become inert."

"Thank God," Burns said, his shoulders relaxing in his starched tan uniform. "So things *will* get back to normal soon."

"Not quite." Gridley snapped back, "Some elements, such as cesium, have a half-life—the amount of time it takes for it to become half as radioactive—of days. Others, like plutonium, which many of the Soviet bombs were made of, have half lives of about nine hundred *years*. So it all depends on how much of the heavier elements there are in the ecosystem now. And how the earth can deal with them. Through the purification of rain, wind, disintegration. Whether it can at all."

After more questions, the president said, "Thank you for your report, Doctor Gridley. It's a chilling report, but one we all had to hear, so that we all know the score and plan as best we can for whatever future there is."

Later, after chow, Sturgis lay in the bunk, deep underground in the middle of the desert. Above him, a whole continent heaved with the agony of nuclear devastation. He was still tired, but couldn't stay asleep. He was too troubled. He found the Scotch bottle, slugged down the last few fingers of it. His mind drifted to Robin Adler, his wife.

She was out there somewhere. Was she still alive? Would he see her ever again? What was she doing right now?

If only he could know . . .

He felt so alone. Even his dog, Excalibur, who should have been here, was missing. A technician Sturgis had run into while searching for the lovable pit-bull earlier, had told him that the dog had run off. Just a day after Sturgis had left on the Washington rescue mission.

He felt bad about Excalibur, but if any creature could survive, make it on his own out there, he could.

Sturgis switched off the small lamp. In the total darkness he relived better days—Robin holding him close to her, pressing his lips with hers; the dog barking, running around them in the grassy field, the daisies bending with the warm winds, the scent of the fall foliage, blue sky above.

Just a dream . . .

CHAPTER SEVEN

Sturgis walked briskly down the white-tiled hallway toward Carlos Ortiz's room. Taking a deep drag from his Camel, he held the warming smoke in his lungs, flicking the cigarette's lengthy crown of ash unceremoniously to the floor. Taking a look at his watch, a special, heavy-duty Navy piece, he saw he had plenty of time left before he was to meet Van Patten. Stopping in the hallway, he relaxed his hold on the smoke in his lungs, trying to blow a smoke ring like Billy had shown him.

Nothing. The smoke came out in puffs and streams, but nothing that resembled a circle.

Sturgis flicked the butt away in disgust, banking it off the wall ahead of him into the shadows of the hallway. Checking his watch again, he thought, Van Patten doesn't need me for the testing until 1300 hours. I'd just be in his way until then. Making a left in the corridor, Sturgis stopped at Ortiz's door.

"How's Carlos?"

The guard on duty outside the heavy, steel reinforced door saluted sharply, and then whispered, "No change yet, Colonel. He hasn't budged an inch."

Sturgis gave the man a worried look, but told him, "Have to see what we can do about that eh, Paul?"

"Yes sir."

The guard punched in the proper electronic code for the door. It waited its standard three seconds, and then pulled back into the wall, giving Sturgis three seconds to step inside before it slid back into place. Inside, the room was dark, except for a dimly illuminated wall clock. "Please leave the lights off," said Ortiz. Sturgis did.

"Carlos?" he called out softly in the near darkness.

"Colonel." The voice that came back through the darkened room was weary, flat, dead. "We movin' out, sir?"

"No. We're not going anywhere. Not for a while. We're home, Carlos. Time to relax. Sleep. Eat. Get drunk. Now, why don't you take off the C.A.D.S. suit. Come with me, we'll get some women, have a drink — What do you say, pal? You did the fighting — you're as tough as any damned man in this outfit — now get the few rewards we got left to give you."

"No rewards, better not, sir. It's best to be ready, sir. The enemy is always near."

Sturgis moved forward to the center of the room, to where Carlos Ortiz had stood since they had made it back to the C.A.D.S. base — to where he had stood for over forty-eight hours in his armor. Refusing to emerge from his velcron/titanium/plastic sheath, he had remained in the same place, in the same position for two days. The base doctors had coaxed him; his friends had begged him. But he hadn't moved.

The ranking psychologist at White Sands, a woman, Dr. Sheila de Camp, had recommended Sturgis not visit Ortiz. She had predicted such a visit would be demoralizing for the soldier, to be seen in such a state by his commanding officer. Sturgis had accepted her verdict for two days while she and the others had tried to desensitize, psych-out, and finally force Ortiz out of the seven-foot stack of super-strong armor that he now seemed to call home. Finally Sturgis had decided he had waited long enough.

Only problem — now that I'm here, Sturgis thought in the darkness, what the hell do *I* say that's supposed to make any more sense than anything else they've already thrown at him. Still, he had to try. Maybe the direct approach.

Staring up at the ominous metal giant before him, Sturgis looked into its reflecting green eye. "Okay, Carlos — stop fucking around. Get the hell out of that thing."

"No disrespect, Colonel, sir. I don't think I should."

"Why not?"

"I have to be ready, sir."

"For what?"

"For the Russians, sir."

Sturgis continued to argue with Ortiz, going around in the same circles the head shrinkers had. Dr. de Camp had told the C.A.D.S. team commander that the basis of Ortiz's problem was a fear of taking off his armor. She had said the rigors of the mission, after days of living in his armor, of it being his only protection, in many ways, his only home, Ortiz was now terrified to take his armor off. The C.A.D.S. unit had become a symbiotic part of him. Beyond the cybernetic link-ups; Dr. de Camp felt sure Ortiz was now psychologically dependent on his suit for emotional survival, unable to feel secure outside of it—a kind of regression into infancy with the suit his security blanket.

Sturgis argued with the trooper to no avail. Everything he said just brought them around to the same point—Ortiz *had* to stay in his armor because he *had* to be ready for the Russians. The metal behemoth refused to release its hold on the man within it, no matter what kind of order or logic Sturgis used. And then, the C.A.D.S. commander realized he had been working from the wrong angle. Smiling to himself, he pulled himself atop a utility table and relaxed. Sitting back, resting his shoulders against the wall, he pulled his Camels from his shirt pocket, lighting one and dragging deeply.

How stupid could I be? I've been playing this as if I thought Carlos *is* a coward, as if that woman with her graphs and charts would know more about what went on out there than *I* do.

"It's Driverville, isn't it Carlos?" Sturgis finally said softly.

At one of their rest stops on the way to D.C., when they had split up into two groups, one to guard and one to get some sleep, a party of escaped inmates from a nearby lunatic asylum had gotten the drop on those who were supposed to be doing the guarding. Carlos was one of the ones who let the crazies get by—he was one of the ones who almost made them

86

all die.

Five minutes. Keep that head shrinker out of here for five minutes, and I'll be able to get through to him. "That's it, isn't it, Ortiz?"

Quietly, in between drags on his cigarette, Sturgis began again, working at getting a brave man to realize he was not alone in his fear, in having fucked up. And that he didn't have to atone. For no sin had been committed.

In the medical lab facilities of White Sands base, Dr. Sheila de Camp sat at her desk, going over the reports on the recently returned C.A.D.S. troopers. She was still an attractive woman, despite the bags under her eyes from too little sleep, and the slight tremble she had developed in her lips from going too many days at full tilt. Before the C.A.D.S. team went out again, she would be damned sure that each man was mentally fit for duty.

"Dr. de Camp . . ."

The woman turned at the nervous voice of her second-in-command, Dr. Peters. "I thought you weren't going to give Sturgis access to the Ortiz man," Peters said, walking up to her desk and taking a mint from a bowl she always kept stocked on the front of the long, ancient work desk.

"I'm *not*. The man's a killer. That's all he knows how to do. He wouldn't have the slightest notion on how to heal someone."

"But," Peters half croaked, "He's in the Ortiz room right now!"

Dr. de Camp sat bolt upright, her blue eyes snapping fully open like laser reflectors. "That bastard." She stood immediately, shoving her chair away with the backs of her legs. It rolled into the middle of the floor, but de Camp didn't notice. She was already heading for the door. "That macho lummox may twist everyone else's orders around to please himself—but not mine! Not this time!"

The doctor stormed out of her office, crashing the swinging door backward against the inner wall. She marched for the living quarters, walking so fast that Peters could scarcely keep up with her. Her hands were shoved deep into the pockets of her lab coat, in tight fists wanting to punch, to strike out.

She hit the main corridor just as Sturgis was coming out of the room. As the bay guard stepped aside for the colonel, de Camp shouted: "What do you think you've been doing in there, Mister?"

"Your job," replied Sturgis harshly. Carlos Ortiz walked out behind him, looking tired and sheepish. He had not shaved for so many days that his normally neatly trimmed beard had begun to blend in with his stubble.

He said, "I'm sorry I caused you so much trouble, Dr. de Camp. Colonel Sturgis explained everything to me. If you don't mind, I think I'd like to get some of that sleep everyone's been trying to force on me."

The doctor dismissed Ortiz curtly. He wasn't the one she wanted a piece of. As the half-asleep trooper stumbled out of the way, de Camp rammed her index finger into Sturgis' rock hard mid-section. "What the hell did you do to him? You could have ruined hours of my detraumatization process. I *told* you to stay away from him. Damn you, I told you!"

"You also told me you'd have him out of his C.A.D. suit in six hours. You told me that two days ago." Sturgis blew a fog of smoke in the woman's face, trying to create a circle, but never quite reaching it. She made to slap the Camel from his mouth, but he stepped back out of her range, and then batted her hand away with his own. De Camp yelped slightly, shoving her stinging fingers into her mouth.

"You—you dare strike me?" she asked standing at her haughtiest.

"You'd better learn to get past your own problems before you try to cure anyone else's, lady."

Sturgis tried to leave the room, but de Camp stepped in his way. "What the hell is that supposed to mean?"

The C.A.D.S. commander stopped himself from shouting back at the woman. "Look, de Camp," Sturgis said, taking a long, tired breath, "many of my men have come back from the trip greatly demoralized. They've seen stacks of the dead as high as buildings. For days, for weeks, they drove past burnt fields and parks, through disintegrated towns and cities, over melted bridges, across smoking deserts, and through treeless forests. Not once did we ever lose sight of the effects of the Russian attack. The bombings have left millions of burned, blinded, and poisoned victims. Have you ever seen the flesh peel right off the body like rotted meat—seen mouths, teeth, explode out in blood as the dying cough.

"The team saw what remains of great American metropolises: burning, twisted, exploded ruins of cement shards and slagged girders, littered with broken glass and the vaporized ashes of the dead. Most of my men are in their early twenties. All of them firm believers in the power of the U.S. They had returned to their base, knowing that their country was no longer inviolate—no longer the strongest nation on earth. It had also made clear to them that the only thing that might possibly stand a chance of stopping the brutal Russian invasion was the C.A.D.S. team. It was a heavy burden, a very heavy burden, de Camp, knowing that the future of the entire world—if any—depends on us. Carlos Ortiz wasn't the only one of the men it got to. *The realization that it was all up to them!*

"Listen Dr. de Camp," the commander continued, "Your mistake was in thinking that any man who freezes up is a coward—that to be brave you have to always be an unemotional type. You pegged Carlos for a coward because that's what you think of all of us. I know I'm scared. I'm scared I'll never find my wife in all that death and madness out there. I'm afraid the Russians are going to win, and take everything that ever meant anything to us, or that would have meant something to our children. And I'm most scared of the mistakes the C.A.D.S. unit makes. The ones it has made, like in Driverville, and the ones it will make."

Sturgis stared at de Camp, his barely open gray eyes locking hers. Dropping his butt to the floor, he crushed it out. "*Help* my men, doctor. Don't condemn them for doing their jobs. I know you don't mean to hurt anyone—but you'd better learn to be a military doctor, and damn fast. The time is past for keeping the wildmen in line. You'd better start listening to what our men say. Not try out theories on them. Hell, we'll have to go out again, and again and again. And fewer and fewer of us are going to come back each time; it's going to be your duty to tell the ones that make it back that they did a swell job, and that every mistake we make is just that. That we are human, fallible, and that it's okay."

Tears started to well up in de Camp's eyes. She knew Sturgis was right. Since the war, she had stayed hidden in the White Sands underground base, safe and insulated from all of the destruction outside. She had shielded herself from the horrors all around her, refusing to truly acknowledge them. When the C.A.D.S. team had returned with the president, C.A.D.S. suits covered with shell marks and blackened scorings, with dried muck and blood, something within her had snapped. Deep down she had withdrawn from them, as if *they* were the enemy. Putting her hand up on his shoulder very softly, she whispered, "You're right!"

The C.A.D.S. commander stopped short, not knowing what to say. He had been shouting at the woman in anger, not realizing that anything he was saying would actually get through. But it had gotten through—had broken down the walls in fact. Flustered, he began to apologize profusely, but de Camp stopped him cold. "No! You don't have to say anything. I've been turning away from the present situation because I didn't have the strength to face up to it. Maybe I still don't. But I think you are right, Colonel. I'd better try to change that. It's my duty to overcome my own fears, to offer whatever real help I can give."

Sturgis looked at his watch. De Camp said, "You're

91

due at the test cave, aren't you?"

"Yes," Dean said, "Demonstration of some new gizmos to add to our collection."

"May I come, to watch the suits in operation?" she asked a little shyly. "It might help me to understand what these boys are feeling when they get in them, and when they have to get back out."

"Sure." Sturgis agreed with little hesitation. He smiled at her for the first time.

Sheila de Camp felt more awake, more like a woman than she had in months. This masterful, violent man was so compassionate, so understanding, so — so handsome!

Sturgis opened the swinging door for the doctor and the pair of them headed off in the direction of the test cave.

Dr. de Camp waited with Van Patten behind protective shield-glass in the massive C.A.D.S. base tent cave. The cave was actually part of the Carlsbad Cavern system. Although the well-known Carlsbad area was some hundred miles to the southeast, the same natural forces which had created the one had created the other. What primal series of events, cave-ins, earthquakes, flooding, whatever, had separated the two was now impossible to say.

Nor, in the middle of World War III, was it very important. Van Patten thought nothing of using the staggering beauty of the caverns for targets. There was no questioning the logic — it was something which had to be done. You couldn't test such weapons on the surface and not be detected.

Sitting in one of the white plastic observer's chairs, Van Patten reclined with his fingers knotted behind his head. He manipulated rows of dials, turning on the TV monitors throughout the cave, as Billy Dixon, who had volunteered for the day's testing, moved into view. Van Patten hit the intercom, slipped on a set of headphones, indicating to de Camp, who had come alongside him to do the same.

Checking his level, he asked, "Is that you, Billy?"

"Yeah. What you got for us today?"

"Drones." The scientist's voice came in clearly through Billy's helmet. "Your suit has been re-fitted with an improved track-system. I want to see how they hold up under combat conditions. Let's check with the machine guns first, shall we? Each target will move at different speeds."

Billy moved to the center of the cave, waiting for Van Patten to launch the first of the drones. Seconds later, three black, flying discs buzzed in at the trooper. De Camp wondered how he could see them. The few lights within the cavern created more shadows than illumination.

Inside the suit, however, Billy tracked the movement of the drones with the computer analysis screens on his visor. Ordering his suit's internal systems to "target 3 drones," he pointed his left arm and said, "Rapid fire." Instantly the machine gun built into the armor of his left arm cocked. While he used his visor screens to sight the first drone, the new laser trackers homed in on all targets, waiting for his signal. The moment the blue screens before his eyes turned to red, signalling that the laser sighting had the first target locked, Billy turned his left wrist a bit counterclockwise triggering his machine guns.

9mm shells trailed through the high cavern, cutting the first drone in two. Bits of metal exploded outward, spitting about the cavern. Wheeling quickly, surprising de Camp with the speed with which the massive suit could be turned, Billy lined up his second target, flicked his wrist and blasted it from the air. Turning again, he caught the third flyer in his screens, waited for the red, and then fired. The last drone exploded in mid-air, shells ripping through it before the falling halves of the first drone had finished falling from the air.

"How's that, Doc?"

Van Patten looked over the computer screens before him, checking their measurements of the effectiveness of the new C.A.D.S.-suit tracking system. The actual outcome had been different from his computer predictions, but only marginally. The closeness of prediction to actual performance pleased him. His expectations had seemed too high. He had difficulty accepting such perfection being created by his own hands, but the evidence was in.

As the tests continued, trooper after trooper came forward, going through each situation Van Patten had prepared. Fuentes put the mini-hawk darts through their paces, emptying his arm holders into both walking and flying drones. The ¼" thick 8' long steel darts spun the drones like children's tops, pinning them to the stone walls of the test cave.

Tranh then grappeled with a robot in a type of elephantine hand-to-hand combat, slamming their massive bulks against each other. Blows which could crush girders, slam holes in concrete walls the size of car doors, bounced off the smooth coating of the C.A.D.S. armor, leaving little or no damage. Van Patten watched the meters which were measuring the always cool Vietnamese's pulse and respiration rates rise and fall. He knew the robot was putting his all into trying to topple the C.A.D.S. man, but it simply could not be done. The C.A.D.S. suit contained Van Patten's latest modifications, more armor, and a gyro-emergency system. It was undefeatable!

De Camp watched in amazement. When Sturgis came out to test the enhanced E-balls, the woman hid her eyes as the blinding flash of a battery of the armor-piercing explosive balls blew out whole sections of the cave wall. Rock showered in all directions. An elephant-sized boulder slammed into Dean's suit, but the shock resistant bondings which coated it reduced the bone powdering contacts to the slightest of bumps to the man inside, as the suit automatically spun out of the way of the object.

Peeking through her fingers, de Camp watched as Sturgis turned his arm upward and then fired more E-balls at the ceiling. Explosions thundered through the test cave, hurting the ears of the observers even through their protective head sets. As de Camp and Van Patten watched, truck-sized slabs of rock fell from the cavern ceiling, heading directly toward Sturgis. Before they could hit, the C.A.D.S. trooper hefted his LFP flame thrower and showered it upward into the rain of rock so that it ignited into a burning coating of liquid, flaming plastic. Still the suit held.

The observers watched the pile of rock in the center of the test cave, watched for long seconds. Then with a sudden burst, Sturgis shrugged the flaming rocks from his armored body like drops of water.

"Well, Doc," he called into his communicator, "I like this new armor, definitely stronger armoring from heat. I was able to take every bit of it."

"Go get out of your suit, Sturgis. I think we have all the live tests we need for the time being," Van Patten said with a smile on his usually cool face from Sturgis' praise.

De Camp turned to the scientist. "What do you mean 'live' tests, Dr. Van Patten?"

Suddenly, Sturgis entered the observation bunker. "He means it's time to bring up 'Charlie'."

"Correct," Van Patten answered.

Before de Camp could question what they meant, a huge multi-armed robot came onto the floor of the test cave, its 20 wheel feet navigating around and over the heaps of debris, some of it still flaming from Sturgis' grandstanding. The robot moved easily, despite the appearance of being off-balance due to the weapon strapped to its right arm.

"See that white titanium weapon, the size of a Sub-Thompson, with the row of colored lights on its side?" Van Patten said to de Camp. "It's the new LWA, or Liquid Wave Amplifier. In lay terms, I suppose one could describe it as a laser beam submarine gun. It can be adjusted from a tight, almost needle-fine beam to a plowing track the width of a house. We need Charlie because there is one adjustment we haven't been able to make yet, though. We haven't been able to piece together how to keep it from exploding. It overheats."

Sturgis said nothing. He had been fascinated through the other tests even though they were mere modifications. He already knew how well the C.A.D.S. armor worked. He was aware that Van Patten's tests were important. If the scientist was to improve the tracking, firepower and armor of the C.A.D.S. suits, it might give them just the edge they needed. As far as Sturgis was concerned though, the truly important test was the next one. A new super-weapon. The C.A.D.S. commander was desperate for the LWA to succeed. As his team's suits were now, they were fairly invincible. The more they worked with their suits as a unit, the more combat they saw, the better a team he and his men were becoming. But although they had been able to turn every force they had encountered so far, the war against the Russians had barely begun. The odds they would be facing in the future would be ten times, twenty times, a thousand times what they had faced so far.

Sturgis wanted the LWA as an equalizer. The Russians even had their own version of the C.A.D.S. team — The Gray Suits — powerful but primitive compared to C.A.D.S. — but *nothing* like the LWA! He watched the technicians making their final adjustments from his spot in the bunker, making sure Charlie held it tight.

The compact white weapon did not look like a gun. It actually did not look like much of anything Sturgis had used. It had something that looked like folded modular wings on both sides. Van Patten said, "Those are power cells. Sort of like ammo magazines, only for light-power, not to contain bullets."

"Let it work," Sturgis spat. "Just let the fucking thing work."

"Colonel," called Van Patten, "We're ready."

Sturgis crossed his fingers. "Then get on with it," he snapped.

Charlie the robot stood in the center of the test cavern. Unsettled dust from the previous tests made the atmosphere of the cave hazy. Controlling the robot through remotes, Van Patten drove the robot into a deep part of the cavern. And fired. A white narrow beam as powerful as a runaway jet slammed into the rock, gouging out red hot bowling ball sized chunks as if they were nothing. It melted a hole three feet deep in the limestone!

Now wanting to move the LWA like a wand, Van Patten moved Charlie's arm in a side-to-side motion, digging the laser through the rock wall like a stick through the snow. Fissures cracked in all directions, the wall splitting and toppling on itself, waves of stone and rock dust splashing across the test cave floor. Super-headed chips exploded outward, crashing into the cavern walls. "Good thing we're watching this through Charlie's eyes," de Camp gasped.

It was impossible to gauge the damage being done by merely watching through the "Charlie-vision" screen. Flying stone and dust and smoke made watching the beam's path impossible. Van Patten, following the readings on his console screens, however, had a very good idea of what was happening in the chamber. "It's hot. The overheating problem. Damn! It may work out in time, Colonel. Charlie's arm temp is not bad, the LWA is hot, but—no vibe registrations, temp balance is improving, the new fan must be keeping the dust out this time—the generator is . . ."

Van Patten continued to read off data, but Sturgis said, "Let's fire again."

98

The LWA continued to turn the bowels of the test cave into a molten ruin. Sturgis hoped his prayers would be answered. So far the LWA had held up to the pressures.

"The LWA has a vibrational 'kick' to it," Van Patten said. "That accounts for the jerk in the viewer every time Charlie fires the thing. The kick is no more powerful — *Oh no!*" Van Patten began stabbing at buttons on his console, but it was too late. Although he was able to kill the energy trail slicing up and down the walls, something had gone wrong internally. The overheating process had gone wild inside the LWA. Already, two C.A.D.S. troopers were moving forward with coolant spreaders, hoping to dampen the building reaction swelling in the LWA. The instant Van Patten had triggered the cavern's blue-light warning flashers, they had moved out, spraying Charlie's right side and the weapon strapped to his right arm down with the freezing liquid gas in their spreaders. But it was too little, too late.

"No good," said Van Patten, "it's going to blow."

And then, as if hearing the scientist's prediction, the LWA glowed sun-red as the sprayer crew ran for their lives. A blinding flash suddenly lit the cavern and left everyone with stars in their eyes. Charlie's arm disappeared in the flash, but when the blinding light faded, the monitor still worked. Only scarred metal and burning wires remained at his shoulder. Charlie was built as tough as the C.A.D.S. armor. His smoking, ruined body told the story of the testing — the LWA simply was not a safe weapon for combat. Van Patten pushed the button to return Charlie's remains.

Van Patten began to talk, but Sturgis waved him to quiet. The C.A.D.S. leader barked, "Don't give me excuses. I don't need them and I don't want them. When I go east against the Reds, I *need* the LWA! We all need it — bad."

"What do you want from me, Sturgis?" The pockmark faced scientist waved his arm toward Charlie's burning side. "Doesn't that show you that the LWA is just too unsound for you and your men to use?"

"It shows me you think-tank boys aren't doing your jobs. We *need* those lasers! Work on it twenty-four hours a day — two shifts — you're close man — I can feel it."

"And we need parts — and equipment!" Van Patten yelled. "Supplies and men. And more hours in the day, and then more supplies and more hours! But do you know what I have — *nothing*! There's nothing new coming in here, Colonel. There are no contractors delivering anymore — there are no appropriations, or a Congress to give them to us, or, or anything — damn it!" The tall scientist rose from his chair shaking with futile rage. "We're supposed to be researchers; well, we're not. Right now, we're just your miserable repairmen. And all we have is what's on the truck. We can't go back to the shop anymore."

Sturgis kept his fist at his side. Knowing the man was right kept him from decking him, but it didn't keep him from wanting to. The C.A.D.S. commander had wrapped up a lot of his future hopes in the LWA. He didn't like being told his hopes were impossible.

"Then that's it, huh?" asked Sturgis.

"Not quite," responded Van Patten. Reaching

under his console, he pulled another LWA from concealment, handing it to Sturgis. He pointed to a new light meter on the weapon's side. "See this? This is an internal sensor. Let's step outside."

Both men headed for the bunker door. Dr. de Camp chose to stay indoors. Outside, in the settling dust, Van Patten explained, "As long as this row of lights stays in the blue, the weapon is fine. As it moves over into the red, however . . ."

"Yeah, I get the idea." Sturgis stared at the meter. "But the lights on your board inside went from blue to red instantly. What good will that do me in combat?"

"The lights on the console weren't designed to pick up what this meter does. I had to jerry-rig part of the panel for this new reading. Without the proper supplies, I ended up with what I think is about a ten to twenty second warning of overload. By the time the board in the observation room knew Charlie was in trouble — he was already over his head, but this LWA is different."

With some of his hope returning, Sturgis said, "Guess I should try it out then. You go back inside." Sturgis snapped down his visor.

Van Patten stood his ground. "This test is for keeps, Sturgis. If I'm not here to watch you, the test isn't valid. Besides, I have faith in your ability to distinguish between red and blue."

Sturgis looked at the usually overly-serious scientist, scowling at the man's joke. Van Patten chuckled, and then said, "Go ahead. Try it. I'm about as certain as one can get that we're safe."

"Well, doc; believe it or not," answered the

101

C.A.D.S. commander as he hefted the LWA, "your word is good enough for me." He squeezed off a burst. Ruby light played out in a wide arc, slicing backward through the cavern rock in the distance. Sturgis quickly narrowed the beam, bringing it rapidly down to a one-foot wide level. Keeping an eye on the blue light shining alongside the LWA's surface, the C.A.D.S. commander alternated from bursts of power to steady streams, causing an even greater amount of damage to the surrounding cavern than Van Patten had with Charlie.

Minute after minute he slashed the walls with laser swords, cutting deeply into the rock formations, almost daring the LWA to go into the red. The several times he coaxed it to the barest of pinkish flickers, he would cut back, trying to anticipate how soon he could cut the power back in without going over into the red. After ten minutes' testing, he asked Van Patten: "Well, what do you think, Ace? Can we take our toys out to play with us next time?"

The scientist shrugged his bony shoulders. "Two small problems, Colonel. Firstly, even if we had a supply of LWAs with the light meters in stock, I'm really not sure I'd be all that eager to turn them over to you. I hate killing our own men. But I only have *this* one equipped with the overload lights—and I don't have more NX-3 diodes to make more. The Exrell Corporation was supposed to deliver thirty dozen of the super-diodes the day before the nuke attack came. Their truck never showed up."

Sturgis frowned. "This is it? Just this *one*? Are you telling me that the only metered LWA in the base is the one I've got slung over my shoulder? Come on,

Van Patten, just how long will it take you to convert fifty more of them?"

"Forever." The scientist ran his hand up the side of his pock-marked face. Shrugging again, he continued, "We don't have the *parts*—as I've told you—to convert. In another few months I might have five or six . . . *might*, I said. You find that last truck of components we never received someday, and I'll fit all your boys out. But until then, or some other miracle, it's just this one LWA. Comprende?"

"Yeah. I understand. I'll tell General Knolls to get a task force together to track down that missing truck. Guy might have had a breakdown, laid over a day somewhere, and when the war came, just left it on the road between Silicon Valley and here. If so, we'll find it. But I want to head out of here soon, and I want at least *this* LWA with me."

Before the pair could say anything further, de Camp called from the doorway of the booth, "Hey, you two; it's past mess call." Waving her hand toward all the fallen rock she finished, "If you two are done with the redecorating, you might want to take a girl to dinner. What do you say?"

"Oh, no," declared Van Patten. "I'm afraid I have another test group coming in any minute now. I had no idea it was so late."

"Colonel?" she asked.

"Yeah, sure." He told her, "Just give me ten minutes to take a shower and I'm all yours."

De Camp agreed, thinking to herself, If he weren't such a difficult man to like, I might ask him if he wanted company in that shower. Not voicing her opinion, however, she merely contented herself with sitting and waiting as Sturgis de-suited, passing the time by wondering what it would be like to soap the back of Colonel Dean Sturgis. The more she thought about it, the more she thought it might be fun to find out.

CHAPTER EIGHT

Lieutenant Brian Martel, communications officer, night shift radar scanner, sat far underground monitoring the computer terminals of the huge White Sands Communications Center in the heart of the secret military compound. In the days before the war, the wide cinderblock room was just for storage. Now it was filled with an array of pulsing high-tech equipment.

A bevy of computers lined the walls, and above them tracking screens, linked to mini-cams outside, scanned the horizons. Rows of teleprinter machines stood ready to spew out written messages, decoded — if any ever arrived — from friendly sources around the globe. But aside from an infrequent crackle of interference that quickly faded into nothing, the Communications Center had been ominously quiet since the hour of the Russian attack.

Still, Brian Martel worked, and worked hard, his oversized earphones strapped to his head, his hands spinning the dials on his receiver. He sent out constant streams of communication. *Nothing*. Nothing except bands of buzzsaw-like transmissions — the impossibly-scrambled Soviet military transmissions. Not really expecting to accomplish any de-coding of the bizarre radio chatter, Martel worked to keep from going crazy.

Things had gotten tense at White Sands.

The base population was now well over maximum due to influxes of desperate civvies and fragments of a New Mexico National Guard unit. The constant thoughts of friends and relatives lost, choking on their own blood, lying unburied in heaps, burned in everyone's mind. Already six cases of suicide had been registered and a suicide watch was in effect. One of Brian's fellow com-staffers had plugged himself with a .45 just the other day, leaving a note saying he was sure his wife and kids were dead.

But Brian worked. He was a first-rate communications expert who had graduated at the top of his class at West Point. The war had snuffed out all of America's communications satellites, and the radioactive dust surging across the continent, plus a variety of Russian jamming devices, had caused massive interference for any radio traffic.

He had built a receiver he hoped could de-scramble the Soviet military broadcasts. It was a mass of clipped together wires, tubes, and circuit boards.

He had stayed up two days in a row to build it. Probably, he thought, it would merely blow the fuses. But hell, he had lots of those. He'd give it a try.

He took off the big earphones and crawled under the table and plugged the wire-mess in. Then he came up again, and took the feeder cable and attached it to the receiver. He tuned the receiver to the most powerful Red broadcast, and put on the headphones.

"My God," he exclaimed. He was listening to Russian being spoken. He patched in the recorders, the computer printer began printing out a transcript of the broadcast, translating it into English. His eager hands tore a sheet from the printer: Weather, radiation readings at different locations — even ship-to-shore messages being forwarded! He made sure the printer had plenty of paper and then listened, fascinated, to the results of his creation. What should he do?

He glanced up at the clock. It was 3:30 a.m. Van Patten would be sleeping. But he had to tell somebody! *Sturgis*, he thought. Of course! Colonel Sturgis would appreciate this. He's the only one who acts like he's in control, who seems to know what's really going on. Brian liked Sturgis. He liked the way Sturgis handled that Fascist bastard Clearwell and his gang. He had heard that Sturgis was slated to lead another mission. An attack on the Russians. Brian wanted in on that. Maybe if he showed Sturgis the information he'd get on the list. Martel duped a cassette of the Reds speaking.

A quick ride up the elevator to the barracks level and a trot down a white arched hallway brought him to Sturgis' quarters.

Martel rapped at the door.

"Open," came Sturgis' voice. He entered. Sturgis lay on his back in fatigues, one hand behind his head, the other hoisting a cigarette trailing a thin line of smoke to the bare bulb glowing overhead. Sturgis smiled. He pursed his lips and let fly a row of small smoke rings at the bulb. To his right in the narrow aisle between his bunk and the pale wall sat Fenton and Billy on opposite ends of a bench, a game of poker laid out between them. A glass of scotch occupied Fenton while Billy nursed bourbon. To the left of Sturgis sat Tranh leaning back in a shaky wooden folding chair, his feet on the foot of the bunk. He was throwing tiny darts with uncanny precision into a board on the far wall.

"What's up kid?" Sturgis said as Tranh walked to the cork board, collected six darts and returned to his seat, rocking himself back and forth. "You're Martel right? Communications? A wizard, or so I hear. Well?"

Brian stammered. These guys were his heroes, the men the base had their hopes pinned on.

"It's just that I got this intelligence sir," Brian began. A lump formed in his throat as Tranh let fly with a flurry of darts each landing in a neat circle around the bull's eye, the last hitting dead center.

"What sort of intelligence kid?"

"Well, it's like this, Colonel. I developed this receiver you see, and suddenly I find I'm able to cut through all the interference out there. Not only that, but I tied in a new modem I put together, and suddenly I'm tied into the Russian pipeline, and I'm descrambling their stuff like a breeze. Maybe they're getting a bit careless or something. Don't expect anyone to be listening in. Anyway, I think I've got some pretty hot stuff," he said, producing the cassette.

"For instance, this is off a satellite link-up between Moscow and Washington. I'm not one hundred percent sure of my Russian but I think the stuff's top grade info. Something about the 'Charleston project' being ahead of schedule. Facilities in excellent shape. Full mobilization of army of occupation imminent."

Sturgis crushed his cigarette, placed the cassette in his little recorder and listened to the Russian voice:

"Comrade Bukarov, you must not let the Resistance form. It will be harder to overcome if it is concentrated. Small scattered bands will be a minor problem now. It will be another two to three weeks for build-up in Charleston. We create a superforce to cut the U.S. in two. It will be the army of occupation for the east of the Mississippi. After we finish the east, we move west and occupy the remainder of the continent. But you, Bukarov, must first crush the Appalachian resistance."

"This is pretty rich stuff," said Fenton, looking up from the hand Billy had just dealt him.

"Charleston huh?" said Tranh van Noc, pulling out an Exxon U.S. road map and tacking it to the wall with four of his darts. "Yeah, it makes sense," he said. "But I would have chosen New Orleans myself. They could have used the Mississippi waterway to occupy the country. Russians never did have any good military strategists. Just come at you with massive equipment and numbers."

"Have you shown this to Williamson and Van Patten?" Sturgis asked. "Or General Knolls?"

"No sir," smiled Martel. "Just you guys. And don't

worry, I've got my equipment recording and printing out everything while I'm here."

Sturgis frowned and grunted. "What else you hear?"

"Some numbers on their troop movements. Third-world reaction to the attack, lot of weather reports and rad readings filling the air waves. Looks like things are about as bad out there as we expected. Oh yea, some interesting bits about a submarine called *The Lenin*. They called it a command sub—and mentioned some Red name—Veloshnikov?"

"Veloshnikov!" Sturgis said. "I've heard of him—a hardline bastard. Probably had a lot to do with this war starting." Sturgis ejected the cassette and handed it to Martel. "Go get the printout kid. Whatever is translated. Bring it right to the president, G-3 Area. One of his aides will take it to him. Code word is *Garland*. That'll get you in the first door. Tell them I sent you personally."

"Colonel?"

"Yes, Martel?"

"I'd appreciate it if you'd consider me when you make up your list for the attack force, sir."

Sturgis stood up, patted the young officer on the back. "I'll do what I can, Lieutenant. But really, none of us knows what's going to happen yet. It's all up to Williamson and that bunch. I got a big mouth kid, but I'm still just a colonel. And barely holding on to that sometimes. Don't mistake me for a big shot. Don't mistake me for the head man here. I still follow orders. Now go!"

"Yessir. Thank you sir," said Martel, then he went

out the door and closed it.

Sturgis sat up and studied the maps Tranh had pinned up, especially the East Coast. "So it's Charleston, huh?" Fenton craned his neck to see but Billy held him to the poker game.

"C'mon Fenton, plenty of time for all that. Play out the hand."

Fenton shrugged and studied his cards while Sturgis and Tranh traced lines this way and that across the continent.

"We'd cross here," said Sturgis. "And hit the Appalachians here, then cross here. We should be able to get to the eastern mountains of Tennessee undetected, with any luck. From there we're only three hundred miles or so from Charleston. Billy?"

"Flush," said Billy, laying his hand before the disgruntled Fenton before stepping over the bunk with his long legs to Sturgis' side.

"Yessir," he drawled, his hands finding his back pockets as he hunched and focused his keen eyes on the map.

"You know this area?" Sturgis asked, pointing to South Carolina.

"Sure, Skip. My grandpap's house is right about here," he said, pointing to a spot in the Cumberland Mountains. "Should I phone and have granny put supper on?"

"Ain't no granny," said Fenton absently, immediately regretting the remark. "Sorry," he said quickly. "That was stupid."

"Forget it," said Sturgis.

"What about Charleston, Billy?" Tranh asked

111

quickly, trying to gloss over the grim reminder of what lay ahead of them, a landscape of devastation.

"I know Charleston pretty good too," Billy said.

"What do you think of this approach to the city?" Tranh asked, indicating a line from the mountains of eastern Tennessee southeast into Charleston with his finger.

"Probably makes the most sense. That'd be the last place the Rusky's would expect us from. That's all hill country and pretty rough. A regular force—no Tri-bikes—would find the going hard. My bet is that the hill people wouldn't stand for no Russians walking around in their pretty hills. But they'd welcome us. My mother's family hails from Tennessee."

The phone rang. Sturgis picked up.

He shot a few quick 'yes sirs' into the receiver, then hung it up.

"General Knolls wants the Inner Circle for a meeting, and he's in a hurry. If you guys can desist from your card game for a while."

Sturgis rang up Rossiter and Roberto in their room. "Hey, warriors, General Knolls wants us. Pronto."

Billy put his hand face down. "Mr. Fenton MacLeish of Her Majesty's Black Guard, I will take your money later." Fenton, Sturgis and Tranh rode the elevator together to G-3. A marine guard checked their names off on a clipboard and they were ushered in from the hallway into the G-3 security area by two guards. The space they entered was a massive, cathedral-like cavern room.

A large circular table with two dozen seats, some occupied, some not, faced them.

112

The seats to the left had rows of generals and admirals, the new Joint Chiefs of Staff. Sturgis recognized Van Patten and several of the men he had rescued from the White House bunker including Admiral Turner, CIA Director Quartermain, General Abrams of the Air Force, and the acerbic, red-haired General Burns, Chief of the Army. Rossiter, Dixon and Fuentes were seated too. The president was seated at the far end of the table. On his right was Gridley, the old white-haired science advisor, and on his left sat Jerry Morton, the president's aide-de-camp. Fenton, Tranh and Sturgis found seats alongside Morton. Knolls rushed in, clutching a folder, and winked and sat next to Sturgis.

As soon as everyone was seated, Williamson rose and addressed the gathering.

"Gentlemen, I've called this meeting at this ungodly hour to report that we are now in possession of solid intelligence relating to the location and intention of the Red invasion forces. We know that the Russians are landing in force in Charleston, South Carolina, thanks to a young genius named Brian Martel—a new Edison. The Reds intend to support a vast army of occupation from the Charleston camp. Monitored broadcasts indicate a massive buildup of personnel and equipment and some sort of new construction and a gigantic naval vessel in the harbor itself. Gentlemen, with this knowledge, I must give new consideration to Colonel Sturgis' plan to launch an immediate C.A.D.S. equipped attack eastward. Plan 'Tech Battleground' as Sturgis called it, aimed directly at the Soviet's jugular, must be implemented."

Van Patten shot to his feet and slammed his knuckles onto the table. "Begging your pardon, Mr. President, but such a plan would be sure suicide. We'd do nothing but lose our last remaining effective force. The C.A.D.S. unit is no longer a big secret to the Reds. They can pull off a rescue mission sure, or even espionage. But to send a lousy one hundred men into the jaws of the enemy, even if they are C.A.D.S. forces, would be a disaster. First of all, they'd have absolutely no air cover at all. And even a C.A.D.S. suit can't take a direct hit from a MIG air-to-surface missile. Secondly, if the build-up is anything like we have heard, the Russians will be able to take their losses indefinitely and still destroy our troopers one by one. Then where'd we be? At least now we have White Sands. With the entire C.A.D.S. force as a defensive unit, we're practically impregnable here. And we're growing every day, we can build a whole civilization right here, underground!"

"Unless they choose to drop a few dozen h-bombs on our noggins," Sturgis said emphatically, "Just what's to stop the Russians from doing that?"

"The simple fact that they don't know where we are, Colonel. We need no heroics here. Just why are you so anxious to march off to battle?"

"I figure that's just what we do need about now," he replied. "Some heroics. It's too late to be careful, Mr. President. If we're ever going to get our licks in in this war, we better get going. We're missing out on everything. Besides, I don't exactly relish the thought of starting a whole civilization of *mole*-people.

People are already starting to get pretty neurotic down here, holed up underground all the time. It just ain't healthy."

"There's not much that *is* healthy in the good old U.S.A.," interjected Admiral Turner. "We all have to realize that now. Our first requirement right now, Mr. President, is survival. Pure and simple. I'm not a scientist. And I don't think I'm any more or less scared of battle than anyone else. But I'm practical too. And I hold that we're best off holding up right here at White Sands until we're back on our feet."

"And just how long do you expect to hide out here? Weeks? Months? Years?" asked Sturgis.

"But Admiral," President Williamson said, "just what is the advantage of holding up here at White Sands? What do we have to gain by that?"

"We can gain time to consolidate, to regroup our forces. For instance, if the men we sent out to find the missing Exrell Corp. truck succeed, we can build 50 more LWA's. And we have several jets—"

"But not enough *fuel* to get half of them across the country, let alone back," remarked General Abrams of the Air Force. "We were caught with our pants down on that one, along with everything else."

"True," said Turner. "But there's some fuel at bases in California. We could send a truck convoy out there, secure the fuel, and get back here with it. In the meantime we can get that Lieutenant Martel working on contacting militia units with his equipment. I figure we could get a sizable air force together, plus a good sized militia. Maybe we could organize enough to hold a line at the Mississippi River. At least save

115

half the country in, say two months."

"You're dreaming, Admiral," said Sturgis. "You've been reading too many adventure novels. There's not going to be any civilian militia or makeshift Air Force to match the Soviets. If we try, *that* would be a suicide mission, not the C.A.D.S. commando attack. C.A.D.S. is an armored high-tech radiation-shielded unit. Ready to fight *now*. If we don't strike a blow quickly, before the Reds deploy a couple of million troops—before they settle in, we'll be *beaten*. As far as the missing supply truck—it's a needle in the haystack. The Reds would like nothing better than for you to collect up all the scattered military supplies around the country in one nice tiny package for them. You heard Martel's tapes? That's just what they want. They want us to be slow about counter-attacking them. They're counting on that. And say we did collect forty planes together, or fifty, and even through some miracle got fuel through to them. Do you suppose you'd get within five hundred miles of Charleston, or any Russian base? They'd scramble eight hundred MIGs to meet you in no time. And if you shot *them* all down they'd have sixteen hundred to meet you at the next stop. You forget pal: They still have their industrial might intact, as far as we know. We're operating on scraps and there ain't much of that.

"We've got to play our trump card now, or we're out of the game for good. We've got to implement my plan, code-named *tech battleground*."

There was a long pause as Sturgis' words sank in, sighing through the cavernous room.

116

"I'm afraid Colonel Sturgis is correct, Admiral," Williamson said, then looking at each of the other joint chiefs in turn. One by one they all looked down and stared at their clenched hands. They all remembered too well how they hadn't believed the Russians had actually been attacking. They had no desire to hold back Sturgis' plan. Van Patten sat with his arms at his side, deflated. Finally he slouched to his seat realizing he had lost. A show of hands was for Sturgis' plan.

"Now," said Williamson, "what are the details of 'Tech Battleground,' given that Charleston is the new target?"

Sturgis looked at his watch. "We muster C.A.D.S. forces by 8 p.m. We travel by land all the way to avoid radar. We'll need complete surprise. I need the cream of the Omega Force, on Tri-wheelers, and a Rhino. That'll leave one hundred C.A.D.S. troops to defend the base, together with your regular forces. My officer staff the same as always, Tranh here, MacLeish, Billy Dixon, Rossiter, and Roberto Fuentes. And," he added after a second, "I'd like to take Brian Martel along if possible as my chief communications man."

"Impossible," said Van Patten. "Martel must stay at the base to work on his receiver. It's vital that the president and joint chiefs be informed of developments on all fronts. Martel's device is our only hope for that."

"I agree with Van Patten on that," said Williamson. "We need Martel here. He'll be able to accomplish much more working at the Communications Center

117

than on a battle trek."

Sturgis had to nod. He had done his best. "Of course sir, I understand," he said. "I'm confident that the C.A.D.S. force could execute a complete surprise attack at Charleston. One-hundred C.A.D.S. troops loose in one city is a hell of a lot of firepower. I believe we'll be able to sabotage their naval vessels in the harbor. I plan to scuttle their whole fleet *from underneath*, before we even open up on land. Wipe out their naval support. Our equipment operates underwater."

"All right, Sturgis," said Williamson, "I have the utmost confidence in you and your men. God knows I wouldn't be here if it wasn't for you. Put *Tech Battleground* into operation immediately. Gentlemen, let's give the colonel our full co-operation and wish him the best of luck on this most hazardous mission."

Sturgis stood and saluted, receiving a salvo of praise from the assembly of generals and admirals. Then Sturgis and his team turned and left.

They rode the elevator to the barracks level and walked through the corridors toward Sturgis' quarters. Down the hall Sturgis could see the slim figure of Brian Martel approach as they turned a corner. A small lump formed in his throat. Usually Sturgis wasn't bothered by such things, but he knew it would be hard to break the news to Martel that he wouldn't be with the expedition. He knew how much it meant to the kid. Even in the brief moment he had spoken with him before, he could tell that Martel was extremely excited at the prospect of heading out. Sturgis didn't exactly know how to break it to the guy that he couldn't go.

"Tranh, I'll see you later. I have to talk to Martel."

Sturgis continued down the hall after leaving Tranh at his door and met Martel.

"C'mon," he said to the kid, who could tell with one look what was up. Sturgis, his arm over the smaller man's shoulder, led Martel down a flight of steps to the engineering level where the C.A.D.S. suits were stored.

"You're *too* good kid," said Sturgis as he checked on his C.A.D.S. suit. "You know, they won't let you go. We need you here. The U.S. comes ahead of individuals. We all have our job to do. How about suiting up and going out to check out the systems a bit anyway?"

Sturgis could see that Martel was near tears. Suddenly he was secretly glad the kid wasn't going with them. The young man suddenly seemed a bit unstable to him. There was a thin line between genius such as his, and going off the deep end.

"No . . . no thanks," Martel stammered vacantly, staring off into space and walking away.

"Don't let it eat you kid," Sturgis called after him. "Like I said, we all got our jobs to do." He watched as the kid disappeared into the elevator, heading down.

Sturgis suited up, rode up to the staging area at the top level of the base, just below the surface. He boarded one of the Tri-wheelers kept there and, after getting the all clear from the rad-man, passed through the decontamination chamber that had been set up between the outside and the base.

119

"Rad reading," Sturgis ordered his suit's computer. The readings danced across his visor, showing a "moderately dangerous" level, meaning exposure outside the C.A.D.S. for over an hour or so could cause permanent health damage. He shook his head. Rad readings in the area were constantly on the rise due to unusual winds from the regions struck in the east. Surface activity had been curtailed as much as possible both to prevent detection by the Soviets and to prevent radiation poisoning. C.A.D.S. suits were required by anyone with clearance to leave the base.

Sturgis rode at top speed in the direction the C.A.D.S. force would be heading, constantly scanning his radar sensor for signs of an enemy jet overhead, or perhaps a column of Russian tanks rumbling through the neighborhood. One never knew what to expect in devastated post-WWIII America.

Eating up the smooth desert landscape at a brisk 80 mph, Sturgis thought of what lay ahead. His mind seemed to be speeding along faster than the Tri-wheeler.

Robin, according to the note she had left for him at their Virginia farm, had headed for the Stony Mountain Monument Park in Georgia. He knew she would wait there as long as she could for him.

The mission's objective — Charleston — was less than 500 miles from Stony Mountain. If there was any way in hell to cross that distance without jeopardizing the men or the mission to reach her, he sure as hell would.

For the rest of the check-out, his thoughts were of Robin and little else.

Sturgis was back at base in 45 minutes. After parking the Tri-bike and slipping into his black coveralls with the Omega symbol emblazoned on its breast pocket, he was walking to his room when he met technician Wilson. "You looked worried son. Hang in there, okay?"

"Yes sir. Up to seven suicides now, sir."

"Seven?" said Sturgis.

"Yes sir. That Martel. Communications man. Electrocuted himself down in the Comm Center just half an hour ago. Just after you left, Colonel."

CHAPTER NINE

In the still, black harbor of Charleston, South Carolina, a huge metallic monster rose up slowly from the midnight water. It crested the surface like a giant whale. Then, a thick rod rose in the air and a mechanical eye fixed itself on the once-mighty city. The nuclear command submarine *Lenin*, the largest sub in the world at nearly three hundred meters in length, had arrived to claim the shores of America.

Inside the sub, eyes pressed against the periscope, Supreme Marshal Mikael Nikolaevichy Veloshnikov could barely contain his satisfaction at the gruesome scenes of death all around him in the harbor. Even from a distance, the death was visible in the night-scope: Black and green putrefying bodies scattered like broken dolls across the docks and decks of the useless American warships. Many of the bodies still bore tatters of their military uniforms. Obviously they had been annihilated as they scrambled frantically to their commands. Killed in the twin flashes of two Soviet neutron missiles. Cooked from the inside by intense radiation, their blood boiling out their mouths. A pretty picture, pretty enough to frame.

The U.S. military alert had come too slow, too late. Charleston's superb harbor defense system—the Patriot and Pershing II missiles, the submarine and destroyer flotilla's sonar and radar, the Phantom II and Eagle fighter jets at the nearby airbase—were worthless in the face of the two neutron bombs launched from coast-hugging missile subs.

With relish, Veloshnikov imagined what it must have been like for the terrified Americans. He envisioned the scenario. First the attack sirens. Initially, no one believed it. Despite their constant preparation and training, Veloshnikov knew the Americans never really believed the Soviets would ever attack, would ever willingly start a nuclear holocaust. Besides, it was Christmas Eve, and the capitalist Americans were busy indulging in their greedy habits of buying useless objects and stuffing their faces.

During the alert, precious minutes and seconds were, no doubt, wasted while military commanders went up the chain of command to verify it. Only then the U.S. military scrambled to their posts. Panic and pandemonium erupted in the sedate, civilized streets of the genteel South. Those who had no idea what to do—the complacent, overstuffed, overweight civilian population—tried to stampede to safety. The military personnel made a laughable attempt to man battle positions in their futile efforts to stop the bombs before their searing, blinding inferno turned Charleston into a massive cemetery, a death-museum of funeral ships and buildings.

Yes, that was how Veloshnikov imagined Charleston's final, desperate moments. He wished he could have witnessed its death throes.

"How is it, Supreme Marshal?"

The voice of Veloshnikov's second-in-command and captain of the submarine, Ilya Ivanovitch Guriev, interrupted his reverie.

Veloshnikov grunted. "Most satisfactory, Captain Ivanovitch. Most physical structures appear to remain in excellent condition." That was the beauty of the neutron bomb—it could destroy life without destroying buildings, making it perfect for the conquering army to step in and set up operations with a minimum of inconvenience. A few bodies to sweep up, a little broken glass—and the radiation, of course, to shield against. But no rubble, no charred ruins of any consequence. And neutron rads fade quickly, Veloshnikov was pleased.

"And life?" asked Guriev. "Are there any signs of life?"

"Only the rats and the sharks that have come for the feast." Veloshnikov pulled himself away from the periscope. "Would you like to see?"

"Thank you, Supreme Marshal," Guriev said enthusiastically. He, too, was anxious to see the effects of the neutron bombs. The idea that bombs could wipe out humans without destroying their dwellings seemed incredible to him.

Guriev grabbed the handles of the periscope and gasped as he surveyed the death scene in the harbor. Then he composed himself. He was a citizen of the Soviet Union, a member of the victorious forces, an officer of the mighty sub *Lenin*. He must conduct himself coolly, not act like a schoolboy watching a peepshow. "Interesting," he said.

Veloshnikov ran his fingers through his dark, wavy

hair and slapped his middle. At 57, he was fit and trim, having worked hard to avoid going to seed as did so many of his male Russian contemporaries who had too great a fondness for vodka. He felt every inch the conquering general, and very soon he would at last set foot on the hated soil of America.

"We're going ashore," he announced. "Tell the landing party. I will ride the launch, in forty-five minutes."

"Yes sir! Right away, Supreme General." Guriev barked orders for the periscope to be lowered, and hurried off into the bowels of the giant sub.

After a few moments, Veloshnikov followed Guriev out, wending through the metal innards of the great beast *Lenin*. The nuclear-powered attack submarine was the flagship of the Soviet submarine fleet, built at the Sudomekh Shipyards in Leningrad. It plowed the world's oceans with a 625,000-ton displacement, armed with twenty SS-20 nuclear torpedos and every conceivable defense. Fully equipped and stocked, it provided a self-sufficient environment to its crew for up to two years, meaning the *Lenin* could outlast virtually any adverse conditions. That's why it was the operations center, the hub for the great last war. It was invulnerable.

Veloshnikov walked through the sub until he came to the *Lenin*'s Naval War Command Center and entered its wide hatchway. Before him, a giant map of the United States was lit up and displayed on a screen. Color-coded dots indicated the phase of the Soviet take-over. The map was littered with black dots indicating all the cities that had been bombed and subdued. Red stars showed Soviet bases and beachheads. Veloshnikov found the one that marked Charleston. A preliminary landing party had already searched the city and declared it devoid of life, had measured its radiation level — still quite high one month after the bombing — and had scouted sites for the Soviet command center that was to be established here.

A few green dots were sprinkled over the map. They were known pockets of American survivors and resisters, armed and undoubtedly dangerous, most in the Appalachian Mountains. Some were known to be only ragged bands of wild thugs scratching for a primitive survival. Other groups were more organized cells of patriotic fanatics trying to make a last stand. Even if they all were on the verge of dying from radiation sickness, they had to be eliminated as soon as possible. The Soviets could take no chances on even the slimmest resistance movement gaining momentum.

Veloshnikov observed the green dot not too far from Charleston, somewhere in the Blue Ridge Mountains. Hate blossomed in his heart. Finding and eradicating these vermin would be his first priority, after setting up a well defended headquarters.

"Death to you, fools who dare to fight back," he muttered. "Every one of you will be tracked down and exterminated."

The Soviet launch plowed through the eerie, still coastal waters. From the forward and vertical view-cameras projected on a screen, Veloshnikov could see the awesome, heavy cloud cover hanging over a nearly dead world. The land, sea and sky were still in the grip of nuclear trauma. Sickly gray-green clouds

127

billowed in the sky, sending down a radioactive drizzle. No birds graced the air currents. The sea looked dull and oily, the currents broken occasionally by the fin of a shark that had survived the radioactive bombardment. Sharks and rats and cockroaches — what appropriate survivors in the New World, thought Veloshnikov. Survival of the fittest, the most vicious creatures.

The land, as the launch drew nearer, had a frozen-in-time look to it. The closer Veloshnikov and his crew got, the more details bloomed into view. The magnitude of the horror became apparent. Entering Charleston's once bustling harbor, the launch slowed, giving all on board ample time to view each passing scene.

Warships and merchant ships, now ghost hulks, rocked gently at the docks. None of the warships had been able to get out of the harbor before the bombs went off; indeed, few even left their dock slips.

American flags hung in ribbons from the masts of every ship, symbols of an arrogant nation whipped to its knees. "Captain Guriev," Veloshnikov began, using the formal address instead of his subordinate's first name and patronymic, "make sure these ridiculous American flags are replaced at the soonest opportunity with the hammer and sickle. Have a task force named to make these ships operational."

The bodies of the dead were bloated like pus-filled balloons. Many had been ravaged by the scavenging seagulls, or rats, their flesh gnawed and torn away, bloody hunks of it left behind as the predators had

.become sated.

The stench. God, the wind smelled dreadful, thought Veloshnikov. Beyond endurance. A combination of neutron blast, fire, decay. Bodies that had been rotting in the recent thaw. He was thankful they were well away from the ships.

He shifted, covering his nose with a sleeve. Guriev and the others in the landing party were silent. Guriev looked like a Roman general at a victory march through Gaul. A good soldier he was, but a bit too serious, too posed, too filled with his own importance. Such a man could be dangerous.

A couple of the men, the juniors in the crew, looked distressed and were struggling to hide it. Gutless, sniveling worms! the Supreme Marshal thought, his brain burning in disgust.

Veloshnikov turned to the men, his fury showing, his clenched fist raised. The offending juniors cast their eyes downward in fear of his wrath.

"What's wrong with you two?" Veloshnikov fairly shouted into the wind of their swift passage. "Is the sight of war too much for your weak stomachs?"

Everyone in the launch turned to stare at the two offenders, who looked at the deck and shook their heads.

"Eyes forward!" snapped Guriev. "Show respect!"

The two men looked up at Veloshnikov, now more fearful of punishment than of the death scenes on all sides of them.

"I asked you a question!" roared the Supreme General.

"No, sir," they mumbled.

"No, sir what!"

129

"No, sir, the sight of war is not too much for our weak stomachs," one quavered.

Veloshnikov fixed them both with a steely gaze. "Captain Guriev, I want both of these men assigned to special detail after we land. Put them in charge of body disposal. I want a full report within twenty-four hours of landing on how they plan to collect and dispose of all the dead in Charleston."

"Yes, sir, Supreme General!" Guriev made a smart salute.

"And the rest of you better keep in mind that we are *still* at war. America's regular military is destroyed, but the land is infested with idealistic resisters who will make a useless but determined effort to stop us. When you look at the destruction around you, feel glad about it! If it hadn't been for our preemptive strike—for our superior strength and intelligence—this could be *your* hometown instead! If any man feels differently, he will be sent home in disgrace to keep the women and grandmothers company!"

"Yes, sir, Supreme General!" chorused the men.

Veloshnikov made a mental note to put the two junior men under observation for further signs of weakness. He would tolerate no defective men in his command. This shameful behavior would go in their dossiers.

At the dock where the launch was to tie up, the leaders of the preliminary landing and scouting party waited to greet Veloshnikov.

"We have inspected the entire city and it is secure," announced Colonel Yuri Molokin, saluting as Veloshnikov stepped ashore.

Veloshnikov grunted. His anger at the two snivelling subordinates still hadn't dissipated. "Is that *all* you've done since you got here?" he sneered.

"No, sir, not at all sir," responded the blond colonel, puzzled at the general's testiness. "We've identified several sites for the base and have prepared for your inspection. The bodies have been sealed in this area — to — "

"Very well. Let's get on with it."

Captain Guriev assigned several men to stay with the landing boat and dispatched the hapless snivellers to attend to a body disposal plan. Only Guriev would accompany the marshal and Molokin on the land tour of inspection.

As they walked along the decks, avoiding sani-bagged bodies, Veloshnikov forgot his anger and took in everything around him. The drizzle had lifted and, even though the sun had yet to break the clouds since the bombing, the view around him was clear.

America! He had set his own feet upon this despised, enemy soil! Not as a visitor, or as a captive, but as a *conqueror*. It was revenge at last, and the taste of it rose up sweet in his mouth.

They got into a U.S. Army jeep salvaged from the depot, and the Soviet driver began the journey through the streets of the city, placing a hammer and sickle flag on the front fender.

The streets were desolate. Charleston was a ghost town. The office buildings stood ready to embrace a bustle of workers. Goods displayed in windows awaited shoppers. But none came. None would ever come.

A traffic jam of cars, trucks and buses filled many

of the lanes. Doors hung open, indicating their occupants had abandoned them in panic. Some occupants still sat, bony fingers clutching their steering wheels, black faces like death-masks.

Veloshnikov turned to Guriev in the back seat. "I want a body disposal report in twelve hours, not twenty-four. We've got to burn these bodies as soon as possible, or we'll have a terrible pestilence problem on our hands."

Indeed, bodies were everywhere. The population of Charleston proper was 80,000, and it was safe to assume that the majority had died in the greater metropolitan area. Some undoubtedly had staggered off to the mountains, but most were here, polluting the streets and buildings with their decay. The preliminary Soviet landing party, unable to arrive until the radiation level had decreased, had been able to get rid of only a small percentage of human carnage. It was going to be an immense job.

As they drove, rats skittered among the bodies and the piles of garbage. Veloshnikov could see some flesh remains crawling with cockroaches, the other invincible survivors of the cataclysm. A hundred million years old—and they would outlive man!

Molokin, sitting in the back seat and brandishing a PKM automatic rifle on his knee, occasionally levelled it at a rat and blasted the creature apart with a burst of 7.62-mm fire.

"The Americans affectionately called South Carolina the Palmetto State," Molokin remarked, acting like a tour guide. "This street here—East Bay Street—used to be called Rainbow Row. I imagine because the homes here were supposed to be elegant in their day."

132

Veloshnikov surveyed the townhouses. Imagine, these huge structures for only one family each! Why, in Moscow several families would be thrilled to share such quarters. The waste and greed of these capitalist dogs was disgusting.

"Palmetto State!" Veloshnikov stifled an impulse to spit, an impossible act in an anti-rad suit. "I claim this land in the name of Russia! It is now the *People's* State of the Union of Soviet Socialist Republics!"

Few of Veloshnikov's subordinates and peers understood the real reason for his intense hatred of America. It had little to do with Soviet ideals, loyalty to the Motherland, or anything of the sort. He hated America and everything it stood for because it was America that destroyed his beloved family.

Involuntarily, his mind slipped back to those awful days in Hanoi in 1972, before the Americans finally gave up on the Viet Nam War and pulled out. Veloshnikov had been a military attache assigned to Hanoi. How young and idealistic he was in those days! He'd come home one day to find his house smashed from an American bombing raid—his beautiful wife and two precious children dead. He'd never stopped hating the Americans since, and had vowed revenge. It took more than twenty years to get it, but it was worth the wait.

"Look out!" a shout filled the air.

The jeep careened to a stop so sharply Veloshnikov was almost thrown out. But he seized the dash and hung on. He heard Guriev behind him crunch into the back of his seat.

No sooner had he gotten his bearings than Veloshnikov saw the cause of the ruckus. A strange creature—the pathetic remains of a radiation-sick human—was lurching in the street in front of them, waving an M-16 American automatic rifle. The creature was screaming out unintelligibly. Its red eyes were wide and vicious-looking, its exposed flesh covered with running sores. Before any of the Russians could react, the wretch began spraying bullets at them.

A horrible scream cut through the air above the sound of the bullets, and Veloshnikov saw the driver, his smart dress jacket suddenly wet with bright red blood, topple out of the jeep onto the pavement. The marshal ducked as low as he could behind the dash and pulled out his own pistol. There was an answering burst of fire from Molokin.

For an awful moment it was impossible to tell which weapon would triumph. Then the bullet-riddled attacker—what was left of him—crumpled to the street.

In the smoke-filled silence that followed, Molokin got out of the jeep and crouched beside it, surveying the street and the buildings around them for signs of other attackers. Guriev, after assuring his commanding officer that he was unhurt, did the same. At last they satisfied themselves that there were no more ambushers. They dragged the driver's body to the sidewalk. A recovery team would be dispatched to pick it up.

"The attacker was a man acting alone," Molokin announced calmly to Veloshnikov. He and Guriev climbed back in the jeep. Molokin took the wheel.

"I thought you secured this city and reported no life," Veloshnikov said icily as he put his pistol back in the suit holster.

"We did, Supreme General, sir," Molokin said, an anxious note in his voice. He did not want to incur the famous Veloshnikov anger, nor have an official reprimand entered into his file. "This man undoubtedly was an outlander — someone hiding out in the mountains outside the city. An aberration."

"Indeed? And how do you explain his penetration of the security system you supposedly established around Charleston?"

Molokin squirmed, "The force here is very small, sir, pending the arrival of the *Lenin* and backup troops from the carrier *Kiev*."

"I see." Veloshnikov was silent a moment, reflecting on this inexcusable laxity, and the need, more urgent than ever, to eradicate the mountain resistance. "Do not let it happen again, Colonel Molokin. Ever!"

They resumed the official business at hand — the selection of a site for the Supreme Soviet Command Headquarters. Molokin's men had identified a number of potential sites, but the final decision was up to Veloshnikov.

". . . the municipal building, the seat of local government, of course offers fine facilities," noted Molokin as they drove past. "Would you like to inspect the interior?"

Veloshnikov shook his head. "Perhaps later, but first I want to see all exteriors. The headquarters must be grand to behold. A place to invite dignitaries."

Nor was the supreme general much impressed by the office buildings, the performing arts center, the public library, the old Dock Street Theatre, or the charmingly historic but woefully inadequate powder magazine.

"What else is there?" he demanded.

"Homes, Supreme General. Perhaps a mansion—?" To Molokin, the soft luxury of a mansion seemed inappropriate for a command base, which required desks, computers, telephones and other services that would be needed. But who was he to say?

He headed the jeep out into the suburbs, where deceivingly serene lanes were lined with live oaks, birch, beech and maple trees. Many had lost their foliage, giving the scene an odd wintry look that was further emphasized by the gray pallor of the sky. Long strands of Spanish moss still hung from a few huge boughs of live oaks. Veloshnikov had to admit that Charleston must have been a beautiful city. But it would rise to even greater beauty and glory under the hammer and sickle!

"Stop!" the supreme general suddenly commanded. "Stop here!"

Molokin screeched the jeep to a halt. They were opposite a magnificent ante-bellum mansion, its great columns and huge coach lanterns creating a spectacular entrance.

"*Tara*," whispered Veloshnikov. Once, as a boy, he'd seen a black market copy of the film *Gone With the Wind*. He'd never gotten over his awe of the mansions possessed by the Southern American genteel. And now, right in front of him, was one for the taking.

"Tara?" asked Guriev. "What is Tara?"

"A place in Georgia you never heard about," answered Veloshnikov, leaving the captain to puzzle out what he assumed was a reference to Soviet Georgia.

Veloshnikov got out of the jeep and approached the graceful home. "The base will be here," he said. "Code named Tara. Order the anti-radiation shield to go up immediately."

An inspection of the interior revealed ten bodies—three adult men, three adult women, three children of varying ages and an infant. They were huddled together, still clutching one another. They smelled.

A movement in his peripheral vision caught Veloshnikov's attention. It proved to be a black-and-white cat. It had somehow managed to survive the radiation but appeared to be staggering on its last legs. The pitiful remains of its fur stood out in dry tufts against its inflamed red skin.

The supreme general hated cats. He yanked out his Tokarev and with a single, well-placed shot splattered the cat's brains all over the wall.

The structure and contents of Tara were in excellent condition. Food had rotted in the kitchen, but the shelves were stocked with many canned goods that might be free of radiation.

Veloshnikov barked out orders as he went through the house, Guriev and Molokin following behind. ". . . dispose of these bodies and disinfect the premises immediately . . . the communications center will go in here . . ."

Everywhere, the signs of a life of luxury greeted them. It angered Veloshnikov. The extravagant waste was appalling, and it would give him great satisfaction to commandeer this place for the State.

When they reached the master bedroom suite upstairs, the supreme general was staggered by the ostentatiousness of it—a king-size bed covered in rich blue velvet; heavy satin curtains gracing floor-to-ceiling French windows; an enormous crystal chandelier; white carpeting; and ornate antique white furniture. A 30″ television set! Off to one side, not one, but *two* baths, done in exquisite white marble with gilt fixtures. Not even royalty deserved to live like this!

"This room will have to do for my quarters," Veloshnikov announced.

In a subdued but rich oak-panelled library, the supreme marshal found a bottle of *Southern Comfort* hidden away in a steel filing cabinet. He tested it with his miniature Japanese made radiation meter and found, to his delight, that it was clean. He tucked the bottle under his arm.

CHAPTER TEN

The atmosphere at White Sands was charged the next night as everyone hurried about to help prepare the attack force. Sturgis had met with General Knolls and the president and showed them his roster of troopers for the C.A.D.S. attack force.

When the list was finally posted at 7:30 am, the men crowded around to learn their fate. Some were excited at the prospect of going, others despondent at not being chosen. The next minute, those chosen to go would be indifferent, while those staying behind would be thanking their lucky stars. No one knew quite what to feel anymore.

The motor pool bristled with activity as every Tri-wheeler was inspected and serviced. The underground cave's proving grounds thundered with weapons checkouts. Food and water, provisions to last 100 plus men for 20 days, were packed, and each man given his rations to store in his Tri-bike. In all, the special package included about 30 pounds of food and 4 gallons of water. These represented minimal require-

139

ments, and Sturgis hoped some supplies could be secured en route. In addition, each man was required to carry his ordnance package, about 480 pounds of firepower including rockets, Electro-balls, 9mm machine gun ammo, and darts for the Tri-bikes and the C.A.D.S. suits. Finally, the remaining storage space in the Tri's was filled by having each man carry one or more pieces of special equipment or machinery needed by the expedition. These included everything from axes and tents to drills and fuses. The men were issued spare parts for the C.A.D.S. suits and Tri-bikes. Six of the Tri-wheelers were fitted out with small trailers full of supplies to be used on the first leg of the journey, when they would be travelling over even terrain and would not require too much maneuverability.

The C.A.D.S. suits themselves were given a thorough testing. Each suit represented a level of technical sophistication that far outreached that of the Apollo space flights. One by one the computer chips that operate the weapons systems, communications systems, sensors, strength actuators, jump and hover systems, and environmental controls, were tested. Then, the systems themselves were inspected. Each suit was put through a rigorous two-hour field test, inspected again, refitted with armament, and recharged. As the suits left the engineering plant each trooper picked up the C.A.D.S. unit he was to wear.

The men chosen for the mission gathered here and there, checking out their Tri-wheelers, or just gabbing and smoking. They were the cream of the crop, America's finest young men, patriotic, intelligent, fit. And proficient in high-tech combat. These hand-picked warriors had esprit de corps not unlike that of the pilots of the Royal Air Force who had fought and won the desperate Battle of Britain. The men of the Omega Force knew that their mission was even more important than that great battle. And they had another reason for attacking the Reds. Revenge.

Every C.A.D.S. nuke-trooper had lost people dear to them in the Soviet first strike. Most knew they had lost not only their families and friends, but most likely their homes, their neighborhoods, their towns—virtually blown off the face of the earth in a swirling million-degree maelstrom. The C.A.D.S. nuke-troopers licked their chops at the prospect of wielding the awesome fire-power of the C.A.D.S. suits on the Soviet enemy. The more the better.

As the men lined up for medical check-ups and inoculations Danny Magee, a diminutive weapons expert and part time wise-guy from Brooklyn started kidding "fatty" Rossiter that he was getting a bit overweight.

"Look at that stomach," he called out. "How in hell you going to get into your C.A.D.S. suit, Ross? Somebody better bring along a can opener in case you get *stuck*."

Rossiter had adjusted to the barbs, the first-rate engineer chuckled along with the others, then, in his suit he casually walked over to the quaking Magee, lifted him up by his neck with one hand, and hung him from his belt on a nearby coat hook. Magee kicked and struggled like a bug to the amusement and delight of the entire crowd. By the time he worked himself free a good belly laugh was had by all.

The muster of troops continued at a hectic pace

141

throughout the day. Sturgis met with the squad as a whole at 2 p.m., telling them they would leave that evening in order to afford themselves the cover of darkness for the first couple of legs of the journey. He did not want their departure to be noticed by a Russian MIG casually zooming overhead.

Next Sturgis began meeting with the men in smaller groups, detailing to each man what was expected of him on the mission. The men were told what to do in case they were captured or separated from the main force. At all costs, the suit must be destroyed in case of imminent capture, they were told. And of course, if any knowledge of their mission was leaked to the Reds, they would all be doomed. Therefore, knowing that the enemy would stop at nothing to extract information, each man's suit was equipped with a built-in cyanide injector. "Painless; quick," Sturgis said. "But before you commence your own self-destruct, make sure you set the destruct codes in the computer to make the C.A.D.S. suit a bomb ready to go off if anyone attempts to open it and find its secrets."

Finally everything was beginning to come together. Fenton and his technicians pulled the Rhino out of the motor pool and drove it into the cavernous main exit ramp. It was about 5:00 pm, just before dinner and about three hours before scheduled departure. The schedule called for dinner at 5:30, then the men were to relax and rest before meeting at the ramps at 8:00 pm.

The nuke-troopers began driving their Tri-bikes out onto the concrete floor, and into position with the Rhino. Then they dismounted, congregated around the big RV-like battlewagon, smoking cigarettes and shooting the breeze. The atmosphere was at once tense and relaxed, uncertain and electrified. Finally, to everyone's relief, the bell rang announcing chow.

The entire White Sands population filed into the base Mass Hall. Even the less serious hospital ward patients — rad victims mostly — some with ghastly reddish blotches scarring them, attended. The C.A.D.S. Attack Squad sat at a long table along one wall. The president sat at its head, the troopers were fifty on a side. In all there were 600 people gathered, all craning to see the squad members.

Once everyone was seated, the stewards began bringing in the food. White Sands was now probably the best supplied facility in the U.S., simply because it had doubled as an agricultural center. Also, because it had a deep underground well system, it had a more than ample supply of uncontaminated water.

Steaming potatoes and yams, a small garden salad, with fresh baked rolls hot from the oven, and delicious apple pie was served, followed by plenty of good coffee. There was no meat. The men made short work of the victuals. Those in the A-1 C.A.D.S. Force knew it would be some time before they tasted good fresh food like that again.

Before long, General Knolls stood, and after the room had quieted, introduced President Williamson. The president stepped up to a small podium behind which an American flag had been painted on the wall. He rummaged through some 3" × 5" cards.

"Fellow citizens. Tonight we have all shared a meal dedicated to the brave men chosen to undertake the second official mission of the Omega Force. Their first mission was an unqualified success. Myself and my emergency staff owe their lives to them. And if there is an America left today, symbolized by the office I hold as a duly elected representative of the American people, it is because of the bravery of these C.A.D.S. men.

"But that was a rescue mission. An attempt to pick up the pieces after our nation and people were victimized by the greatest crime in human history: the wanton and intentional attempt to destroy an entire nation and its people in one chilling day. Citizens, I must speak plainly and bluntly. All across the American continent the radiation is *still* killing Americans. *140 million dead* is the estimate, I am told. My family, most of your families are among them. The East Coast is being occupied by Soviet troops. America, a country of generous people, a nation that has tried to live up to the slogan "Freedom for all" is *down*. Down but not *out*. There is still hope that it will rise once more.

"We made mistakes. America's leadership, perhaps, put too much faith in our 'invincibility.' It was just too easy to grow less watchful, because it always happened to the other guy.

"I ask you to keep the faith. We will prevail in the end. We have real hope. Our American ingenuity, our mastery of technology, our bravery, vitality, has provided us with the power of the C.A.D.S. Omega Force. It is in them we must place *all* our hope for the present. Colonel Sturgis will lead a mission, calculated to deal a fatal blow to the army of occupation that we now know is massing on our eastern seaboard.

"If we can prevent an army of occupation from taking root in America, *then* we have preserved our liberty.

"We shall mend our homeland. That is my pledge."

With that, Williamson raised his glass filled with the last ration of champagne that White Sands, and perhaps France, had to offer, "To the C.A.D.S. Attack Force, to their victory." Scattered applause, then wild clapping ensued. The Omega Force, the Joint Chiefs of Staff, and the White Sands staff raised their champagne glasses too. They all drank the toast slowly, to savor it.

Dinner had finished at about 6:30 p.m., which gave the troopers of the Omega Force an hour alone, an hour of reflection before they were to meet at the wide ramp and head out.

Most of the troopers chosen for "Tech Battleground" had participated in the rescue mission Sturgis had led to Washington. They were veterans of WWIII, men Sturgis could rely on. When they had gathered at the ramp, Sturgis had one final thing to say.

Solemnly, he took out a piece of chalk.

"I'm going to draw a line down this concrete floor here," Sturgis said, "and I want to tell you something." Dramatically he drew a line about five feet from the wall, 100 feet in length. He stood up and said, "All of you who volunteer to go on this mission will have to cross this line and stand there, facing me. I want to give those who feel that they are not up to this arduous journey a last chance to stay behind. If you honestly feel your presence might jeopardize our goal, don't come. No one will call you cowards.

145

"If you cross this line," he said, "then I will expect that no matter what the hardship, no matter what I command you to do, no matter how bad the situation looks, you will not go back on your word. Those who cross this line will follow me to the death if need be. Is that clear? Any deserters, any shirkers will be shot. Period. If you come down with rad sickness that is too severe for you to go on, you will have the option of taking a painless cyanide injection, or shooting yourself. There is an outside time limit of two weeks for us to get to Charleston and blow the shit out of it. Nothing is going to stop me from fulfilling this order by the president of the United States. *Nothing.* No one man will interfere with this mission. If I am disabled too severely, I will be left behind, like any other man.

"Now who will join me?"

Fenton was jumping down from the hatch of the Rhino and running for the line. He was the first to cross it. With a wide grin, he saluted. Tranh was just an instant behind him. Then the rest of the inner circle — Billy, Roberto, Rossiter, followed. The ranks grew thick, only a few holding back.

In a minute and a half, most of the floor full of Tri-bikes was empty of personnel. A handful of men, with downcast heads, stood their ground where they were.

Sturgis said, "Well, that's it. You men who didn't volunteer, good luck to you here. I hope you will use your skills to further our cause from this base."

The volunteer force went back to their bikes, sat facing the wide steep exit ramp. Those who hadn't crossed the line were instructed to roll their bikes off the floor to the rear.

At exactly 8:10 Sturgis started moving forward. The huge lead-shielded bunker door rolled open slowly, a gust of cold desert air rushing in. He, like the other inner circle members, wore their repaired but battle-scarred C.A.D.S. suits for good luck. It had gotten them through hell already—

Fenton and Rossiter rode in the Rhino, Billy and Roberto headed 12-man squadrons that covered the flanks. Tranh drove alongside Sturgis, who took the lead. The roar increased as the engines gunned for the climb upwards. The huge subterranean ramp was long enough for the whole squad to line up. Ten rows of incalculable firepower, ten rows of God-warriors of the post-nuclear age. The Rhino came up last, with its twin-bike escort.

Once outside as their Tri-bike geigers began clicking, the entire force slipped down their visors. The visors gave every man's face the same shiny black appearance as the rest of the C.A.D.S. suit.

"How's it look out there?" asked Sturgis through his helmet mike.

"Good. All clear, Colonel," replied a voice from the radar scanning room at the outer edge of the base. "I haven't seen any radar activity at all. Good luck."

"Thanks," said Sturgis.

Sturgis slipped his Tri-bike into gear and the huge spiked rear wheels dug into the dust floor. He sped ahead, into the radioactive wasteland that was America.

CHAPTER ELEVEN

A huge trailer-truck rig with DEKESON'S POTATO CHIPS emblazoned on its brilliant white aluminum side came roaring down the Interstate. Inside, the speed-demon driver gripped the big wheel with work-hard hands. His deep green eyes, hidden behind mirror-sun glasses, were glued to the clear road ahead. He had to get west, to Oklahoma, to deliver his twenty thousand Bibles. To spread the word for Jerry Jeff Jeeters' *Christian Crusade*. But he was worried about finding more wreckage or stalled cars on the road. At 90 plus miles per hour, it would be hard to stop the big truck.

His name was Rusty Anders, his CB nickname was Crusher. That was because he was a big man. In Cattauragas, Kentucky, he had won the bear-hug contest at every state fair for years.

He hadn't been a "religious" man until now. He had been a beer guzzling brawler. A womanizer. But Jerry Jeff Jeeters, the People's Reverend, the only

American the Reds let use their television station in South Carolina, had changed him.

Rusty smiled. In his earphones, attached to his Sony Walkman, he heard the blasting song "I Can't Drive 55." True enough, for the message had to be spread, people had to understand Reverend Jeeters when he read scripture. Yessiree.

What was that ahead, dipping in and out of the heat-fog on the road? Some sort of dark objects. A whole mess of motorcycles. He hit the big airbrakes. Sparks flew from the grinding cylinders, calipers grabbed and carved gouges in the brake drums. He didn't know if he could stop in time. They were all across the road, these strange black riders atop their odd motorcycles. And they were coming at him at about the same speed he was approaching them.

Cursing, he worked the gearbox, slamming the tortured stickshift down into lower gear, double-clutching the rig down two more. All the time, standing on the big air brakes.

The cyclists were hitting the brakes also, and smoke was pouring from their big tires as they skidded to a halt. It was over. The truck was stopped. So were the bikers, a mere ten feet from each other.

Rusty jumped down from the cab of the truck, his big pump-action .12 gauge shotgun cradled in his arm. He figured them to be some sort of Russian rad-suited squad. Too many of them, only one of him, but maybe he could take a few of them with him to hell. He raised the gun, then lowered it. The strange black suited men on the odd bikes had American flags painted on their shoulders.

"Hello," Sturgis said. "You can put down that gun, mister. We're American, and I'm pretty damned sure you are too, seeing the way you look."

Rusty Anders did just that. In a half hour, Sturgis had explained most of what C.A.D.S. was about to the trucker, as they sat and talked at some rest stop picnic tables alongside the road.

Anders explained that he was a worker in the Army of God of the Reverend Jeeters.

When Sturgis asked who that was, Anders told him that Jeeters was spreading the holy word, courtesy of the Russians' satellite TV hookup, all across the nation. Anyone with a dish on their roof or lawn could listen in to his revelatory messages.

Sturgis didn't like the sound of that and said so: "This Jeeters—is he some sort of commie? How come the Reds are allowing him, and only him of all Americans, on their network?"

Rusty glanced at his Mickey Mouse watch. "Well, it's about time for a program of the good gospel message of the reverend. I've got a dish to pick up TV on the top of my rig—and a little TV in the back. Come on around the back of the truck and I'll turn on the program. You'll love it."

Skeptically, Sturgis followed Anders. Anders unlocked the back of the truck and opened it up. Sure enough, floor to ceiling, filling the entire rig, were stacks of bibles and right next to the door was a little portable TV, with wire running up through the roof to the three foot wide satellite dish up there.

151

Anders turned the set on. A thirteen inch color screen lit up with the English words—in red over white "Freedom Broadcasting Network, Hartstown South Carolina." Then Sturgis saw a man in a white polyester suit holding a bible.

The TV screen showed the red faced, trembling Jerry Jeff Jeeters as he actually started thumping the Bible in his hand, writhing, almost frothing at the mouth. "Dear Christians," Jeeters began, "Do you all know that *God* visited our friends the Russians upon us, for we are Babylon, stung by sin and sunk in imperialistic capitalism? *Yea,* Jesus wants to punish us for our transgressions, *yea,* he wishes to deliver us from the unrighteous congress and president to the paradise predicted in the Book of Revelations."

"Why that bastard," said Fenton, "I'd like to wring his scrawny neck—he's a traitor—that's why the Reds allow him to broadcast!"

"Shhh—" said Rusty, "He *pretends*—but the important part is the *code* he speaks. It tells those who know how to hear all the Russian invaders' secrets—*now listen up.*"

Fenton paced and fumed while the mad preacher fell to his knees saying, "Thank you, Jesus, thank you. For giving us our Soviet protectors, for freeing us Americans from the sin of greed and capitalism . . . As it says in so many places in the Bible—As it says in Exodus 15 verse 22, and Psalms 136 verse 13, yea it is true they are our chosen redeemers, the Soviets are the friends that were predicted by our Lord. As in Ecclesiastes 3, verse 7 and again in Isaiah

152

64 verse 1, if you read your Bible and interpret these prophesies correctly. All Christians will *know* the truth." He smiled, his eyes rolled heavenward, he fell again to his knees.

Jerry Jeff Jeeters took off his sparkle-silver sequin jacket and threw it off-camera. He loosened his tie with the crucifix containing the bleeding Jesus painted on it. He took off his shirt, and then stood barechested, beating his breast. "Thank you Lord, for delivering up your people. Thank you. I stand naked before you — and again make reference to your inspired words in the Holy Bible, which all of you out there who still resist our Soviet brothers must consult to see the errors of your ways. I say consult Genesis 12 verse 2, and Psalms 33, verse 12. If you *read* you will know that God is coming. Soon. In his lamb Jesus. Verily. And He will not stop at the Jordan. *Yea*, he will not. Genesis 11 verse 4, yea, and Ezekiel 4 verse 3 say it, they predict it." Jerry Jeff Jeeters leaned his sweaty face into the camera, a tear forming on his left cheek. "God said it, clearly in Job 1 verse 22, though it must be read with Isaiah 7 verse 14 and Hosea 11 verse 1, to be understood by all the faithful. For you must locate your soul and come forth from it, be baptized in his name by fire in order to be saved against the hordes of mammon. Read Isaiah and Hoseah and say his name, praise his name. I know this for I have seen it in Luke 20 verse the same. I felt it in my heart."

Jerry Jeff Jeeters retrieved his tie and jacket and put them on again, without his shirt — apparently in a

153

holy daze. He collapsed into a leatherette recliner and put on his pince-nez reading glasses, picked up from a small table. He held the Bible close to his chin, and began reading, "Take heed lest you forget the lord—"

"We can stop watching now," said Rusty. "This is the part where he doesn't give any more messages. Let's get out our Bibles, gentlemen, and have a good ol' country prayer meeting."

Rusty began handing out a stack of New Revised Standard Version Bibles he had taken from the truck. "Now gentlemen, let's look up the *code*."

Sturgis was skeptical, but he stood there and flipped the pages with Rusty. "First Exodus 15, verse 22—let's see, Rusty said. "Led Israel onward from the *Red* sea." So that's probably *red* as a key word. We'll check with the next line. What was it? Oh yes, I jotted it down here—" he looked at a notepad he had been writing on while the mad "People's Preacher" had given his insane traitorous blasphemy on the little TV. "Psalms says 'Who divided the *red* sea . . .' Yes, gentlemen, the first word of Reverend Jeeters' sermon is definitely *red*. Now the next word—turn your pages, gentlemen, and praise the lord."

Sturgis turned as Rusty indicated, to Ecclesiastes 3, verse 7 which said, *"A time to rend and a time to sew."*

"What's the magic word there?" Sturgis asked.

"Look up the next reference to be sure," said Rusty. "We check Isaiah 64, verse 1, which," he flipped pages, "says 'Oh, that *thou* would *rend* the heavens and come down . . .' "

Fenton shouted out gleefully. "He means *rend*. The word here is *rend*."

"Praise the Lord," said Rusty Anders. "Now to speed things up, I'll flip through and do the rest of the words . . . take a seat, or have a smoke, gentlemen . . ."

Before Sturgis' Camel was finished Rusty announced, "Jeeters indicates that the *reds are planning to rend* the *nation*. Probably the Mississippi is the dividing line — can't be sure, but Jeeters usually picks passages — if he can — that give other clues. The message also indicates — though Jeeters used two words to make up the city's name — that *Charleston* is their main base now. Genesis 11 verse 4 indicates they are building a city for themselves, and plan to expand from there. I'll play the videotape I made of his program later and try to draw other indications from his speech."

"I shall always carry my Bible with me from now on," Fenton said. "Your bloody Jeeters is brilliant! And to think I wanted to wring his neck for being a traitor. He's a bloody hero, that's what he is. Imagine! Using the Red's propaganda drive to pass messages to the resistance. Incredible!"

"And dangerous," said Sturgis, crushing his cigarette out on the macadam with his big boot. "The man is facing death. One of these days some sly Red bastard is going to pick up that book none of them is allowed to read — the Bible — and then Jerry Jeff

Jeeters is going to be tortured to death very, very slowly. The Reds don't like people who pretend to be on their side and fool them. We should say a prayer for the People's Preacher and wish him good luck. Anybody have any objections?"

Nobody did. And there, in the barren western desert, in the middle of a road that would have been zipping with traffic just a month and a half earlier, 100 C.A.D.S. troopers and a ruddy-faced trucker named Rusty Anders stood behind a truckload of Bibles. They bowed their heads and said a prayer silently for the true American hero who pretended to be a buffoon, for Reverend *Jerry Jeff Jeeters*.

A coyote howled in the far hills, and that seemed to signal them to raise their heads and get about their business.

"We have to move on," said Sturgis, "But we thank you for the information. Go and spread the gospel. Distribute your Bibles. You're doing good work."

Sturgis gave Rusty directions for White Sands, and the password, plus a note. "When you're all done in Oklahoma, go to White Sands. I bet they could use this information about Jeeters."

"And so will we," said Fenton, shaking Rusty's hand. "We'll pick up a TV in the next room, and carry it in the Rhino, make sure we hear the gospel too. Maybe he'll pass on some more information we can use as we head east."

Rusty was roaring off down the Interstate before they were all mounted up, tooting his highway horn in a final salute. They watched the big truck roll over a hill, then the C.A.D.S. team headed off in the opposite direction.

At least someone else is doing something, thought Sturgis, as he eased his bike up alongside Ortiz's. The old American derring-do is not gone. With people like Anders on our side, maybe we can turn the tables on the Reds yet. And then go about restoring what's left of America.

He felt better than he had in days. Hope. There was still hope that the Reds would be pushed out of the United States.

CHAPTER TWELVE

The caravan was a sight the likes of which those who beheld it could hardly believe. Moving along the highway at a slow, but constant, pace, it wound its way through the plains, defiant of all around it. The lead vehicle was a United States Army tank. Not one of the newest, certainly—but big enough, and fierce enough to command the respect the word "tank" always had. It plowed forward smoothly, smashing through crude barriers set out by an Arkansas National Guard unit before they died.

Behind the tank came a row of school buses; still school-bus-yellow, still covered with large red flashers and official black letter warnings about passing laws, but with other, non-regulation attachments as well. The ten buses had been modified into war machines—steel decks had been welded to the tops of some, mounted platforms to hold machine guns, or mortar men; one even held a battery of anti-aircraft guns. The bus windows had all been plated over with metal panels; some were hinged, but most had simply been welded on, all of them with gun slots burned out of their centers.

In the middle of the buses rode two armored cars, each with the name Exrell, Inc. painted on the sides. They rode as quietly as the rest of the caravan, looking as menacing as all the other vehicles, more so since they both had heavy caliber machine guns poking from their tiny gun ports, whereas most of the bus windows only sported rifles or small caliber machine guns.

The only vehicle in the silent parade which didn't appear deadly was a long, dark gray Rolls Royce riding comfortably in between the two armored cars. It was instantly recognizable to any who saw it as one of *those* cars, with a bar, and a television, and air conditioning, and all the other possible comforts one could hope to have.

The car, in fact, had been redesigned by its owner. Originally, it had not held a converter bed, nor a refrigerator, one capable of making its own ice yet. The Rolls had been adapted for what its owner was sure would be its new life sooner or later—that of mobile home. In the back seat of the car, the owner in question, Morris 'Pinky' Ellis reclined against a stack of pillows, going over an inventory log. One of his fat hands clutched the dog-eared list of his supplies, a list constantly being updated. The other hand was in the grasp of Morgana Pinter.

Morgana had at one time been too good for Pinky. Seeing her at a party in his former place of residence, Philadelphia, he had approached her with an interesting, if somewhat undignified, proposition. She had declined, loudly. Morgana had created quite an ugly scene, causing Pinky no end of embarrassment. Something Pinky did not forget all the time he was planning for *the end*.

Pinky had known something would happen in America; something devastating had seemed just around the corner — another, larger A.I.D.S. plague, or the final collapse of the economy, or even nuclear war — and he had wanted to be prepared for it. As head of Exrell Inc., often described as the world's largest conglomerate, a few months earlier when such labels had meaning, he had gotten advance word from Ambassador Dobrynin of the "imminent destruction of Philadelphia." He was not told exactly what kind, but told to go 20 miles away, fast. And take cover. Pinky had been pleased. It *did* pay to do $50 million worth of illegal, high-tech exporting business with the Soviet bloc! Pinky didn't know Dobrynin informed him because, after the nuke attack on the U.S. the Reds wanted Pinky alive to expedite the retrieval of certain valuable semi-conductors and diodes his Exrell Corp. manufactured.

He had been given the message 10 minutes before the missiles were launched — 35 minutes before Philadelphia was vaporized by a 5-megaton hydrogen fusion bomb.

It had not been time enough for the puffing fat man to put his entire survival plan into operation, but it had given him enough time to survive. Calling in his private army of security guards from around the estate, (he managed to find enough of them, despite the holidays) he got his small fleet rolling.

They had all assembled in his underground garage, each of them loading supplies, weapons, et cetera, they knew they were to bring if Pinky gave them the "special" call. Two of them brought Morgana Pinter.

161

Her wrists and ankles cuffed, her head bagged, and her nervous system relaxed by a healthy dose of qualudes, she was thrown at Pinky's feet. The fat man pulled the bag from her head and let her know what was happening.

Instructing his men to take her cuffs off, he asked her if she wanted to go with him — or die. Morgana had looked Pinky in the eyes and known he was telling the truth. She had been part of the high rolling set too long not to recognize the look of a man who was holding all the cards. She told Pinky she wanted to survive — that she'd do anything to stay alive.

The fat man had then put his hands on the woman's shoulders. Even in the chill of the unheated garage, his palms were sweating, marking her as his possession.

"Anything I want, you know you'll have to do."

There was no hesitation.

If a man with a lot of supplies, guns and men said he planned to survive, then she planned to survive with him — even if that man was Pinky Ellis.

As soon as she agreed, he told her, "Then get on your knees."

She hesitated. His beefy hand snaked out and slapped her. Two of his rings scraped her face. "You're coming, you do what you're told. Whatever, whenever — understood?"

She knelt down before him. He felt powerful, important. The woman at his feet had always been so haughty — so unapproachable. Now this debutante, this child of *haute* society, wasn't so high and mighty! She was suddenly *nothing*. Young, attractive, privileged Morgana Pinter was a slave to do his bidding.

162

He unzipped his pants.

When Pinky was six, he had stolen apples from a neighbor's yard. The neighbor had seen him, and told his parents, who had punished Pinky, not so much for his crime, but for their embarrassment. Several weeks later, he had taken the neighbor's cat, chained it to a pole, and then soaked it with gasoline. Throwing lit matches at it, he had worn a special kind of gleeful look on his face as he'd watched the cat catch fire, then dash madly in one direction, then the other, trying to run up the pole, rolling in the dirt, then finally dying. That same gleeful look returned to his face as he urinated on Morgana Pinter, and everything she represented to him.

Two of his men loaded her in the back of one of the buses while Pinky laughed. One found a grease covered T-shirt for her to try to use to dry off. Five minutes later, the caravan had rolled away from the outskirts of Philadelphia. They hit the freeway in plenty of time to beat the clogging traffic jams which would snarl all movement only twenty minutes later. They made it to Pinky's northern emergency shelter with two minutes to spare before the bombs fell. They stayed sealed in for 10 days.

After the radioactivity dropped to a level to permit movement outside, the band had begun moving again, first to pick up the armored cars, second to pick up the tank. Following a diagonal line across the country, they raided each of Pinky's previously established blockhouses for supplies as they moved toward their final destination, the fat man's hidden fortress in Mexico.

Now, in the spacious luxury of his Rolls, Pinky put the inventory log aside to pay attention to Morgana. She kept his right hand tight in hers; she teased it with her tongue and teeth, rubbed it across her body, letting the fingers of it close over first one breast, then the other.

Running the fat hand down the front of her body, she danced his fingers over her stomach, and then ran them in between her legs. She shuddered in response to his fingers on her thighs.

The last month she had seen the bodies, the dead and dying, an ocean of blood. She had witnessed the burning of corpses, a hundred deaths, a thousand murders committed by Pinky's ad-hoc army.

All around her, radioactivity was eating away at people and plants and animals and water. The weather was a nightmare from some bad horror film, except that it never went away; unrelenting cold and clouds held the whole world prisoner. Acid rain fell which burned the skin; lightning came out of the clouds and split trees, boulders, buildings, anything in its path. The earth cracked open on occasion, for no reason anyone in their group could discern, to spew forth a rotting gray ash in gushing great arcs two hundred feet high.

The only thing keeping her from a life like all the dying wretches she had seen by the thousands over the past two months was her ability to please Pinky Ellis. If being his toy meant not joining the rest of the dead on the other side of the Rolls Royce's doors, then that is what she would be.

"Pinky," she whispered, "let's draw the curtains,

164

and make it dark in here."

"Why?" asked the fat man.

"Because, sweetie, you brought me along for fun, didn't you? We should be having some."

Pinky reached over and caught hold of the leash leading to the studded collar around the woman's neck. He was about to chastize her; he was the one who gave all the orders, made all the moves. She was nothing, and had to learn it. Still—maybe she had simply learned who the boss was and was just trying to please. Maybe he could afford to be gentle this once.

A sudden ringing cut his attention. The captain of his security was calling from the first bus. The call meant one of only two things—either there were easy pickings ahead—a small town or encampment they could raid, something they had done a number of times already—or trouble. Pinky's hand closed on the receiver built into the seat in front of him.

"What is it, Harris?"

"I don't know, sir." The small man strained to see down the road into the desert ahead of him. "A couple of miles down the road, sir. Looks like a lot of motorcycles, or something. Fifty, a hundred—can't tell for all the dust they're raising."

Pinky shouted, "Are they military? Jesus fucking Christ; are they ours or theirs?"

"Can't say, sir. It's too dark. Can't really see much, sir. Like always."

Damn cloud cover. Damn storms. Damn fucking trouble. Always something. Life just is never too goddamned easy. "Don't go any further," ordered the fat man. "Pull the buses into a defensive ring. That

165

box formation we used when we slugged it to those hospital workers in Kentucky. Hurry up."

Sitting back, Pinky's mind raced. If it was military, even his fire power might not stand a chance, not if they attacked right away. His boys needed something to give them an edge.

Reaching behind him, he pulled a pillow free and then ripped the white silk cover away. He opened the door of the Rolls, forcing his massive body upright.

"Pinky . . . ," called Morgana, "what's happening? Is it some sort of trouble?"

"Well," wheezed the fat man, "we'll find out, won't we?"

Slamming the car door behind him, the man steadied his rotund form in the cold darkness. Moving toward the front of the caravan, one mushy step at a time, he accepted a parka from a servant. By the time he had dragged himself to the front of the defensive block of vehicles his men had set up, the unknown force had arrived.

There were a lot of them, strange armored figures, dismounting from large three wheeled motorcycles. The fat man's jaw dropped as he took in the dozens of black metal encased warriors arrayed in front of him. They could be from anywhere. They might even be another corporate venture, some place that had Pentagon contracts — didn't that last board meeting have some project . . . combat radiation suits . . . post nuclear war weapons . . .

Pinky started waving his pillow case. "White flag!" He screamed again and again, whipping the casing back and forth in the slight breeze. "White flag. Friends!"

166

The apparent leader of the group moved toward the fat man. Opening his visor, the man within the ominous looking black suit told him, "You can stop screaming." Reaching into his utility belt, Sturgis pulled forth a pack of Camels. Shaking one loose, he lit up, taking a deep drag. The fat man had stopped waving his flag. Coming closer, Pinky shouted, "They're Americans, boys. He's one of ours."

The impossibly round man came toward Sturgis. The C.A.D.S. commander marveled at how round the approaching figure was, wondering if the parka was making the man look bigger. Could any human being really be that fat? At a time when most people had no food at all, the man was an impossibility, and an obscene one at that. Sturgis surveyed the fat man coldly through his squint.

"Greetings. Hello." The fat man waddled right up to the C.A.D.S. commander. "My name is Morris Ellis, but my friends call me 'Pinky.' "

"Good morning, Mr. Ellis . . ."

"Pinky, call me Pinky, son."

"Okay, Pinky. I'm Colonel Dean Sturgis of the United States Air Force. I'd like to ask what all this," Sturgis waved his arm, indicating the fortified buses and the tank, "is about."

"Protection, soldier. Protection bought and paid for. I've got receipts and everything."

"You can't buy heavy military equipment for use within the borders of this country."

"Com'on now, Colonel. This is a new world we got here. Let's be realistic about what's going on. We're from Philadelphia. Ever heard of it? It's a smoldering cinder back on the other side of the Russian border

167

of this country. If anything, you should be thanking me for taking it out of their hands."

Sturgis blew a puff of smoke into the frosty air. He looked down at the fat man, wondering what could be going on — where the man was headed, what kinds of trouble he might have caused, or be planning. The fat man did not strike him as the self-sacrificing type. But still, he asked, "I'd like to enlist the help of you and your men."

The fat man laughed. "For what, Colonel?"

"For fighting the Russians."

"Com'on now. Seriously. Does this look like the body of a soldier?"

Sturgis dropped his cigarette belt. "No. Quite honestly, it doesn't look like the body of anything I've ever seen in my life. But that's beside the point. There's a lot of people around here who could use the kind of protection you're carrying. I have a feeling they could use the supplies you have. What do you think, Pinky? Use your men and equipment, help set up fortification for the villages west of here."

"I think you're ripping my heart out by the juicy strings. Give me a break, will you? Com'on, level with me. What are you and the knights of the round table here up to? The war is *over,* the Reds *won*."

Sturgis eyed the man carefully, taking darting looks to both sides, wondering if he was being set up. Seeing no movement out of the ordinary from any of the buses, he said, "I'll tell you what we're up to. We're going out to make some trouble for the enemy."

"Ahhhh," scoffed the fat man, "why bother? Throw in with me. I've got plenty of supplies stashed away all across the country. Never knew where I'd be when the end came, and let's face it — I'll bet you knew just like me the end was coming. America had caved into the blacks and the homos and welcomed the penniless refugees to our shores with big open arms. The idea of democracy is a sick joke. Screw the United States. There is no more United States at all. We *have* to get along with the Russians. Make a deal, work *with* them. Come with me and the boys. Be my general. Nothing will be able to stop us. The Russians will treat me — and you — right."

Sturgis laughed. For the first time in he could not remember how long, the C.A.D.S. commander howled. Standing beneath the black slate of the never-ending twilight, surrounded by the signs of a world gone mad, he laughed at the preposterous fat man until his sides hurt.

Pinky pulled back in on himself. He had thought he could get through to the military man. He had never thought to find any idealists *after* the bombs had fallen. Hating Sturgis for his embarrassment, he shouted, "What's so funny? What are you laughing at?"

Catching hold of himself, Sturgis smiled. "I'm laughing at *you* Pinky. I'm laughing because in one breath you condemn American freedom — a freedom you used to make yourself rich. And in the other breath you embrace totalitarianism. You're a piece of slime, Pinky, pure concentrated unadulterated slime."

Walking back toward his Tri-bike, the C.A.D.S. commander yelled back to the fat man.

"You're too ridiculous to talk to, fat man. You're like some sort of post-atomic humpty-dumpty!" Then, with a final chuckle, Sturgis added "Go on,

Pinky. Take off for whatever rat hole it is you plan on stuffing your fat self into. I've got work to do."

Sturgis stepped up onto his Tri-bike, unaware that the fat man had not heard anything he had said. All the man could think of was the laughter, the fact that the man in the metal suit had laughed at him in front of all his men; had made him to be a fool. Waddling back behind the front line of his buses, Pinky looked up into the face of his captain.

"What should we do sir?" the man asked.

With Sturgis's laugh still ringing in his ears, the fat man answered, "Kill them."

Pinky's men had been poised for battle. Seven times they had come across unknowns, and had routed them all, from biker gangs to a lesbian karate-school band. They had even mopped up an Ohio Highway Patrol, but only because the jerkoffs had attacked them. The fat man's men were tough, and dedicated. Like all good soldiers, they obeyed orders without question. The tank turret moved, taking aim at Sturgis.

"Jesus Lord, Colonel . . ." shouted Ortiz. "*Look out!*"

Without hesitation, the C.A.D.S. trooper threw himself at Sturgis, knocking him from his Tri-bike. At that second, though, the tank opened fire, striking Ortiz squarely in the back. The tank shell ripped open the black armor, barely pausing as it ripped through the man inside the suit and splattering his guts across the highway.

The rest of the C.A.D.S. unit stood in shock for a moment, even as the machine guns within the buses opened fire on them. Suddenly, Sturgis ran forward,

170

ordering "Waste them, C.A.D.S.!"

Pulling the new LWA from his shoulder, Sturgis thumbed it into action, pulling the trigger and zeroing-in on the turret of the tank. The amplified laser burned through the side of the housing, biting into the chamber, exploding the shell ready to be fired. The turret flopped upward in a volcanic eruption of smoke and blood, large slices of human meat falling from the sky.

Across the highway, the rest of the C.A.D.S. team charged the buses. Machine-gun bullets bouncing from their armor, Fenton and Tranh took aim at the side of one, both firing an E-ball at it. The side blew out instantly, sending Exrell security men flying in all directions, spraying trails of red. On the other side of the tank, four C.A.D.S. members, trying to conserve precious heavy-ammo, ran under the hail of bullets. Reaching the side of the bus, they drove their metal hands into the side and began to lift. Despite the weight of the bus, and all the extra plating which had been welded to it — despite the men and supplies and heavy arms within it — it began to rise as all the muscle-assisted systems of the C.A.D.S. suits reached their limits. Those within were thrown sideways as the vehicle lurched upward.

"One — two — three!" Billy shouted over the mike and they all thrust simultaneously, sending the bus crashing over on its side, folding into a smoking crushed accordion of death.

Roberto shouted, "This is for Ortiz, my buddy," and fired an E-ball into a broken open window in the bus. The blast was contained by the heavy plating around the vehicle making it a crematorium for those inside.

Keying his jet pack, the West Virginian shot up over the field of combat and picked a target, showering it with liquid flaming plastic as he descended. Billy's hot goo stuck fast to the bus he had picked, eating its way inside, oozing down the protruding weapons and on in through the gun slots from which they protruded. Men tried to leap from the emergency door of the bus, only to become mired in the pools of flaming death dripping from the roof and sides of the vehicle. They ran screaming, burning, into the distance.

Crawling back into his Rolls, Pinky clutched at his heart, hoping the exertion of running back the fifty odd feet to it would not be too much for him. Wheezing hard, he fumbled for the receiver in the back of the seat in front of him.

"Harris!"

"Mr. Harris is dead, sir," answered a voice Pinky did not recognize.

"Screw him then," growled the fat man. "Get us out of here. Blow some holes in those bastards out there and get us out of here."

The remaining men, having realized how tough their opponents were, had abandoned the light machine guns, breaking out their heavier equipment. From one armored car a volley of portable rockets went flying, four of them zeroing in on one C.A.D.S. trooper. Unlike the others in the area who jet-packed up over the missiles, the man fumbled for his manual control instead of merely giving a spoken order. The missiles slammed into the suit, spinning it around, flipping it over, and then blowing it across the landscape on both sides of the highway. Sturgis cursed. He couldn't afford to lose men!

Roberto, coming around the side of the armored car, sent bullets through the same window, then dropped a grenade after the men who had killed Maniss. The only things to come back out of the window were smoke and pieces of flesh.

"Destroy them," came Sturgis' voice. "Stop them all—quick. We can't afford any more losses."

"Rather," came Fenton's thick accent, "easier said than accomplished."

Now Roberto had run into trouble. He was pinned down by the bus with the anti-aircraft guns. The firing crew chewed up the scenery around the C.A.D.S.-man. He barely escaped death only by continuing to move faster than Pinky's marksman.

"Hold on, Roberto," came Sturgis' voice. "I'll bail you out!"

Bounding across the desert, the C.A.D.S. commander came up behind the heavily armed bus, blowing in its back door with a Hawk-2. The fat man's crew did not panic, though. Several of the Exrell security men leapt through the door in bullet-proof flak jackets, with heavy caliber automatic weapons. The trio lay down a pattern of heavy fire which forced Sturgis to flatten out. A concentration of their fire had run up his left arm, actually stinging him within his armor. Realizing several such armor-piercers could severely damage his C.A.D.S. suit— and him, Sturgis shouted into his helmet com, "Someone bite the sky and wax that trio pinning me down!"

Horner and Beck, who had been working their way

173

up over the dunes behind their leader, hit their jet packs. Taking advantage of the fact that Sturgis was drawing the heaviest of the fire, they shot upward into the open, and then blasted down at the men gunning for their commander. The flak-jackets worn by the security men turned back some of their shots, but not most. 9mm slugs tore through their bodies with devastating efficiency, eating through their steel helmets, and the soft brains underneath to erupt through the necks of the men and drill into the fallout dust.

Sturgis was up and running before the men hit the ground, charging the heaviest armed of the buses. He crossed half the remaining distance between himself and the bus when suddenly, the big ack-ack guns which had been keeping the others pinned down began to swing in his direction.

"Mother of Christ!"

Sturgis barely leaped to the side in time as the ground where he had been and would have been disappeared, cratered by tank fire. The C.A.D.S. commander landed roughly, his boots losing traction on the loose sand, spilling Sturgis onto his side. The tank wasted no time in taking advantage of the C.A.D.S. commander's difficulty and bore down on him. His computers, working automatically, flashed a P.D., probability of destruction, warning; 0.9. Sturgis knew if the gunners zeroed him, that his time was up.

He moved his legs, digging in, pitting his servo-mechs against the slippery sand. Knowing he could not jet upward from the on-your-back position without almost certainly being hit, he tried to get back to his feet, hoping to avoid the deadly shells by getting close to the tank and under their line of fire. Unfortunately, when he tried to lift his 200 pounds of armor, his boot found a chuckhole hidden beneath the dust which toppled him a second time, leaving him completely exposed.

The C.A.D.S. commander, knowing he could not stand in time, strained his arm around to line up a shot which might save him. And then, when his arm was almost half-way to lining up with its target, the top of the tank disappeared, blowing upward and outward in a fierce inferno of electric fire.

Fenton's group, no longer pinned down, had moved forward and blasted the tank with a volley of E-balls which disintegrated the heavy guns, their operators, and the entire back half. As Sturgis freed his boot and got to his feet, his C.A.D.S. troopers finished off the remaining buses with any fight in them. Those still firing were destroyed in a matter of minutes.

The last bus tried to run; Tranh fired a mini-Hawk dart into one of its front tires. The driver tried to compensate but turned the wheel too sharply; the buses had been redesigned for combat and defense, but not for maneuvering. Without hesitation the war wagon fell onto its side and then rolled over. Two men jumped out. Billy covered the pair with liquid flaming plastic. They became living bonfires.

Seeing how badly things were going, Pinky had his chauffeur drive the Rolls Royce behind a copse of burning fir trees, away from the killing field.

Morgana Pinter seized the opportunity of Pinky's distraction to lunge for the door. Pinky grabbed her by the waist and dragged her back. "You're staying with me, you bitch," he snarled.

Pinky shouted orders over his pink phone as the car sped away toward an intersecting road and safety.

"Don't surrender," he ordered. "Keep firing. A gold bar to every man who kills one of the enemy. Keep firing."

There were two armored cars and one of the buses still left. The C.A.D.S. troopers ignored the fleeing Rolls, choosing to attack the hostile targets first. It was as Pinky hoped.

The bus flew up twenty feet rear-end over as an E-ball found its gas tank. Billy tore the door off another and jammed both his arms in through the entrance, filling the interior with machine gun fire. Tranh and several other C.A.D.S. troopers overturned an armored car, using their combined strength to simply tear the flooring away from the toppled vehicle, exposing those inside for quick elimination. Roberto, screaming "Die *mothers*," fired an E-ball through the front window-grid of the other armored car, exploding it from the inside; a stew of blood and steel.

Billy exclaimed, "Sturgis — the Rolls is getting away!"

"We'll catch him easy with our Tri-bikes, let's finish here first."

After a few more volleys, the battle was over. The surviving soldiers of the millionaire's army knelt in the sand while the dozens of black armored suits closed in around them. Sturgis walked up to one of them and asked, "You boys had enough?"

With downcast eyes, the man nodded. Sturgis

looked around him. "How about you others?" All agreed they had had enough.

"Now," Sturgis asked, "What the hell am I supposed to do with you? I have no room for prisoners."

"Don't kill us," the man pleaded, "let us go. You can have the gold—all of it. Just let us live—okay?"

The C.A.D.S. team noticed the gold bars blown from the back of the armored cars for the first time. Roberto and Billy moved forward, entranced by the sight of what months earlier had meant a king's ransom, but now was of questionable value. Starker said, "Gold! Double stamped, Grade A, government inspected gold! We're rich!"

"Rich as anyone," Wilson shouted. "Rich as emperors, as movie stars, as kings—we're as rich as God, man!"

Sturgis walked forward. "Shut up, both of you."

Starker put his arm up, aiming at Sturgis. "Damn it, sir. We're rich! I ain't never had nothing but leftovers! Never! This makes us the boss—this is our ticket, Colonel. Ours."

Wilson backed Starker, covering Sturgis, yelling, "We deserve it, man. We do all the damn work, and if we win this damn war, you know what's going to happen to us—we're going to get a pat on the head, and maybe promoted one level—those of us that don't die with our guts blown all over the insides of our walking coffins."

The C.A.D.S. team began to split in two directions—some behind Starker and Wilson, more behind Sturgis. Most stood pat, not knowing what to make of the exchange coming over their radios. Tranh moved to Sturgis' side, as did Roberto and Billy.

Tranh said, "Is this why friends died, blown into little pieces—is this why they're lying back there on the road, shot down so you can become just like the toad that killed them?"

Starker shouted, "Listen. I'm not saying we quit. I'm not saying we don't do our duty. But how long will it take us to just *bury* this gold, and leave it 'til after the war's over? Like a prize, for the ones who make it?"

"Or as a lure to gnaw at all of us," added Sturgis, "pulling at our guts, tearing at us to desert, to run and start digging it up. Use your brains, man. The war killed any use for gold! Haven't you heard, money's no good anymore. And if it *is* any good, it's only good on the black market, for trading against bales of hay, and racks of chickens—the rich life is gone, kid. That swimming pool, martini-mixer, trip-to-the-Riviera stuff went up in radioactive smoke just like everything else we ever wanted, or cared about."

The young C.A.D.S. trooper threw his arms down, screaming into his com-link, "Then why bother? What are we fighting for? What's the goddamned point of it all?"

Sturgis said, "There *is* a point, man. We just have to keep fighting the Reds. We kill them or they kill us. That's it. Period."

Fenton strode up beside the C.A.D.S. commander. "We have to go on for those who can't, Starker. We have to hold the line, give the rest who may have survived time to get into action against the Russians. We've all lost family. I may have lost my whole country—everything I ever knew may be gone, nothing more than glowing, deadly char—and I don't even

178

have any way of knowing."

"Then why both to fight, man," asked Wilson. Taking off his helmet, the young blond man shouted, fighting back stinging tears, "Why take the abuse and fight and die for nothing? For damn, stinking, nothing?"

"Because it's not for nothing," said Sturgis. "You want to know what we should do with this gold? I'll show you."

Walking over to the still kneeling security guards, the C.A.D.S. commander told them to get up. Once they were standing, he asked the one who had been acting as spokesman for the group, "Why were you guys working for that fat slug?"

The man explained how Pinky had formed his survival squad. He told Sturgis how they had run from Philadelphia, and the things they had done along the way, the bad and the worse. "We just did what we were told, you know? There didn't seem to be anywhere to go, anything to do—any point in not just heading for Mexico with Mr. Ellis and trying to survive. I know it sounds lame, but there just wasn't anything better. You know?"

Sturgis nodded. He knew. He understood the despair that came from feeling helpless. He'd fought it every day since the war began.

"My name's Deke Powers. Maybe I've done some stuff since this all started that I'm not too proud of, but I heard what you said, and I'd like to join you. I don't mean in a suit, or anything like that, just whatever you think I could do. You tell me, and *I'm your man.*"

Before Sturgis could say anything, the other three

security men came forward, all saying the same. Shamed, Wilson and Starker stood aside, refusing to look at any of the other C.A.D.S. troopers. Those few who had moved behind them to back their play for the gold now deserted them.

Sensing a mood he wished to exploit to end the rebellion, Sturgis said, "Listen to me, *everybody*! There's nothing more to be said over what happened here. A fat greedy bastard started all this, and maybe he woke something in us that wasn't too pretty—forget it. I mean it now. *Forget it!* Maybe if *I'd* been the first one to look at that gold, the first one to see that gold—I'd have been the one to go greedy."

Sturgis pointed down the road. "Pinky, in his elegant Rolls, is racing down the highway. At the kind of mileage those gas-eaters get, he ought to be in the middle of nowhere when he runs out completely. He'll have *nothing*. That's what greed buys you. What will he do? Eat his gold? Pour it in his gas tank?"

"But we *can* do something useful with it."

As his men crowded around at the suggestion, Sturgis continued. "We can send this gold to the resistance. You all know there are armed Americans resisting the Russians. They will use the gold to get any weapons they need on the black market. The gold would help them a lot more than it will us. What do you say?"

Wilson shouted, "Who needs to be in a higher tax bracket? Give it to the Resistance."

Starker followed, "To the Resistance."

And the others, and then all the C.A.D.S. troopers, were shouting the three-word slogan over and over in the middle of the desert amid the burning remains of Pinky Ellis' caravan.

Sturgis said, "I've had the audio from Jerry Jeff Jeeters' TV show on while we were travelling. The computer helped me decode his 'holy' messages. There's a drop-point for donations to a rebel group called the Revengers. Do you think you could get this helpful bit of hardware to them? Plus the gold?"

Powers reached down and grabbed up the gold bars he had guarded in the truck earlier. "We'll do our best."

Sturgis detailed a number of them to righting the bus with the least damage to see if it could be made road-worthy again. It turned out to be fairly sound, needing only a few minor repairs, most of which was bending metal with C.A.D.S-powered hands!

Other troopers were put to gathering what supplies might be still intact in the other buses. In their suits they could rummage through the still burning vehicles with little worry of danger. Powers and the other security men stripped the wrecks, even to the point of draining the gas tanks of all the remaining fuel.

While the others wrapped up the last of the work, Sturgis checked the map. There were many more miles to go yet. Too many.

CHAPTER THIRTEEN

An exhausting, 150-mile trek through western Tennessee's rugged Cumberland Mountains had brought the C.A.D.S. Team into the Appalachians. Now, as the murky greenish sun broke over the distant horizon, they came to an abrupt halt at a 100 foot wide canyon that wasn't on the map. It stretched for miles in both directions.

They stared across the awesome gap before them. Evidently, it had been formed as a result of earthquake activity brought about by the bombing. The canyon was clearly a new feature to the landscape as its cliffs were sheer and denuded, while huge trees tottered near the brim, their ragged root systems half-exposed. At the bottom, a mighty underground river had been channeled within the confines of sheer granite walls. Sturgis peered across the 100-yard wide gap. He knew the squad could cross by jet pack but the Tri-bikes, the Rhino, would be somewhat of a problem.

"Fenton, what have we got in the way of suspension cable?"

"You want something that'll get the Rhino across?"

"You got it buddy."

"Well, maybe. Just maybe. We've got enough nickel-cadmium steel cable to crisscross, let's see, one, two . . . I guess we could get three strands across. That might just do the trick. That's if you can get supports equal to the task on both ends."

"Time Fenton. How much time would it take?"

"Three, maybe four hours. The Tri's are no problem really. But the Rhino's a 50-50 proposition, due to its weight."

"Let's go," said Sturgis. "Tranh, you and I'll cross over and attach cable on that end. You guys get busy over here. The rest of the troop chop some trees and cut some boards for a bridge. What'll we need, Fenton?"

"Look for some nice solid granite," Fenton said, rummaging through the Rhino's supply bin for hardware—all of which could be linked up to the suits and worked off their power unit. "A nice flat spot about ten feet from the edge," Fenton continued, "sink these steel rods about four feet into it. Use the rock drill. You can set it for the exact diameter of the rods and it'll dig you out a hole in no time. Then drive the rods in and I'll hop over and harness the cables to them."

Sturgis nodded. Taking the rods he jumped across with Tranh who carried the drill. Within an hour they had set up supports and Fenton had stretched three lengths of suspension cable across the canyon and began testing each line. Soon, the expert team had put down boards and were driving their Tri-wheelers across the precipitous chasm to the other side where the Omega Force was already forming up and prepar-

184

ing to move on. Finally, everything was across save Fenton and the Rhino.

"Okay, Sturgis," he said over his speaker. "Here we go. Keep your fingers crossed."

The Rhino was driven to the very brink of the cliff and Fenton drove its front wheels onto the bridge. He was busy inching it out on the creaking makeshift bridge when he heard a murderous, blood-curdling scream from behind. It was an attack party, apparently made up of local folk. They were dressed in tattered rags and buckskins, but were armed like professionals—M-16s! They opened fire on the Rhino. Fenton had opened the hatch on top of the Rhino to get a better look. Now a grenade hit him square in the chest. His suit withstood the blast but the impact succeeded in blowing him off the Rhino and he plummeted down into the canyon. He righted himself in mid-air screaming out *"Jump"* to his suit. The jet pack activated, stopped him on a dime and he started back upward toward the canyon ledge. But then Sturgis and several other C.A.D.S. troopers had reacted. Sturgis ordered covering fire. "Don't fire to kill—they're Americans. Maybe they think *we're* Reds!"

One of the mob irregulars opened fire on the empty Rhino with a bazooka and the blasts sent it twisting half out over the chasm. The front of the vehicle was secure, but the rear wheels worked free and the Rhino dangled precariously.

Sturgis directed Billy to lead a detachment of 12 Omega Commandos against the mob on the far side while he and Fenton along with six other team members tried to push the Rhino back onto its perch on the makeshift bridge.

Billy and his squad quickly dispersed the attackers with a volley of machine-gun fire, eating up the dirt around them like a plow. The rag-tag marauders scattered wildly, dropping their weapons. Seeing the C.A.D.S. team floating up on their jet packs and their bullets bouncing harmlessly off the suits had sent terror into their hearts.

Meanwhile Fenton and Sturgis coasted alongside the Rhino. Fenton fumbled with the hatch, which was bent shut. He couldn't get back in. Sturgis looked around and could hardly believe his eyes. Now a trouble was brewing on the other side of the canyon. The C.A.D.S. column was being set upon by an even larger armed group. Both sides of the bridge were under attack by locals. Sturgis' men were under intense fire from automatic weapons.

"Scan," he said. Instantly the screen estimated the enemy's projected development. How had they arrived so unexpectedly? Just a few minutes before, he had scanned the area and seen nothing for a few miles.

Just then a howitzer opened up on them. The first and second shell damaged the bridge moorings on the western side, the others fortunately went wild.

"Damn," Sturgis yelled, "forget about not injuring the screwballs. Take out that howitzer!"

Billy's voice radioed "I've got it on my screen—and I'm hitting it with a mini-hawk—jetting up over the thing and firing down."

Sturgis heard a huge explosion off over the ridge on the western side of the bridge. He saw a figure jetting back across the chasm through the smoke,

186

waving its arms. "Got it, Skip. You want me to waste some of their infantry?"

"No. That's enough. Pin 'em down with some fire until we get the Rhino across the bridge," replied Sturgis. "If anyone opens up with a bazooka or another howitzer though, go after them."

Sturgis saw that the bridge would last only minutes more. The cable was slowly slipping. "Fenton, Roberto, everyone—give me a hand. Use your jet packs for help. Get under the Rhino and push her back onto the bridge."

Five of them struggled to push the heavy vehicle back onto the precariously rocking makeshift bridge. Fenton cursed and swore like never before, with such foulness that even Sturgis was amazed. It seemed to help his work, though. The Rhino inched back onto the boards.

All of their jetpacks were on empty by the time they had accomplished their herculean task. Once the Rhino was steady on the bridge, Fenton managed to open the hatch. He climbed in and recklessly drove across to the other side. Now at least all the equipment was safe. The remaining men, including Sturgis, ran after it, crossing the quivering bridge. Sturgis was the last across. It fell seconds after he made it to the other side. Sturgis saw that Tranh and his men had pinned the attackers down in a primitive hill fort made of recently hewn timber, just over the ridge.

"What's the story" he asked, coming alongside Tranh.

"Locals. Lots of them—they seem to be irradiated—half crazy. Sickly bunch, hair falling out, but they're game. And organized. They got some sophis-

187

ticated weapons too. We took some shots from bazookas and a mortar shell. Lost a Tri-wheeler and a few of the guys have minor damage to their suits. Nothing we can't handle though. Should we go on in?"

Sturgis said "No!" He stepped forward and spoke over his mike, his voice amplified 100X.

"You men inside the fort," he said, "listen to me. I don't know who you are, but I know you must be Americans. Listen, We're American also. Air Force Special Forces. My name's Sturgis. Colonel Dean Sturgis. Do you read me?"

"How do we know you're Americans?" came a husky voiced reply from behind the stone and timber barricade.

Sturgis knew his force could easily demolish their defenses and so said in a relaxed voice, "We're friends. Trust us fellas. What do you want us to do to prove we're Americans just like you?"

There was a pause and then the voice said "How many base hits did Ty Cobb get in his career?"

Sturgis smiled. He actually knew that one. He replied "367."

Slowly, after a silent pause, the gate to the primitive fortress swung open and three men emerged, followed by a band of armed warriors. Billy and Sturgis stepped out into the open and held their hands out in friendship. They approached the band slowly, cautiously. Sturgis knew they had some high-powered missiles trained on him. When they were about thirty feet away, they stopped.

"Greetings, citizens," Sturgis said, raising his right hand. He gasped at the sight of the band before them. Nearly 80 men made up the wild pack, dressed in an assortment of army fatigues, dungarees, and work boots. Some had clothing that was little more than torn rags, but they were armed with regulation U.S. Army issue weapons.

Just about every one of the band showed signs of the nuke disaster. Many were maimed and scarred from cuts and burns. Some showed advanced signs of radiation poisoning — balding heads, blotchy patches of red on their skin, blanched complexions.

One of the healthier specimens, a man in his early twenties, a patch over his right eye, stepped forward. He kept his M-16 at the ready, eyed Sturgis and Billy from top to bottom, and when his eye alighted on the U.S. flag painted on Sturgis' suit, he smiled and extended his hand.

"Welcome," he said. "Sorry about the shooting."

Sturgis and Billy opened their helmets so the men could see their faces, then shook hands with the man.

"I'm Dean Sturgis, Colonel, U.S. Air Force. This here's Billy Dixon. Who're you fellas?"

"I'm Bart McCoy," said the eye-patched man. "We're the Revengers. We run the territory on this side of 'New Canyon.' Now tell me Sturgis, just exactly what in the hell is this get-up you're wearin'? I know damned well we made direct hits on your men but nothing fazes you guys. Then you take off, hover like a chopper, shoot like a battleship . . ."

"We represent our country's last organized regular forces. But what about you men? Where'd you get these weapons?"

"We're part of the resistance movement. You savvy?"

189

"Sure. I've had contact with the resistance. How about those boys on the other side of the canyon. They part of your band?"

"No way. That there's Duke Hatfield and his bunch. They been on that side of the river since before Tennessee was a state, and now I wouldn't doubt it if they don't consider themselves a part of the U.S. at all. Never was a one of that bunch that could be trusted. We spend more time keeping them at bay than anything."

"You mean you're at war with that bunch over there?"

"Well, since the quake split the mountain there ain't been much conflict. We picked up all their stragglers that was caught on this side and I guess they did the same with ours on their side. I lost my own brother over there. All we do now is snipe at each other occasionally nowadays. If we had a half dozen of those suits of yours we could really take the battle to 'em. Other than that, we've had a couple good fights with a few squads of Cuban Reds passing through from the east, but they weren't much to handle. Most of them wasn't even armed right. Just old Russian rifles."

"Cubans?" asked Sturgis. "Did you interrogate them?"

"Why . . . no . . . killed 'em," replied Jake, as if he only just then realized it. "Is that important?"

"All right, all right," Sturgis said impatiently. "What's important now is that we *all* start working together. First . . ."

"First we must eliminate the *common* enemy," Tranh said, finishing Sturgis' thought exactly.

"The Ruskies?" Jake asked.

"Right. We have to learn to trust *each other*. Jake, we need your help. We've got top secret orders to execute, and speed of execution is an important factor."

"Now wait just one dadburn minute, Sturgis. It's like you said. We *all* got to learn to trust one another. We're all in this together I suppose. There's a pretty strong resistance movement this side of the mountains and we're an important link in it. Sure, we've all come to battle with each other in one crazy way or another. But somehow we're tryin' to link together. Now there's a few things you oughta know. We've been watchin' the Ruskies set up a huge base in Charleston."

Sturgis did a double take. He was hardly able to believe that this leader of a mountain band had the intelligence to be monitoring the big Sov build-up in Charleston. But so much the better!

"You see," continued Jake, "us hillbillies ain't so all-fired stupid as you might make us out to be. We know all about what's going on in Charleston. And I suppose you fellas want to stop the Reds from doin' what they're doin'—and that's why you're here!"

"Right," Sturgis replied, with new respect for Jake. "Maybe you can tell me also—are there Red patrols up in this area?"

"Plenty. And things've been gettin' hotter all the time. We run into scouting patrols regularly. 'Course their planes is always buzzin' us. We got a few Redeye missiles—Anson here's bagged him three choppers and a MIG. About a week ago they sent an armored column into our eastern territory, about fifty miles

191

away. That was some real action. About two thousand men engaged on both sides."

"Yea," continued Anson, the Redeye sharpshooter. He was a giant of a man, six-foot five-inches, a good 300 pounds. Radiation scars tattooed his body and his hair hung in long thin strands from beneath his large sloppy hat. Sunglasses covered his eyes, but Sturgis could see scarring around them.

"They had six tanks, couple of armored cars. There was some advance fire bombing. Quite a slick operation really. We teamed up with our allies, the Rebels they call themselves. They got a division called the Jeff Davis Squad. Sixty men, all ex-special forces fellers like—I guess—yourselves. They led a suicide attack into the center of the Russian column. Wiped out to a man, but that allowed the rest of the Rebels and us to outflank the Russians and we polished nearly every last one of 'em off."

"So it sounds like there's been some regular action in these parts," Sturgis said.

"Yessir," said Jake proudly. "It's war. Pure and simple. Now you see, Colonel Sturgis. We can appreciate the fact that you men are Special Forces. And you sure as hell have some kind of equipment here. No doubt about that. But there's a lot going on here. As I'm sure you know. In Charleston the Rusky's got some pretty sophisticated equipment unloading. Occurs to me you're just gonna *have to* work with us, too. Listen, Sturgis. We got a bit to talk about. You showed us you can go your way if you want. We can't stop you. But we sure would like to work with you guys when you hit the Russians. We ain't no slouches, and believe it or not, you're gonna need help."

192

"You're right, Jake. How far's your headquarters from here?"

"Jest about eight miles. And it's in Charleston's direction. Bring the whole gang and we'll thrown a hoe-down for 'em."

"Great," chimed in Rossiter, who had joined the bunch. "What's for dinner?"

"Well, if you like, we got a whole mess of canned hams and tons of smoked turkey meat. There's a cannery down in Wolena that we helped ourselves at. Will that do? Plus jars of peaches, some cranberry sauce in tins . . ."

"Sounds incredible," Rossiter said.

When they got back to Fenton at the canyon's rim, they saw that the Britisher had the C.A.D.S. force all set to go, mounted up on the Tri-bikes, in formation.

Billy returned just then by air, landing close to Sturgis slowly on the nearly invisible blue-white flame of his jetpack.

"What's up over there in those hills?" Sturgis asked.

"Strangest thing Sturg," the southerner replied. "The men over there call themselves Hatfields, and they've been feuding with just about everyone in these parts, for a long time. Anyway, there's a good two thousand men, they say their village is about six miles south of here, on that side of the canyon. Lot of 'em are suffering from rad poisoning. Their chief man, this guy Duke Hatfield, told me about an attack by about sixteen Russian choppers. They raided their village. Sounds like a pretty good encounter went on.

They lost a couple of hundred guys before escaping into the woods. Russians finally took off after burning most of their village. What'd you find out?"

"This group's part of the Resistance. They may be some help to us. Charleston is definitely East Coast Red HQ."

"And we're gonna go wreck it?"

"Right. But we'll need a lot of help. Head back over and tell their chief man to pick his best five hundred troops and get ready to cross over to this side. Tell him we've got to work together against the Russians. Make him understand. No more feud. Take ten men with you, Billy. Stay in touch by radio. I'll leave Fenton with the Rhino and ten men on Tri's waiting for you on this side."

Sturgis jumped on his Tri-wheeler and he and Tranh sped to the head of the Omega's column where the Revengers had clustered.

"Have your men come aboard with my men on their Tri-wheelers," Sturgis told Jake. "The rest can follow us with a rear guard." He pointed to the Hatfields' side. "We're all Americans. The Hatfields are coming too."

"Now listen everyone," Sturgis called out through his voice amplifier. "We've got to all forget this petty bickering and think of ourselves as one nation, one people, faced with the greatest threat to our existence ever. If America is to survive, it's up to none other than us. There's no one to pass it off on. The history books of the future, if there *is* any future, will record what we do. If America is to not disintegrate into a collection of petty states to be picked off one by one by the Russians, it'll be because of us."

"He's right," called out Jake. "The Hatfields are welcome to our camp. The three-hundred-year old blood feud between West river n' East river folk is hereby ended. Ain't never been anybody able to figure out what we was fightin' about in the first place."

"Good," said Sturgis. In a few minutes, the columns of the Omega Force, joined by the irregulars, formed up behind Sturgis and Jake and moved swiftly through the mountain passes to the Revengers' mountaintop fortress.

The Revengers' secret camp, known as "Camp X" appeared suddenly at the edge of a high mountain cliff, surrounded by ice strewn peaks. The log built fortress itself was tucked against a steep granite cliff formed when a mountain split in two—probably during the recent quake activity. It was so camouflaged that it was difficult to see from the air. Jake said the heavy lead content in the rocks throughout the region rendered the area ideal for the maintenance of rad-proof housing. A series of guard checkpoints were passed and Sturgis marvelled at the sophisticated weaponry guarding the stronghold. He reckoned that even the C.A.D.S. force would have a difficult time assaulting the place due to the narrow defile caused by the opposing cliffs of the split mountain.

When finally they gained entrance to the fortress itself, they found themselves in a honeycomb of caves.

The tunnels were very narrow. At first the men walked upright. Then they had to crouch. Finally they got to a narrowing where the C.A.D.S. force could no longer advance due to the size of the suits.

"Listen, Jake old buddy," Sturgis said, "couldn't we just parlay outside here, so we don't get our fat metal backsides stuck?"

"You just might find our little cave interesting, Colonel," Jake replied. "Besides, believe me, we'll be comfortable in a minute. And safe. Why don't you just hop out of the contraptions and let your hair down a little. You're among friends here."

Sturgis decided to go along with Jake's suggestion. He posted a couple of men at each end of the chasm, a couple at the retreat's entrances, and five men just to watch the suits. The rest took their suits off. When they finally reached the inner part of Camp X, Sturgis had to admit, he was fascinated. A good mile inside the cliff the Revengers had a vast arena studded with brilliant crystals of every color jutting from walls and ceilings. It was beautiful, this hidden amethyst city. And totally unexpected.

"This was a huge crystal dig for years," Jake said. "We all worked here all our lives, cutting quartz crystals and shipping them to 'Artsy' stores nation-wide. The nuke-quakes opened more caves. We found we could move most of our operations down in here. And there's practically no rads."

Mining lamps were scattered about giving illumina-tion. The cavern was crowded with people, a good percentage afflicted with serious radiation poisoning, but a fair representation of healthy folks too.

"Tell your men to make themselves comfortable here. We'll be settin' up for a big meal soon, and there'll be plenty to eat and drink, and dancin' to boot. But let's you and me and your top lieutenants here go on and have a talk. There's a couple a boys down there you might want to meet."

Sturgis dispersed his men who found their way into the company of a variety of country gals who were busy setting up tables. Fenton, Billy, Tranh, and Roberto all eventually joined Jake, Sturgis, Anson, and the chief men from the Hatfield clan in the "war" room, a larger cavern deep in the ground. They all had to crawl through a second maze of tunnels to get to the place.

Sturgis was impressed. For a rag-tag bunch of irregulars, these simple folk had organized themselves into a highly efficient and effective unit. Their bucolic attitude and clothing concealed a sophisticated unit, uniquely adapted to the brave new world they were now all a part of.

The officers gathered at a large table littered with maps and reports, and introduced themselves. Jake was the first to address the gathering.

"Men, I think we all pretty much know the real story here. The Reds are landing in force in Charleston and God knows where else. From what we see Russia is making a base from which they'll be capable of landing a huge invasion force. All we got is a bunch of pitchforks and a few rockets we gathered up from an arsenal here and there, so the best we can ever hope to do is take a few Reds with us. I say we help Colonel Sturgis take the fight to 'em before we all die of radiation poison. Get these here boys in these space suits to lead the charge just like the old Jeff Davis Squadron did, and hit 'em with everything we've got. Why, I bet we could gather up three thousand fighting men to throw at 'em in a human wave. It's the only way. We may as well go out in a blaze of glory. We got a chance to win now, anyways."

Jake's men cheered loudly and raised their arms and their fingers in V-signs, "Victory!"

Next Duke Hatfield stood and addressed the group. "Now I say that's just plumb crazy. Everyone knows we'd get mowed down in a pitched battle. That's just what the Ruskys would want us to do. No sir. I ain't a gonna send these good men to die. We plan on retirin' to the hills and fightin' it out forever if need be. What we need is a guerrilla war, wait the Russians out until we can get more organized."

Anson jumped to his feet. "I knew you Hatfields was cowards. Jake shoulda never let you cross into our territory."

A general imbroglio was about to erupt when Sturgis yelled for quiet, expecting his voice-amplifier to kick in. It didn't, for he didn't have his suit on. He cleared his throat and raised his own strong voice and boomed, "*Cool it*, you men. We've got to pull together! Now listen up!" Sturgis took a deep breath and looked each man in the eye, one by one.

"Jake, Duke, you both have good points. There's something to be said for each of your plans. You're a good soldier Anson, and I'd be proud to fight with you. But try to remember we're all together now. Listen men, the Omega Squad is acting under the official orders of the president of our country. *He* has approved *my* plan for attacking Charleston with the C.A.D.S. unit acting alone. But we can use you men in a diversion. Because you've lived around here — most of you — all your lives, I'm counting on you men to get us close to Charleston undetected. Then I want a big attack to the north, using Hatfield *and* Re-

198

venger groups. Meanwhile we'll slip into Charleston harbor in a way that the Reds will never suspect."

"No good," Jake said, shaking his head. "We've been planning a hit on Charleston for weeks now. A lot of us already got killed getting together the information and collecting the firearms. We're all chompin' at the bit. Look at us. Those Russians have killed us all. We're all dead men, all burning up with radiation, so are our wives, children. Our whole country's destroyed. We want in on this, Sturgis. We deserve our *revenge*."

"And you *are* in on it, Jake. We all are. We all have our jobs to do. If it was you who was trained to use the C.A.D.S. suits, it'd be your job to use it. As far as the intelligence you've been gathering, that will be a great help to us now . . ."

Sturgis continued for a half hour, finally convincing all that they could best serve America by following the *Tech Battleground* Plan.

"Now I want to see what information you have on what's going on in Charleston, block by block, Jake," Sturgis smiled.

"Well, Bringle here just got in from outside Charleston last night. Talk to these fellers, Ed."

"Got quite an operation over there," the tow-headed man said as he bit on his pipe. "I was in on the recon—and the boys and I tell ya, them Russians got a big landing going on there, enormous. They're unloading twelve to sixteen tanks and heavy transports every day. I'd estimate two full army divisions already disembarked. Enough ships to make the U.S. Navy turn green with envy. My dope says the top man's a General Veloshnikov. Top man—we got these photos."

He handed a folder to Sturgis who eagerly grasped it. The pictures showed Veloshnikov surveying the unloading of ships, and a mysterious tower in the harbor, something like the conning tower of a submarine, but huge. Too big though to be a sub.

Bringle went on for a half hour detailing everything he'd found out on his reconnaissance mission to Charleston. He had a layout of the Russian camp. They had taken over a plantation — Tayland — Bringle had drawings, guard schedules, everything. Jake coached Fenton and Tranh in the local contacts, codes, checkpoints and routes off to the side.

Now, armed with the wealth of intelligence about the Russian operations in Charleston, Sturgis was anxious to head into the fray. But he sensed that it was important to Jake that they stay for the hoedown. He had said they were brothers, now he could prove it with good Southern hospitality.

"And now gentlemen," Sturgis said rubbing his hands together, "let's get to that country hoedown you've been promising all day."

A huge smile crossed the lips of Jake and his men, and the latest meeting of America's ad-hoc citizens army came to an abrupt halt.

The men headed out through the tunnels toward the festive sound of the party in the wood fortress above.

The festival soon was reaching full swing with the Omega Force enjoying the company of the mountain gals, plenty of good food, potent moonshine and a fine array of lively country musicians including fiddlers, banjo pickers, washboard scrapers, jug puffers and a classic wash-basin bass fiddle.

You could forget for a moment the horror . . . Sturgis thought, all of his men had shucked their suits and joined the dancers.

Two banjo pickers broke into a speedy version of "Duelling Banjos" that had the crowd hopping. A wide area in the middle of the dirt filled with dancers. Sturgis and Billy stood up on a table in the midst of the fun as a fine broth of a gal with a buckskin halter top and tanned leather skirt brought several mugs full of moonshine to them. Sturgis couldn't help but watch as the loose flaps of the girl's rustic top opened wide as she set his mug down, affording him an ample view of her firm young breasts. She was gone as quickly as she'd come and Sturgis could only gulp nervously as she disappeared into a back room.

He chugged down the moonshine. "Eccch!" he cried instantly. "What is this, eh . . . creation?"

"We call it Deadbear," laughed Jake. "Use it to knock the bears out. They drink it, pass out, then we come up on 'em and skin 'em."

Jake broke into a wide grin. Sturgis couldn't tell whether he was kidding or not. It sure took the breath away. Maybe Jake wasn't lying.

"Jake . . . a personal—important question . . ."

"Well, spit it out, Sturgis. Don't mince words with me."

"Have you got any intelligence reports, I know this is a long shot, but anything from out that way mentioning any one named Robin? She's my wife— should be in Georgia."

"No, I ain't Sturgis. Sorry. But I'll put the word out. If she's there we'll find her. I promise you." He slapped Sturgis hard on the knee.

Just then the young gal who had brought the drinks whisked by Sturgis again, her breast lightly brushing his arm. Their eyes met.

"Could I get you another whiskey mister?" she asked in a deep coquettish voice that turned Sturgis' knees to butter. He looked deeply into her soft blue eyes. Her healthy glow was a rare pleasure to see and Sturgis drank in her vibrant liveliness. Strawberry blonde hair curled easily over her bare shoulders and her features were made more delicate and seductive by the naive nature of her outfit. Sturgis found her irresistible, and simply nodded his head in a dumb yes to answer her question.

Then, without even realizing it, he found himself following the delicious young wild girl throughout the room. The crowd was working into a feverish pitch of fun and excitement. The musicians played ever wildly and now inhibitions were breaking down as the troopers danced to beat the band, filled with soothing moonshine.

Sturgis was soon alone with the country girl.

"I'm Ann," she said, turning suddenly and stopping Sturgis dead in his tracks. "Well, that's my given name. But folks here just call me Cat."

"Well Cat, and how are you coping with this strange new world of ours?"

"Good as any, I guess. Funny, when I was a little kid, I used to dream that one day I'd go to New York City, or Los Angeles, or maybe even Atlanta, and try'n make something of myself. But my daddy married me off when I was fourteen to an old friend of his. He wasn't a bad man. Old. Poor thing. Got hisself killed when the bombs came. Now I just work in the kitchens here and I suppose I'll die workin' in the kitchens here. There just ain't no New York City, or Los Angeles, or Atlanta."

Sturgis was a captive of the woman's animal attraction. Cat's lips curled in fine yet full lines. Her eyes changed from turquoise to green as he watched, sparkling wildly to accent her playful smile. Her nostrils flared when she spoke of New York or Los Angeles. Or Atlanta.

As they strolled around the room her body swayed in a chorus of allure. He followed, drank in her passion, as she led him through the rooms and caverns, out a passage to a grotto tucked in a tiny mountain vale with the moon and stars above, a waterfall trickled into a lily cluttered pool. They were all alone . . . they embraced.

She gazed upon him with growing desire in her eyes. He started unbuttoning, she helped. She quickly undid her garment. Suddenly she was naked and so was he. They lay down.

She lowered her cool flesh on top of Sturgis. Her smell, her firm young body was overwhelming to his senses. For a second he imagined Robin's face overlaid on Cat's.

She leaned forward, kissed his lips with a desperate hunger, and he responded in kind. She began rubbing her body against his, her large breasts and erect nipples pressing against him, sliding across his hairy chest. He could feel her wetness as her legs spread wide apart. She moaned, kissing his neck and shoulders, working her lips down Sturgis' hard muscular body an inch at a time. His manhood stood stiffly

203

now, as she reached for it, gobbling the pulsing digit in her hungry mouth. Up and down the full length she moved as Sturgis moaned. But then she withdrew. She sat up upon him and took in his hot manhood into her love-opening.

Sturgis groaned in wild pleasure as the country hellcat slid herself down on him, and they started moving as one unit.

"Oh—oh—its—good—good," she mumbled.

They began slowly, increasing speed and intensity, lost in a reverie until they reached a crescendo together at last.

She opened her lips, "Ohhh!" she moaned, shivering with pleasure. At the same time Sturgis released his enormous pent-up reservoir. They lay there, afterwards, for a long time, stroking each other, Cat making little soft cooing noises.

Sturgis walked her back to the encampment three hours later. Some of the pain, some of the hurt of the past month was relieved from both of them. Neither would regret the encounter.

CHAPTER FOURTEEN

The mountain resistance fighters led Sturgis to the top of a ridge from which he could survey the Charleston harbor and the sprawling city through Telescopic mode. Under maximum magnification, Sturgis saw that the town was a beehive of activity. There were great numbers of Soviet vessels of every description in the murky waters. Freighters were piled up in the sea further out, waiting for their chance to unload. They rode low in the water. *Heavy stuff*. Tanks, probably. The Reds would need masses of tanks to head west.

There were too many targets for the C.A.D.S. team to take on. It was a suicide mission, but a necessary mission if the U.S. was to survive.

Sturgis thanked the resistance leaders for their help and they left, heading to begin a diversion in the north.

It was 1700 hours. The C.A.D.S. team would move down into the jaws of death after it grew dark, leaving the Rhino and a small squad behind to guard it. Sturgis saw a spot behind some abandoned warehouses near the waterfront where they could stow their Tri-bikes. Then it was 100 meters on foot, in open sight of the docks, before they would reach the water, and walk out into it. Seventy men in seven-foot high black armor, trying to get to the water *unnoticed*!

General Petrin had started to become quite accustomed to life in what had been known at one time as Washington, D.C., the capital of the United States of America. Having set up his headquarters in a Georgetown mansion, Petrin had begun to prove what he had always suspected, that a little of the capitalist good life never hurt anyone.

He headed for the building's den, on the first floor. The previous owner had been an extensive collector of VHS video tapes. If the man were still alive, the general would have commended him on his taste. Like many Russians, Petrin's command of English was more than tolerable. Fishing in the large breast pocket of the silk robe he was wearing, just one of several he had picked up in an inspection tour of the D.C. department stores, he pulled forth a gold butane lighter. Cocking the hidden mechanism with one hand, he brought the resulting flame to the cigar in his mouth.

Stepping into his panelled den, which was filled with electronic games looted from an American arcade, he looked around. The art on the pinball machines, art painted on glass and lit from behind, was a marvel of the imagination. But the pinball games were all variations on the same theme. You put your money in and used two buttons to manipulate rubber flippers to keep the ball in play and hit targets with them. But his favorites were the *video* games — one in particular where the object was to maneuver your spaceship and fire lasers to destroy all sorts of space objects, like asteroids. The objects actually burst apart when they were struck! And he liked to beat Kurchiev, his aide, at the game. Kurchiev either couldn't catch on, or was deliberately losing. Petrin didn't know for sure.

Defying socialist puritanism, they both were addicted to any sort of game. The general had said to Kurchiev so many times, "We're both dead if this gets out, so let's keep it to ourselves." The pair had gambled on the horses in England, had visited famous French and Italian casinos, even the one in Monte Carlo, and even played blackjack and poker with an American diplomat Petrin could no longer remember the name of. All on Soviet government funds.

The two had been close for years, a secret well-kept for both their sakes. The Russian high command liked to think they had picked good men to watch over those they had in key positions. Petrin and Kurchiev had made up *minor* infractions for both of them to report to the KGB occasionally. Petrin knew the KGB mind — no officer was perfect. Sooner or later he always did something out of line. It made the Party more comfortable to think they had something on their top people to keep them in check. The intricacy of it all gave the general a headache.

Kurchiev came into the den and made for the 45" T.V.

"Could we watch the Three Stupid Ones?" asked

the aide.

"Of course," answered Petrin. He loved the Three Stooges. So disrespectful, so contemptuous of authority—the general loved to watch them. He also delighted in the fact that the one called Moe wore his hair almost exactly like the premier! The first time he and Kurchiev had put one of the old tapes in the VHS, they had stared in amazement at the resemblance between their leader and the head stooge. They had stifled their laughter for as long as they could, until they had caught each other's eye, and then each had burst out in hysterics, having to hold their sides from the pain of laughing too hard.

As the decades-old comedy started, Kurchiev poured drinks for the general and himself, and then carried them over to their seats. The aide always sat next to Petrin in a smaller, straight-back chair, so as not to look too chummy. The two never knew when an additional spy might not be sent to check them *both* out.

Half-way through "Stooges Folly," the pair heard running footsteps coming through the house. Kurchiev slid his drink to an inconspicuous spot behind Petrin's recliner and then stood at ease next to it. Seconds later, a non-commissioned officer barged into the room. "General, sir. Pardon me, sir, but it is the Supreme Marshal on the emergency frequency. He sounds most urgent, sir. He is, ah, screaming, sir, that he needs your troops right away."

Petrin snapped to his feet, out of his chair before the messenger had half-completed his speech. Running across the polished, darkwood floors of his adopted mansion, Petrin arrived in his communications center in seconds. He took the microphone from the outstretched hand of a nervous radioman and announced, "Marshall Veloshnikov—this is Petrin."

"Petrin!" Veloshnikov's voice was a twisted snarl. He flung his words at Petrin without restraint. "You must assemble the Gray Suits and get them here immediately! Do you understand—*immediately*!" Veloshnikov was screaming, his voice cracking in the higher ranges.

"We are under attack! Charleston is under attack— it is *them*; the Americans in the robot-suits. They're here! Destroying us! You have to get here at once." Petrin had already stubbed out his cigar and slipped from his silk robe. "I would have been killed," raved the Supreme Marshal, "had I not just reboarded the *Lenin* to supervise unloading of antiques."

Petrin scribbled notes to the radioman, giving instructions for his Gray Suit squadron. If he could get through to the airport while Veloshnikov spoke, perhaps the Gray Suits could be assembled and ready to go by the time the marshal stopped jabbering.

"You must not fail me, Petrin," came Veloshnikov's trembling voice. "You must destroy them all this time, do you hear me—all of them, or you will pay dearly. I do not warn you lightly—do you understand me?"

Petrin assured Veloshnikov he would be there as soon as possible, all the while instructing the radioman as to what he needed. Kurchiev entered the communications center with one of Petrin's combat uniforms. Veloshnikov continued to speak, spewing forth contradictory orders in panic. Petrin was formulating his own plan of action, ignoring all of the marshal's orders. Finally Veloshnikov got off the line, and Petrin put on the uniform.

"Veloshnikov is a fool," Petrin said. "He wants me to engage those Black-suited devils to the death, as if this were some sort of epic drama of the revolution, to thrill some backwater peasants. It is only a fool who thinks he can climb to the moon on a stepladder," he mumbled enigmatically to Kurchiev.

"I will do what is necessary to save the fleet—if possible—without sacrificing the Gray-suits. *And* I will capture an American commando! If I take the big Ilyushin jet, I can be in Charleston in a half an hour. We will drop—hit with surprise—out of the sky."

Kurchiev handed Petrin his hat. Then the general left.

As he ran down the mansion's steps he took a parting glance at the partially damaged capital city of the defunct United States. Washington had been hit with neutron bombs, which kill but do not damage structures. It was an impressive city. The commandeered American vehicle zipped off to deliver him to the Dulles International airport, where his giant air transport was no doubt, taxiing into position for takeoff.

Sturgis' hope for complete surprise of the Reds didn't quite come off. The last few C.A.D.S.-members walking into the harbor waters had been spotted. But before the Russians could act upon what they had seen, his men were walking along the bottom of the murky harbor, taking long bounds for speed, their strobe lights and I.R. modes searching for the bottoms of the docked Soviet vessels. And they found them. The plan to use the C.A.D.S.-suits underwater capability — the C.A.D.S.-suits were all water-tight and heavy as hell — was working. But Sturgis heard the distant propellers starting up.

"Computer, analyze engines at vector six," he ordered. The answer sent chills to his spine. "Anti-submarine PT boats, Soviet design. Also unclassified Soviet nuclear submarine engines starting activation."

"Spread out, men," Sturgis radioed. "Come up under your designated targets and blow the hell out of them — before company arrives with depth-charges!"

He wondered about the "unclassified Soviet nuke-sub." It must be that giant half submerged object the Resistance men had talked about. He would love to get a shot at *that*! But for now he concentrated his efforts on his target #1, a huge freighter, still loaded, according to the mountain-men, with hundreds of tanks. Tanks that the Reds wanted for their push westward, into the heart of America. Tanks they would never get to use. He fired one of his precious E-balls. The destructive power of 50 howitzer shells ripped the freighter. Without looking back, Sturgis made for his next target.

In minutes, half the Russian fleet was in flaming ruin. Explosions continued to rock the Charleston harbor, sending vessel after vessel to the bottom. Clouds of salty steam rolled across the bay, boiled up from the ocean by volcanic destruction of Russian engines and reactors. Several nuclear powered craft had been sunk, their atomic piles' heat creating clouds of steam tinting the mad clouds a dozen different colors.

Sturgis, in the water along side his target #2, a Soviet destroyer, surveyed the underside of the hull. He could hear running inside, clunking.

The computer told of hi-rads in the area, but Sturgis and his men were still well protected from it by their armor. The Russian sailors and the soldiers along the docks would not be so fortunate, but that fact didn't exactly bother the C.A.D.S. commander.

Using his jet pack for thrust, Sturgis propelled himself up against the destroyer before him. Gaining the side, he raised his right arm, turned his wrist to the left, and then ordered, "Fire, Grapple-Hawk."

Instantly one of the special Grapple-Hawks installed by Van Patten shot upward, tearing its way through the metal skin of the bulkhead. Reaching up with his left hand, he caught hold of the length of cable trailing from the grapple and began pulling himself from the water.

Three sailors caught sight of him making his way up the side of the destroyer. The one that was armed opened fire with his Kalashnikov submachine-gun. Dozens of bullets rained off his armor in the 20 seconds it took him to reach the deck. None had the slightest effect.

Once on deck with his hands free, Sturgis shot the man down with his own internal guns, almost as an afterthought. More Russians came down the deck, the fire showering the C.A.D.S. suit before them. They fell in rapidly growing piles as Sturgis fired back on them with both arms, 9mm bullets hurricaning over the Reds.

One stepped forward with a grenade launcher. Managing to sight the armored suit quickly, he launched his small missile dead on target — but to no avail; Sturgis merely jet-packed up over the path of the grenade, allowing it to sail out into the bay. A burst of SMG fire took the man out. Gotta get to the bridge, Sturgis realized. This kind of fighting is penny-ante.

The C.A.D.S. commander knew he would run out of ammunition soon if he continued to engage the enemy in a one-on-one fashion. Relying on the immense speed and power of his legs, Sturgis broke into a run, thundering down the deck of the destroyer to what he thought might be the gunnery control center in mere seconds, leaving cleat-marks in the metal deckplate.

Russians died like leaves in autumn before the American's cold fury. Sturgis merely ran over their bodies, knocking them aside with his metal-sheathed arms and grinding them beneath his armored feet. Most of the sailors had only sidearms. It was no contest. Sturgis conserved ammo by merely tossing them far overboard, into the boiling waters of the flaming harbor.

Three Russians tried to block his ascent up the stairs to the control area with a shell-trailer. As he maneuvered his suit up the narrow metal passage, they rolled the dolly over the top stair, sending it crashing down toward the C.A.D.S. commander. Huge shells crashed down at Sturgis, rolling, turning end over end, snapping off the outer railing like a twig.

Hitting his jet pack, Sturgis went straight up, as the trio of thousand-pound shells missed him by only inches. Throwing his weight forward, he landed on the deck several feet from the three sailors. Although they tried to run, the C.A.D.S. leader caught the trio up in his armored arms and then squeezed, quickly— shattering their backs, snapping their bodies in two, splattering blood through the air covering his suit and the deck beneath his feet with red.

Fewer and fewer of the Russians came near Sturgis, all of them finally aware of *what* had climbed aboard their vessel. As he closed with the main hatchway to the destroyer's bridge, he broadcast to his men through the com-link in their helmets:

"C.A.D.S., listen up. I'm aboard one of their destroyers—the *Potemkin II*. Don't sink it, for Christ's sake. I'm going to attempt to take it over— use it to sink that big sub out there in the bay. It's mop-up time, boys."

Sturgis moved into the bridge, heading for the weaponry station. He found four officers within, one of them shouting like mad into a transmitter on the panel before him. Sturgis fired a dart.

The eight-inch dart pierced the man through the chest, went right through him like an arrow, and came out through his back, so it pinned him against the panel, a bleeding butterfly.

Sturgis reached out with his armored hand and crushed another man's skull, jerking the body up and away, throwing it into a corner. The other two officers rushed the C.A.D.S. man before them, trying to topple it by tearing the legs out from underneath. Sturgis lifted the servo-mechanism controlled legs one at a time, shaking the men off like babies, and then ground each of them under his heel, smashing their ribs until they were flattened.

Hurrying back to the control panel, he tried to make heads or tails of the Russian labels, looking for the targeting section. Suddenly, he found it. "Damn," he muttered, not wanting to believe what he was seeing. "Look at *this*."

The controls were all of *United States* manufacture. Reaching down, the C.A.D.S. commander ripped loose one of the made in USA tags. He wiped it clean, and read the company's name: *Exrell Inc.*

Sturgis remembered where he had recently seen Exrell Inc. It was painted on the doors of the vehicles in millionaire Pinky Ellis' strange caravan. Why, that fat pig's equipment had contributed to the Red fleet's weaponry! Pinky Ellis must have known if his corporation sent classified components out of America, betraying his country and helping to bring it to doom. Pinky was just the kind of guy to do something like that. To get a business quarter or two of higher profits. Maybe the obese pig was on a roadside at that moment, puking his guts out through his mouth and nose from radiation sickness. Or maybe he's comfortable somewhere, selling out more stuff to the Reds.

"*And I let him go.*" Suddenly Sturgis realized he had made a grave error. Pinky could help the Reds locate many of Exrell's hi-tech products. I should have *killed him*, and I *let him go!*"

But now, the U.S. origin of the Soviet weaponry was to Sturgis' advantage. Sturgis knew how these tracking-targeting gizmos worked.

Forcing his anger aside, Sturgis finished punching in the data he was reading off the panel's radar screens. He had almost target-computed the big sub. Damn, the gigantic thing was moving, pulling out of the harbor. But he had it laser-locked into an inescapable radar cage.

The one I killed on the way in must have radioed them what was up, the C.A.D.S. commander thought. Well, big deal. Another few seconds and they're one for the history books themselves.

Suddenly his suit's Blue Mode lit up, warning him that a mass of the enemy were moving down the hallway toward him. Before he could finish programming the destroyer's firing computers, four grenades came flying into the control room, thrown by unseen Reds. The bombs were useless against the C.A.D.S. armor, but unfortunately, not against the room and the computer.

Before Sturgis could do anything to prevent it, the grenades went off with blinding force, ripping apart the computers he needed to fire the ship's 15 inch guns.

"Damn," he spat, running out into the hallway. He knocked sailors aside in all directions, squashing them without even trying, running over them in his efforts to get outside again. He could barely squeeze through some of the hatches, his bulky armor scraping at a dozen points as he pulled himself through some of the tighter spots, bending the steel plates.

Once out on the upper deck, he used his jet pack to set himself down next to one of the main guns near the stern. Thanks to the shallowness of the bay, the sub had not been able to submerge to any great

216

degree yet. He could not see it unaided, but with the Geometric Identifier in his suit he was able to keep the craft perfectly pin-pointed.

Tearing the doorway off the gun's manual-control room, Sturgis tried to reach the controls, but found he could not fit into the room. Desperate, he grabbed the left side of the door frame with both hands and pulled, stripping back the four-inch steel side wall with only the slightest effort. Seeing that the manual controls had not been fouled up, he turned and raced to a trailer of shells against the opposite bulkhead.

No Reds were left on the vessel to oppose him. Unhampered, he bent down and grabbed hold of one of the massive shells on the cart. Normally, the 2,000 pounders were loaded by four men with a mobile hydraulic lift. Not having the time to waste, however, the C.A.D.S. commander strained his suit's remaining power, slowly lifting the massive explosive to his shoulder. Crossing the deck, he pushed up on the oppressive weight, inserted it manually in the large gun before him, and then slid it home.

Once the shell was placed, he bolted the muzzle door and headed back into the control room. He could see nothing of the *Lenin* through the continual steam, and the spray and debris constantly being flung into the air by explosions, but he did not have to. Using the C.A.D.S. tracking-radar, he again spotted the submarine, and used the levers to raise the huge gun. The sub was nearly out of range.

"Only going to get this one chance," thought Sturgis. "Here's hoping it counts."

He hit the firing sequence, sending 2,000 pounds of explosives flying at the *Lenin*. Seconds after the launch, the shell arced down and bore in on the submarine, rapidly closing and then making contact with the aft deck. A blinding flash filled the waters with twisted metal and bodies of sailors. Sturgis peered through the steam, hoping to catch a glimpse of the sub to see if he had done sufficient damage to sink it. He had little luck. The radioactive mists played havoc with the fine tuned components of his armor's computers, until a sudden ocean wind blew a freshly clean corridor of air through the bay. Just in time to see the sub's conning tower slide smoothly under the water. He had just *nicked* the huge vessel.

Anxiously, he said "Red Mode," which gave positions and numbers of his nuke-troopers. He was glad to see the sinking of the Russian fleet had taken the lives of only a handful of C.A.D.S. troopers.

"Okay, you guys — we've been here too long." The C.A.D.S. commander took a final look at the churning waves with his Telescopic mode. He knew another shot would be useless because the sub was far out and way underwater now. "Fall back," he radioed. "We've done just about all we can here."

The Macro-View system in his armor gave him a grid-centered sweep of roughly a five mile circle around him. Statistics flooded the screens of his visor. If he understood the incredibly rapid flow of data rushing past him, he and his men had destroyed 88% of the Red flotilla.

Now 2300 meters above Charleston, in his Ilyushin jet, General Petrin peered down at the burning fleet. His squadron would be in the jump area in less than five minutes. Against Veloshnikov's orders to engage and combat the Americans to the death, the general had already instructed his men with his own, less ambitious, but far more practical plan.

To win against the Americans, he needed to be able to match them. He and his men would fight — no question. Many of them would probably die. But if they could manage to *capture* one of the American suits undamaged — then they would have fought a worthwhile battle.

Petrin lowered his left arm so the men buzzing around him could attach his other gauntlet. Thick gray armor slid over his fingers; solid bolts an inch thick were cranked into place. Petrin eyed the chronometer once more. Three minutes to drop. In the bomb bay behind him, the other Gray Suits were ready, the large Solkniv tank-parachutes needed to slow their descents already strapped on.

Petrin flexed the steel-crushing fingers of his left glove, making sure all the circuits had been properly aligned. "If we cannot take one of the Americans, we will never be able to beat them in the open. Thousands more will have to die before we can tame this land — maybe millions," he confessed to his aide. "Let me bring peace to the world quickly."

And then, Petrin let the aide screw his helmet's face guard in place, calmly waiting for two more minutes to go by.

The American Black suits are a technological *marvel*, Petrin thought staring down at the smoke and flames below. And the leader of the American Black suits is not the child that his political leaders were. How Petrin wished he could someday talk to the man. But that was an impossibility . . .

When Sturgis' 2000 lbs. of flying explosives detonated below the *Lenin*'s waterline, the sub lurched sideways, pitching as if caught in a hurricane. Normally secured objects splattered every cabin and walkway, flung from their restraints by the bombardment. Electrical systems shorted out, sending sparks flying, creating fires in a dozen spots throughout the submarine. Bulkheads were pushed in, salt water flooded into the *Lenin*'s aft fire-control section.

"Seal all compartments!" ordered Veloshnikov.

The vessel's captain obeyed instantly. Throughout the submarine, large water-tight steel doors began sliding into place, cutting the ship into flooded and non-flooded areas. The voices of drowning sailors poured through the ship's internal phones, begging for release, but it was too late. Veloshnikov sat grimly at his command desk, listening as each of the hollow, doomed voices pleaded through the ship's radio, screaming for their lives.

"Damage control!" Veloshnikov asked, trembling. "Is the *Lenin* doomed?"

Static. More static. Then came Gregov's calm voice, "No, Marshal Veloshnikov. The *Lenin* lives!"

CHAPTER FIFTEEN

Sturgis was pulling himself out of the water when the *Potemkin II* was blown to hell. Not willing to leave such a prize behind, the C.A.D.S. commander had wired the remaining shells on deck to explode a minute after he left the immense ship.

He had not had time to run charges below to sink the ship, but he had ensured that enough destruction would take place above deck to cripple the former flagship, create a metal-melting fire that would at least gut her.

As he neared the loading dock, an armored hand reached over to help him ashore. The black hand closed on his, pulling him up with a powerful surge.

"Billy!" exclaimed Sturgis, seeing the decal that said "STP" on the suit.

"Yes sir," answered the West Virginian. Roberto, Tranh, even Rossiter stood by Dixon's side, their huge arms akimbo.

"I thought I ordered everyone back to the evac site?"

"Sure did, sir. But we reckoned to stick tight to watch *you* disobey your own orders and blow the hell out of that commie rust-bucket. We figured with everyone else high-tailin' it out of here, you might enjoy some company on the way back."

"Okay, you're fools, but thanks. Now let's move out before we're all dead fools."

But before he could lead them away from the docks, their alert Blue Modes lit, warning them of incoming enemy forces. Sturgis did a computer analysis of how much fire power he and his men had remaining; most of them had already spent half their ammunition—some were below half. The Rhino's supply of extra E-balls was very low as well.

"Conserve ammo, boys," he ordered. "Looks like we're going to need every bit to get out of here. We've got to hit them on the move. Billy, come with me up this alley—everyone else go around. We'll meet on the other side. Head east back down toward the parking lots on the other side of the warehouses."

While he headed for the alley-way, Sturgis radioed, "Everyone, meet at computer grid five, the two-story warehouse. Wait inside, wait five minutes for the others—no one else shows . . . take off."

Sturgis checked his G.I. (Geometric Identification) Mode to see what was headed for them. Several dozen Reds, heavily armed, many in jeeps or trucks, were coming in on them from all directions. He had picked the correct route to give his men the advantage of cover. But as they reached the halfway point of the alley, two jeeps followed by a pack of Red soldiers rounded the corner, meeting them head on. One of the Reds had a major's insignia on his helmet.

Running in the lead, Sturgis screamed into his external loudspeaker: "I'll take the major!" and

222

charged ahead. Machine gun bullets bounced from his head and shoulders as he ran, quarterback style, straight for the first vehicle.

Seeing the swift dark form racing at him deflecting bullets like rain drops, the Russian driver slammed on his brakes and leaped out the side. Sturgis, reaching the jeep seconds later, scooped the front of it up in his hands and heaved, sending the heavily plated military vehicle flying end-over-end into the frantic Reds aligned behind it. It crushed five men and bowled over the major. Sturgis fired one E-ball at the overturned jeep, creating a blinding gasoline explosion. Burning fuel showered the alley, alighting on the walls of the buildings.

The officer, half-afire, tried to lift a bazooka. Somehow he fired it, screaming in pain as he did so. Sturgis went into Jump mode, jetting up from the shell, the laser-locked 9mm SMG bullets roared from his sleeve-mount and made target. The man's head exploded off and his chopped sizzling body fell to the ground.

Billy threw the remaining jeep at three Reds scurrying away, finishing the lot of them. It was over as swiftly as it had begun.

"Maximum alert," shouted Sturgis. "Where there's a dozen Reds, there's more. We're in for it now! Scan area, all modes!"

Checking his R-mode the C.A.D.S. commander was puzzled to see on the radar—a spinning thread-like shape with objects flying off it. He raced around to the source and understood. It was Roberto. And Reese and Horner had joined him.

Roberto had fired his Hawk-grapple through one

of the enemy and was using the man as a giant mace. Spinning the body at the end of his grappling cable, he used the Russian soldier to knock the others aside. Misfiring weapons did more damage within the Russian ranks than Roberto. The communists shot each other down, trying to avoid their spinning comrade.

Suddenly, the Russian's body broke loose, ripping the guts from it which sprayed, flying into three charging soldiers. Laughing, Roberto reeled in his grappling cable, cursing the rest of the Reds who fled into an alley. The others joined him, cheered by the fact that the Russians had turned tail so easily. All of them except for Sturgis.

"Something's wrong here."

"What do you mean, Colonel?" asked Roberto.

"This was too easy. They brought us together, inside this square for some reason, and then ran off."

The C.A.D.S. commander boosted his Blue Mode to full power, doing a sweep of the entire area around them. Something he could not recognize, fuzzy blips, showed on his screen. Whatever they were—they were near. Suddenly the G.I. Mode screamed out "Armored C.A.D.S.-type suits."

"Christ," yelled Sturgis. "It's Gray Suits!" His radar now was clear. It had been fuzzy because the Gray Suits were dropping through high-rad clouds!

"They're all around us—from above." There were fifty, then seventy of the Gray Suits hitting the ground now. They ran from every corner, every alley, and still fell from the sky!

The C.A.D.S. team members closest to the action diverted to help Sturgis and the others trapped in the square.

"Colonel . . ." asked Roberto, "Are we in as much trouble as I think we are?"

"More, Roberto — more." Sturgis looked up, seeing one of the still parachuting Gray Suits diving for the square. Cocking his E-ball launcher, he radioed, "We're attempting a breakout. We don't have enough ammo and there are too many of 'em."

Lifting his arm, he let his targeting laser zero-in on the Russian, and then fired. The crackling explosive hit, jarring the Russian, shattering the inches-thick chestplate of his combat suit. The electrical force of the E-ball travelled through the soldier's armor, flying upward into his chute, setting it on fire. In seconds the entire chute was a flaming mass, falling from the sky; the soldier fell on one of his comrades, his blazing hot body smashing into those of other Gray Suiters. Adding to the confusion in the square, Rossiter, Horner and Reese jetted into the air to meet the chuters.

Rossiter blasted at two approaching Gray Suits with his machine guns, trading bullets with the pair in mid-air.

"Christ Sturgis," he yelled. "Bullets are even *less* effective against them than last time."

The C.A.D.S. commander's mind raced, looking for a weak spot in the trap which had been sprung on them. As six Gray Suiters came from each of the three directions open to them, Sturgis pointed toward the opening Roberto and Reese had blasted in the warehouse across the square. The pair of vets had made a good move!

"Follow Roberto and Reese," he ordered. "Through that building!"

225

Sturgis and Billy, on semi-automatic firing mode, ran for the gap in the building. Aiming in the general direction of their attackers, the two fired again and again, setting off a dozen explosions each as they headed for the hole. The E-balls cut through the Gray Suits, staggering many, destroying some. Explosions and smoke filled the square, masking their flight to the building. But both of them took a number of cartridge hits. Sturgis could feel the loosening of some of his suit's overused joints. His own reading was up to .0437. He dived into the gap.

"Bloody hell," thought the C.A.D.S. commander. "Much more stress and we won't be able to use our jet packs without shaking ourselves apart." But, temporarily, they were safe. "Quick everyone — find a basement exit, or a back way out of here. *Hurry up.*" said Sturgis.

Rossiter ran back into the gloomy confines of the warehouse, desperately searching for a way out. Sturgis unlimbered his LWA, lining up his first target.

"C'mon you suckers. Welcome to hell!"

He hated to use the LWA's last charges . . . but blasting with the laser he cut down two Gray Suits who lunged into the building, slicing their thick boiler-plate like a sharp knife into a tomato. The Russians toppled and fell, their torsos in one direction, their legs in another — and the sticky tomato of their guts gushing behind. Sturgis pulled back and ducked behind a support girder as the Russians responded. Nine-mm shells tore at the wall of the warehouse, gouging their way through, smashing brick and plasterboard. The C.A.D.S. commander heard the pop of grenade rifles over the din; ducking back further into the warehouse, he narrowly avoided being turned to shrapnel as four of the small rockets disintegrated the room he had been in. The entire front of the building collapsed, thousands of pounds of concrete and girders crashing down as the upper floors gave way. Damn, thought Sturgis, Rossiter was next to me!

Sturgis transmitted, "Rossiter! Where are you?"

The trooper's reply came through Sturgis' headset, "I'm still alive, Colonel, and busy!"

Tracking the man with his suit's computers, the leader of the C.A.D.S. team made his way through the now dangerously unsteady building, well aware that a number of Gray Suits were smashing their way in behind him, searching for both himself and Rossiter. Ignoring the smoke and rolling clouds of dust that hung in the darkness, Sturgis worked entirely through the sensors in his armor, following Rossiter's trail. When he finally found him, Sturgis could see the man was busy indeed.

Rossiter was on the floor, struggling with one of the massive Gray Suits. Again Sturgis was impressed with just how large, how massive the Russian combat armor was. The Gray Suit had to be a full foot taller than Rossiter's seven-foot armor, and maybe 100 pounds heavier. The C.A.D.S. commander went to help his man, when two other Reds moved within range of Sturgis' sensors.

Sturgis whirled but it was too late. Both of the Gray-suit Russians were holding ZA-11 rocket launchers. Sturgis stared at the weapons, looking for some way out of the situation.

Can't avoid those things—they're too fast. Rossiter

can't help. He's got troubles enough of his own.

Behind the others, more Russians came into view, similarly armed. The ones in front made motions with their weapons for Sturgis to put up his hands. Seeing no other choice, the C.A.D.S. commander did as ordered, hoping he was only playing for time. Why didn't they shoot? Of course! They wanted his *suit!*

Billy and Horner had made it out of the ring of Gray Suits. It hadn't been difficult. Petrin had wanted to lose as few of his men to the Americans as possible. Therefore, his only objective was to capture *one* of the C.A.D.S. suits to take back to Russia for analysis, so the American super-weapons could now become *Russian* ones. This did not mean, however, that the two were in the clear. They had escaped the Gray Suits only to run into a column of Soviet tanks.

The pair took shelter in a storage receiving depot. Large burlap squares containing clothing from Korea stood in hundred foot stacks all around them. Rats, not even fazed by the radioactive steam or the war, jumped from bale to bale, running at the sight of the black C.A.D.S. armor. One defiant rodent reared up in front of the pair. It stood nearly a foot and a half tall, and looked to weigh thirty pounds. Billy laughed.

"We ain't got enough trouble with tanks, now the bastards are sending rats after us."

"Yeah," Horner agreed, kicking at the rodent. "Must be the mascot for their shot-put team."

Before they could find their way to better cover, one of the tanks had spotted the two Americans, plowed through the wall in front of them.

They each fired their last E-balls into its guts, exploding the attacker from the inside out. The tank belched smoke in thick, red-black clouds, flew apart with a force that shattered all of the windows in the building.

But other tanks came through the wall seconds later, forcing the two C.A.D.S. troopers to retreat back into the clothing bales. The tanks rammed the first of the bales, sending the gigantic columns tottering, some forward, some backwards on themselves. By doing so the tanks trapped the C.A.D.S. men. The massive two-ton bales fell ten deep atop the Americans.

Outside of the building, the tank commander radioed General Petrin for orders. After briefing the Gray-Suit commander on the situation, he asked "What do we do now, sir?"

"Torch the building, Major, and the clothing bales. The American *suits* can most likely take the heat, but perhaps not the men within them. Use incendiary shells. Keep the area circled. If they come out, destroy them. If they don't, they die."

The tank commander relayed Petrin's orders. In minutes the whole area was a blazing nightmare, too hot for unprotected soldiers to approach, nearly too hot for the tanks. Inside, Billy and Horner lay trapped, unable to move under the veritable mountain of bales. Despite their greatly increased strength, with nothing to get leverage against, they could not budge it. They were going to *fry*.

CHAPTER SIXTEEN

Inside the collapsing warehouse, Sturgis began to raise his arms as the Russians covering him had ordered. They were taking no chances; five of the Gray Suits had moved into position, zeroing their hand-held rocket launchers on him. The C.A.D.S. commander tried to move slowly, not wanting any of the edgy Reds to grow suspicious.

"Okay, fellows—you want my arms up—they're up." With his arms outstretched completely, Sturgis suddenly cocked his wrist and fired a last pair of E-balls into the ceiling, bringing the roof down on everyone. The Russians unleashed their rockets, but missed him. Sturgis used his jet pack to fly straight into the falling debris, which blanketed the Reds in a cloud of concrete and dust.

Rossiter continued to struggle with the Gray Suit he had been fighting with when Sturgis had found him. On his back, the Russian saw the ceiling falling on them. Losing his grip for a second, he allowed Rossiter to slip free. Pressing his advantage, the C.A.D.S. trooper slammed his fist home with all his armored might, shattering the Russian's face plate.

Before the Gray Suit could act, Rossiter cocked his wrist and shouted, "Fire SMG!"

His arm unleased a trail of machine gun fire which took the Russian's helmet off, and his head with it. At that second, more falling debris hit everyone, filling the room with an impenetrable black billow. The Gray Suits, too professional to shoot blindly and endanger each other, began searching the area for either of the Americans.

Sturgis, clinging to a girder above, checked his P.D. Mode—.6439 and climbing. Too much damage. Too many hits. He'd been lucky with the last stunt—most of the larger pieces of debris had missed him on the way down. He hoped they had missed Rossiter as well. Deciding to take a chance, he radioed, "Mickey? Can you hear me?"

The trooper's voice responded, "Yes, sir. I can hear you, sir. I'm okay. I think."

Then another voice came over Sturgis' head set. "Commander—it's Billy. Me and Horner are trapped in this bitchin' death oven by a pile of overturned burning bales. Can't get out."

"Billy," asked Sturgis, "where are you?"

"Coordinate E-1," said Billy. "We never made it out of the building, sir. They boxed us in real neat. It's getting hot. Too hot. But leave us—we'll self-destruct when we can't hold out any longer."

Thinking quickly, Sturgis broadcast back to them. "Hold on—*don't* destruct!" He hoped the Russians could not pick up the transmissions. "I *need* you two guys—Maybe with the four of us being in here, we'd have an advantage. They're expecting just two. We'll dig you out, don't do anything rash."

Sturgis and Rossiter charged right through a burning back wall to the rescue, sending flaming boards flying. Beyond the wall they found fifty tons of burning bales. Aside from the heat, which the computer indicated would not be tolerable for long, there was the weight to consider. You couldn't very well start moving the burning pile, that would just trap them as well as Billy and Horner.

"Billy," radioed Sturgis, "did you think of smashing *down* through the floor below you?"

"Negative, Skip. I tried and can't do it—it's solid concrete thicker than I can handle. Any other ideas—it's getting *hot* man."

"Any E-balls left?"

"None, Commander. Both me and my pal are on empty. Just bullets. Otherwise we would have taken the chance and blasted away."

"Okay." Sturgis responded, his mouth dry. "It isn't safe, but I'm going to use my LWA—even though its warning lights have been on since the last time I fired. It might hold up a few more shots. Try to shove up and fly out on your jet-packs. Maximum power the minute you feel the weight shift. You should feel the vibration, even if you don't hear the laser firing."

"Anything, Skip, *anything*! Start shooting."

Sturgis raised the LWA and started blasting away, working the beam of destruction from the top of the pile of intensely burning bales. The LWA bucked like a pump-action shotgun every time Sturgis squeezed the trigger. He used the narrow beam, cutting deep through the flaming mass, as Rossiter used the few E-balls he had left to blast away the debris left by Sturgis' work.

233

Sturgis cut off his weapon at the last possible second. The LWA had grown so hot that he could feel its heat right through his steel gloves. "That's it, Billy, push up—push like a son-of-a-bitch!"

The bales trembled, then flew up, like lava from Mount Vesuvius. Out from under the pile flew the two trapped men. Their jet packs smashed them right up into the tin roof high above, and through it. Sturgis heard Billy's triumphant rebel yell.

Sturgis, on max-audio mode, heard their metal footsteps on the roof, then a tremendous double splash. *What the hell?* The two men soon came through the door, their black suits covered with streams of water.

"Remembered there was some sort of water-trough outside, Sturg. Sure cooled off. Thanks for the assist," drawled the southerner.

Checking the Blue Mode, Sturgis could now see a large enemy buildup surrounding the building. It included a number of tanks. From a computer analysis of the suit's internal maps, Sturgis picked the best way available for the scattered C.A.D.S. team to withdraw from Charleston.

"Men, we're going into the *water* again," Sturgis broadcasted. "Carry those that can't walk. I'm hooking you all into the map of the route."

On Sturgis' command, and following the linked-up computer's map displays, all the scattered Americans headed for the waterfront. Sturgis said a silent thanks to heaven for the returned steam clouds which helped obscure them from the Russians. Blasting in every direction at anything that moved, they threw caution to the wind, no longer worrying about trying to

234

conserve ammunition. If they didn't make it the handful of blocks to the ocean, all the ammo in the world wasn't going to be of any use to them later. Sturgis ordered, "If anyone's immobilized, take the auto-suicide shot and blow up your suit. No matter what happens to any one man, the others keep going. Nobody stops for anything. Understood?"

"Yes, sir!" a chorus of voices answered. Then Sturgis added, "Go for their face plates, but don't try to shoot it out with a Gray Suit unless you have to. Our mission is accomplished, and we're getting the hell out of here."

The billowing radioactive steam was thicker than ever. They could barely see one another. Although standing just yards apart, Sturgis' radio beam could barely reach the other troopers' helmets through the rad-interference.

"Follow me; the water is at vector three hundred seventy."

Rossiter stumbled out behind Sturgis, barely catching sight of his commander's disappearing armor before the clouds covered it completely. He stumbled after him, hoping to catch up, unfortunately coming under the attention of the watchful General Petrin who had taken up infra-red binoculars on top of the building across the square. Petrin quickly radioed his five tanks about his discovery.

"The Americans are coming out the way they came in. Lay down a maximum field of fire."

Salvos of shells blasted the front of the building where the C.A.D.S. troopers had just been, and a semi-circle around it. The dock collapsed from the force of the blast, the warehouse tumbling down, falling over like an old drunk. Hundreds of tons of girders, cement, brick, and glass dropped, taking several dead and a number of still living Gray Suits with it. The thunder of the destruction echoed for miles in every direction. But the Americans had disappeared—underwater.

Walking on the muddy bottom in their waterproof C.A.D.S. suits, they emerged far away from the sounds of the tank guns.

The computer-generated strategy for evacuation had been successful. For most of them. But not all. Reese didn't make it. Five others were unaccounted for—after the rest crossed the bay. A heavy price.

The C.A.D.S. team assembled just across the bay. Sturgis and the others stopped waiting for those they knew were never going to come. It had been a successful mission, despite the appearance of the Gray Suits. They had come too late in the game to stop Sturgis' total destruction of the Charleston harbor fleet. But 8 of the C.A.D.S. troopers lay wounded.

"Don't leave the bastards anything," Sturgis ordered.

When the cremation of the spare bikes was completed, the C.A.D.S. troops moved out, the Tri-bikes and their riders racing across a farm field, back toward the West. Sturgis had waited a long time for stragglers. Billy asked him why.

"Just a feeling," answered Sturgis. "Nothing I can put my finger on. I'd just feel a whole lot better if all the suits were accounted for—occupants dead or alive."

The C.A.D.S. commander had a sense of foreboding, that had been brought on by the actions of the Gray Suits. Their strategy had been geared to take one of the C.A.D.S. team alive; suit intact. The only question was, did they succeed?

CHAPTER SEVENTEEN

Sturgis' plan was to head south into the swamp-lands to avoid the inevitable squadrons of Reds searching west, out for blood — They'd lie low until the bombs stopped falling — and then they'd see. Billy knew the lay of the land down there, and they had good computer maps. The Revengers believed there were very few Reds that way too. The column of C.A.D.S. Troopers sped at 90 mph southward on US 1A, hugging the Atlantic seaboard. Sturgis knew they were badly exposed to attack by MIGs, but he had to chance sticking to the highway at least until they crossed the Susquehanna River into Georgia.

The sun was high in the sky, but its diffuse rays barely illuminated the broad open road surface. The highway was oddly clear. No abandoned cars or trucks.

To the east and west, the snow covered fields were a gray/white calm. There should be at least ruins of houses and wrecked cars. There weren't. Sturgis speculated that the entire area might have been swept clean by a massive tidal wave caused by a nuke bomb. A few snapped telephone poles alongside the road indicated this. Everyone, everything had been carried off by a sheer wall of water. The raised highway was like a causeway cutting over an immense burial ground. Only the sound of the Tri-bikes' humming engines cut through the deathly stillness of the dimly lit scene.

Sturgis scanned the horizon with his Macro-view function, which provided a five-mile panoramic view of the area. Flat. No cover for miles. Off the roadway, the Tri's would be slowed down considerably in the snowy marshlands, but on the road, they were sitting ducks! He licked his parched lips and spoke into his radio.

"Okay men, we're forty-five minutes outside of Savannah. Hopefully, there's still a bridge over the Susquehanna. Once we're in Georgia we'll be able to find some cover. Check your monitors. I'm feeding you the route now. We'll head for the I-17 bridge south of the city. It's a strong structure according to my data and a good thirty miles from ground zero in this region."

"Once we're in Georgia . . . then what?" asked Rossiter from the rear of the column, about a half a mile back.

"We regroup," he said. "We're going to strike again, but not now. *We'll* pick the time and the place."

"Why not head back to the crystal caves underground fortress?" asked Roberto.

"No go. We're too hot right now. We'd just lead them right to the heart of the resistance forces. Besides, we'd have to fight our way through the thick of Red ground forces. No — we'll regroup down south. The Okefenokee Swamp, down on the Georgia-Florida border. I figure we could find cover there, hole up, and strike back at their weakest points whenever we want. We could move west from there too, back to White Sands if that's what we have to do. Fenton?"

"Yes, Colonel?"

"How are the wounded eight men?"

"Five died, sir. Martino, Blythe, Donaldson, Gerard and Mandell. We were able to strap them onto their Tri-bikes, which have been following us on auto pilot. I think the others will make it."

Sturgis checked his radar. No bogies. They were safe for a moment, so he ordered a halt. The C.A.D.S. team pulled up into formation of four rows with the Rhino in the rear. The men dismounted, stood at the side of their Tri's on the cracked macadam. Sturgis ordered the troopers to set up a makeshift funeral pyre by chopping down the nearest blackened telephone poles. This they did within minutes, using their chainsaw to topple them.

A detail of pall-bearer troopers brought the suited bodies of their fallen comrades up to the piled wood and laid them on it, after removing computer components and weapons.

Sturgis walked up to the funeral pyre and addressed the troopers. 'Men, we gather here briefly, to honor our brave brothers, fallen in battle for liberty. Let their deaths be not forgotten. And let us hope those who fell in Charleston blew up their suits, so that the Red butchers can't get any info they can use."

Sturgis solemnly nodded at Billy, who aimed his LFP at the pyre. A liquid plastic fire erupted from Billy's arm. The bodies were soon consumed. The suits were slag.

Minutes of total silence passed. Then the C.A.D.S. men remounted and sped off, leaving the smoldering ashes behind, a reddish smudge on the vacant landscape.

They rode in a dark mood for the next 20 minutes or so, their senses tuned to their scanners, searching the sky, the road for Russians. Where were they? Waiting? Hiding? Ready to lash out at any moment?

The deaths of their companions had instilled an icy dread in every man in the force. Somehow they had believed all the talk about their near-invulnerability. Until now. Until the rising smoke of the pyre said differently. They were powerful. The toughest bastards who had ever marched into battle — in their suits. But they were human, mortal. When the suit was punctured — they bled real blood, and died like foot soldiers fallen in the mud.

They were within five miles of Savannah and the Susquehanna River crossing when Sturgis broke in on their helmet radios, distracting them from their brooding. "Nothing shows up on my visor on infrared, radar, macro-view . . . Tranh? Could they be fooling our sensors? Do you detect any low-microwave activity on your T-scope?"

"Anything's possible, Colonel, but I read zero. Maybe we're just being over-cautious. Perhaps we don't realize how much chaos we caused. We had them on the ropes back there."

"Still and all," said Sturgis, "I don't like it. Too quiet. We'll move in three groups. Billy, take twenty men and drive on ahead. See if we have a bridge left. If not . . ."

"Then we're up against the wall," said Billy. "Don't

242

worry, Skip. I'll find a route." He tore off at top speed, his tires squealing on the road, passing the column, his squad hitting 130 mph.

In less than five minutes he radioed back.

"We're in, Skip," he said. "I-71 bridge is A-OK. It's cluttered a bit with wrecks and such, but we can make it across."

"We're on our way," Sturgis exclaimed. "Pull up, Fenton. Close ranks. It's beginning to rain; wind's picking up a bit; visibility might get bad."

"Righto, Colonel," Fenton said, gunning the Rhino up with a roar.

Soon the rest of the column of space-age warriors were crossing the wreck-littered bridge. They weaved in and out of the confused mass of civilian vehicles. Sturgis didn't like being exposed like this on the bridge.

When they were safely across, Billy directed them. He knew of a possible concealed escape route—a canal beginning not far from their location. Its path led right into swamp country.

"Our vehicles churn water pretty well, well enough to get us along the canal at any rate," Billy said. "In my younger days, when I used to cruise all over the South, me and my pals, drinking and pickin' up gals like you wouldn't believe—I stumbled on it. We can drive our Tri-bikes right into the water, it's always level to the banks. It's overhung by a mess of mangrove trees—good air cover! It leads right into the swamps. We can pick it up about, oh, 30 miles west of here. Back then it had bugs like you never seen—and even a few 'gators."

"Thirty miles," said Fenton. "That's thirty to forty-five minutes for the Rhino, if the highway's not choked with wrecks."

"Okee — fenokee — Swamp," said Tranh, apparently entranced by the name. "Okee-fen-o-kee . . ."

"It's just a little bitty canal," Billy continued. "In the old days the South was full of 'em. Some of the big plantations has their own canal systems leading right to the levees or railroads. Me and two other guys got hold of a canoe, went miles down the damned spooky thing. We were lost for ten hours and were surprised we found our way out. Most folks don't. It's thick as a jungle back there. We can get to the canal by turning west on Rte. 7, just a few miles ahead."

Sturgis followed Billy's direction, turning the squad off as the southerner had indicated, onto a smaller road.

It still sounded good. A vast swampy wilderness offering plenty of overhead tree cover, and water and mud as protection from ground attack. The Okefenokee Swamp was a good 100 miles from the nearest nuke hit, the rad-level should be better there.

The road was still cluttered with abandoned cars, slowing them down considerably. The rain was driving hard. It was great protection from MIGs, but meant even slower going. Sturgis' lips gripped his teeth. The wind was rocking his normally stable Tri-bike, and the rain was beginning to fill with hail. Monstrous black clouds rolled in above to the sound of thunder.

"Mode Red," Sturgis requested the computer. The visor's screen instantly depicted the column of C.A.D.S. warriors streaming along the highway on a red grid. They were stretched out too far now. Fenton's Rhino was losing speed, almost two miles back.

"Close ranks," he radioed, easing his Tri's speed down a bit because he had to dart in and out among the wrecks. He watched his Red Mode screen as the column closed formation.

One of the C.A.D.S. troopers lost control of his Tri on the wet surface and slammed headlong into a tan Cadillac turned lengthwise across the highway. Sturgis saw the collision on his radar screen. The Tri exploded on impact. The C.A.D.S. trooper was thrown into the air.

"Fire your retros," Sturgis yelled.

The savvy trooper activated his retros and broke his fall, landing shaken but safely 100 yards off the highway.

Another trooper pulled his Tri along and let the man jump aboard, then rejoined the column.

The wind, according to the suit-comp, was hitting 78 mph. A veritable hurricane. He ordered the men to proceed even more slowly.

"Where the hell is the canal, Billy?"

"It should be right at the next crossroad I think — but it's been twelve years — "

"There it is, Skip!" Billy yelled, pointing to a highway water-culvert bridge just ahead in the downpour.

Billy in the lead, the nuke-commando column turned off and, with care, rolled down an embankment one at a time and entered the water. The big treads of the Tri's churned them handily along in the overflowing canal, all without incident. The big Rhino was eased in deftly by the Britisher, and took up their rear. At least, Sturgis thought, with all the trees overhanging them, they were pretty well covered from air-surveillance.

After several hours, the wind and rain died down. They at last reached Okefenokee, a 30 square mile area of wilderness that included some of the meanest swamp land in North America. The canal wound around grassy knolls and islets before losing itself in a network of streams opening into a broad muck-filled lake. Thick, pungent mists floated through the air, masking the banks. The pine and hardwood gave way to mammoth cypress trees. As the mist waned here and there, exposing the banks, Sturgis and the men were struck by the lush vegetation. Vines and heavy underbrush mingled with the net-like roots and over-hanging branches of the cypress. Small snakes and fishes darted through the murky waters. Lilypads carpeted much of the lake. Birds, insects. My God, *life*. Tons of it.

The mist lifted in the middle of the lake and the entire C.A.D.S. unit gathered there, minus Billy Dixon.

"Billy," said Sturgis. "Billy? Where the hell are you?" Interference crackled through in Sturgis' radio.

"Billy? . . ."

The interference continued for a minute until Billy emerged from the mists near the bank, holding a big catfish aloft on a branch he'd sharpened into a spear.

"We'll eat good tonight boys!" he called out over his mike.

"Dixon, you S.O.B. Didn't you read me just a

246

minute ago?"

"That's negative, Skip. I heard some interference on my radio. That's all . . ."

"Something's up, Colonel," said Tranh. "Check your microwave sensors. Look. I'm getting a mass of morse-code like bursts."

"Same here. Any ideas Fenton?"

"Working on it," Fenton replied, furiously spinning dials and calibrators inside the instrument-filled Rhino. "I'm not sure. Might be natural. I think we have some unusual gasses lurking about. Temp's 60 degrees F. The inorganic analyzer's showing a mixture of methane and carbons. No lethal doses. It seems to be a natural phenomenon. Probably the gas is what's warming it up, making it all green. Gridley mentioned such a warming could happen—"

"Swamp gas!" Billy said. "I remember now. It plays hell with radio traffic in these parts."

"We'll have to live with it," Sturgis said. "These suits need a recharge bad. We gotta hook up the suits to the Rhino's generator. Find some dry land where we can hole up. Billy?"

"There's some dry spots up ahead. There's even a little village—an old swampfolks bazaar. You know—like Lafitte's in the New Orleans bayou country."

"Okay pal. Which way to the casbah?" Sturgis asked, hardly believing that anyone would or could live in the midst of the swamp.

"Aw come on, Colonel. I told you all I did was get lost here once. Now I'm supposed to be some sort of guide."

"The best we got. Now c'mon. You must remember

something."

"Damn — let's see. All I remember for sure is there's only one way into the thick of it."

"That's where I want to go," Sturgis replied. "There seem to be plenty of streams heading inland."

"That's the problem. Most of them just turn in and around on themselves. The brush and cypress'll block you most places. But as I recall, we need a stream that heads — from here — east by southeast for about a mile then it cuts off in a blind, a hidden entrance to another open lake like this one. Then I'll start guessing."

"Lead the way," Sturgis said. "With the radio interference, we'll have to stick close. Billy, Tranh, Roberto, and myself will each take five men and pick a stream to the east. Leave markings as you go, there are small buoys in the Tri-bike kits. Billy says it's only a mile or so to the next pond. Whoever finds it, send a man back. Meet back here, in let's say . . . an hour. That should give us enough time. Remember, you have flares if there's trouble. Fenton, you stay here with the rest of the squad. Let off a flare every fifteen minutes or so. And no one goes wandering off. Too easy to get lost in the muck!"

Tranh found his route most promising. He followed an easterly arm of the lake before breaking off down a winding creek flanked by a leafy waterfall of overhanging trees. When the mist parted on the bank, they could see car-lengthed alligators waddle quickly through the grasses and slither into the water. The creek narrowed until the Tri-bikes were virtually scraping against the blockade of trees on both banks. The going got increasingly difficult, but it seemed to

Tranh that the course was not altogether unused.

He had spent years fighting the murky delta and swamplands of Southeast Asia, so the terrain was not alien to him. His senses picked up signs here and there—a broken branch, a hatchet mark on a tree— all the clues he needed as his trained eyes studied every inch of his path.

They were a good mile-and-a-quarter in when he found the entrance to the pond. Billy was right. It was well hidden. But a close inspection of every foot of the bank led to a tiny rivulet winding into a thick grove of cypress. The Tri's just cleared the narrow passage which twisted in a series of hairpin turns before finally opening into a green lake the size of two football fields.

Tranh just shot off 2 green flares when his senses perked to the sound of danger. An ominous humming sound close by. Not Tri-bikes. For the first time ever, his computer said *unknown vehicle*. He shivered.

CHAPTER EIGHTEEN

"Someone's on us," the Vietnamese said, as O'Leary, Catsin and Redburn came up close to him in the thick mist.

"Where's Doyle and Bower?"

"Right behind us," said Catsin.

"There's some—" Tranh said, but an explosion ripped through the cypress grove, followed by a volley of machine-gun fire. Bower came jetting through the grove minus his Tri-bike, bouncing off trees. Next came Doyle, his suit ablaze. The C.A.D.S. suit must have taken a heavy concentration of rocket or armor-piercing machine-gun fire. It was shorting out violently, sending out a hail of sparks. Tranh could hear Doyle's death-scream over the static on the radio as the man crashed headlong into a tree. A hit from a bazooka shell streaming out of the high vines slammed into Bower, severing his chest from his legs. The mess dropped with a splash and disappeared into the mire. Doyles' headless suit lay against the tree spitting out electricity.

More rounds of mortar shells exploded in the water just in front of them, sending out 20-foot sprays of the sludgy lake. The C.A.D.S. team drew into a circle and fired a series of E-balls into the dense mists, sending up dim explosions in the surrounding jungle.

The mysterious enemy retreated and advanced several times, passing by, firing, then disappearing. Finally they caught a glimpse of their attackers as the mist suddenly lifted off to their right. Two groups approached, riding fan-tailed swamp boats. The boats were compact, only about seven feet long and three feet wide. More like giant water skis than boats. On the rear, a vertical row of three immense fans provided the power. They were highly maneuverable, perfect for skipping between the narrow passages of the swamp.

Tranh saw that the boat's pilots sat at the rear, nestled in a crouched position in front of the fans, using a joy stick to maneuver the craft. At the bow stood a gunner, strapped in a wire brace, each holding a bazooka on one shoulder. Some sort of crude but obviously functional missiles were attached to the sides of the crafts, alongside a set of collapsible poles, probably for maneuvering in tight spots.

The men, muscular, half-naked specimens, darting through the mists, were stippled with tattoos and war paint. Long feathers of startling colors and beauty adorned their hair. Their only clothing were their alligator-skin loincloths.

Tranh at last got a clear shot, fired an E-ball at each of the swamp craft, blasting one right out of the water. The other ducked quickly away from releasing

252

two slim torpedoes. The enemy shells sliced through the water and into the rear of Catsin's Tri-bike, throwing him high into the air.

"*Yahoooo*," sang Macoco, Lord of Okefenokee.

"All who come here without permission *die!*" He stood at the bow of his swamp ski "Jezebel," which had the two skulls of their last unwanted visitors dangling from its bow, dipping occasionally in the murky water. Le Tigre, his war-painted boat-pilot, was seated behind him. Quickly men fitted two torpedoes into the spots recently vacated and handed their chief a gourd of rice wine. He drank it down heartily then pulled an alligator cape over his shoulders. His body was a patchwork of exotic tattoos, and heavy ammunition belts crisscrossed his breast. His bald pate glistened with sweat. A razor-edged hunting blade hung in the belt of his loincloth.

"Now me finish off these spacemen," Macoco said, quaffing another rice wine and motioning for his harpoons, which he had stacked one on each side in special quick-draw mounts made for them.

"You follow," he shouted, waving on a flotilla of 6 craft. He sent a second group to circle behind the strangers — cutting off their retreat.

Macoco downed a final mouthful, dribbling the potent fluid down his chest. He let loose a blood-curdling battle scream . . . "*Yahooooooooooo . . . Yip Yip Yip Yahooooooooooo . . .*"

His band joined in, building to an ear-piercing chorus of human-hunters, wolves with pink skins.

Tranh heard the chilling war cry as he shook the effects of the bazooka blast from his head. Catsin

253

had been slammed against a tree nearly 50 feet away, but seemed all right. The cushioning systems of the suit had saved his ass—and his spinal cord. He joined the others, who righted their Tri's and started out blankly across the still waters into the swirling fog.

"You okay, Catsin?" Tranh asked.

"Yea, I think so. Did you get the number of that truck?"

"Listen man, head back to Sturgis. Travel like we did in Charleston. Under water. Can you find the marker-buoys?"

"Sure. But what about you guys?"

"We can't get out of here with the Tri's. These guys are well-armed, dangerous. But we're claiming this turf. Get Sturgis and the rest of the force. We can hold them off. But hurry!" Catsin slipped underwater, jets reversed for weight. In the dark of the quagmire, he walked along the very bottom back toward the creek leading to the Rhino—so he hoped.

Around Tranh and his men, the surrounding mists awoke again with the yapping and howling of the swamp Indians and the whining mosquito buzzes of their fan-tail boats. It seemed as if they were everywhere—yet nowhere to be seen. Tranh fired his jet pack, and hovered thirty feet above the pond. But even on I.R., mist masked the surface. His computer signaled *Low Fuel—Waning Power*. He dropped briskly back to the surface.

"Anything?" said O'Leary. "My screen is clear again, compass just spinning around. These guys move like ghosts, but it *sounds* to me like they're coming from the southeast. There's a din reverberating from the center of the pond."

"Quick, lash the bikes here," Tranh ordered. "Get underwater. Move apart, but not too far. Try to maintain radio contact."

The Vietnamese dropped under water and was instantly lost from sight in the thick lily padded swamp. Frogs eyed him suspiciously, croaking as they jumped away.

"O'Leary? Do you read me?" Tranh whispered in the underwater darkness lit only by the green printouts and grid maps at the bottom of the visor.

"Roger."

"Radio's weak, losing clarity again," Tranh said.

"Is that you, Tranh?" another voice broke over the others, louder.

"Catsin! You're *supposed* to be heading back."

"I am! I'm heading down the main creek now. Surprised you can hear me."

"Wait a minute," said Tranh. "*Infra-red view*," he said to the computer. "Directly overhead!"

Immediately his visor displayed the bottoms of the fan-boats above him, much more clearly than he could see them in the murk with regular vision. After they passed, Tranh said, "I've got it—We have our radios back. The swamp gases must interfere on the *surface*, but the waves travel freely *underwater*!"

Tranh tried to raise someone with the main body, but none of the other troopers had gotten wise to the trick and submerged.

"Keep moving, Catsin," he said. "Try to reach them. Pass the good word about the radios working underwater."

255

On the surface, Macoco and his garishly painted warriors sped to the assault. Scarred faces licked their chops at the scent of battle — and blood. The gunners fondled their cannon and machine guns. The pilots, wise to every square foot of the treacherous swampland, glided the swamp boats in and out of the cypress groves, darting like dragonflies over the surface.

As the regalia of twelve war craft broke onto the open lake, they let loose a barrage of bullets wildly, hoping to hit someone.

"Let's take 'em," Tranh said. The squad picked out targets on their visors and when the swamprats were directly overhead they shot up from the depths, smashing through hulls like they were paper. Three of the craft sank like rocks, their crews disappearing in a flail of arms and legs beneath the green surface.

The surviving swampers roared off en masse. Tranh stood up waist-deep, searching for a target. Suddenly a bogey appeared to his left, sending a cannon shot just feet away. He was knocked over before he could return fire. O'Leary, behind him, let fly an E-ball, but the pilot swerved and was gone. The C.A.D.S. troopers submerged again.

"The damn ponds are too shallow to take 'em from underneath!" said Tranh. "These turkeys are onto us now."

"What do we do?" O'Leary asked.

"You guys hold tight. I'm gonna get me one of those skee-doo's for myself. We need some mobility so we can use our firepower against them."

Tranh broke the surface and gazed across the misty

waters. He checked his radar. Bogeys closing from three directions. On command two E-balls thundered out from under his sleeve, each taking out a fan-tail. He waited for the third boat. He had to take the boat intact.

The fan-tail approached, but buzzed off before Tranh could reach it.

It began another approach, machine gun ablaze. Tranh dived, but the fan-tail stopped on a dime. Its gunner fired his thunderous bazooka into the spot where Tranh just went down. The Vietnamese was slammed about like a leaf in a tornado. He bobbed to the surface stunned. The swamp man swept by and dropped a net over him, dragging him away at top speed.

"Yahooooo. Me got 'em one spaceman!" the leader shouted.

Tranh, enmeshed in the net, came to, and fired his retros with the last remnants of power. The fan-tail jerked to its side, throwing the gunner and pilot into the drink. "Activate dart system," Tranh yelled to his computer. He held his left arm straight out and turned his wrist. A flurry of steel darts from the C.A.D.S. suit ripped the swamp men to shreds, turning them into alligator food. Tranh righted the fan-tail and jumped into the pilot's seat. Within a minute he had mastered the controls of the craft and began cruising the pond in wide figure-eights. With speed, agility, firepower—and the element of surprise, Tranh was able to score two quick hits on the enemy before they knew what was up.

As he cruised by the hidden, parked Tri's, he saw

swampcraft attaching tow lines to them. He picked them off before they even suspected he was the enemy.

A flurry of gunfire erupted just off to his right. Through the mist Tranh saw one of the C.A.D.S. troopers break the surface and let an E-ball fly dead for him. "No!" Tranh yelled.

The bluish crackling merchant of death sizzled just past his helmet as Tranh cut to his left. As he circled into the center of the pond, he came face to face with Macoco, the chief of the swampmen.

The tattooed Indian smiled a broad grin that glistened even through the mist, and would have frozen a lesser man. But Tranh came head on toward Macoco's boat zeroing in with his laser sight. Just as he fired, his swamp craft grounded out on a branch hidden below the surface. He was thrown headlong into a grove of cypress trees. Tranh felt his suit shorting out in a flurry of acrid smoke and sparks, choking him. He quickly zipped out of the sizzling cocoon of death, before it took him with it.

Macoco watched as the thin Oriental emerged from the protective confines of C.A.D.S. suit. The swamp chief gave a war whoop, lifting one of the long harpoons in his right hand, clutching the trigger of his SMG in the left.

Tranh groped his way to his knees and pulled out his long killing blade from a sheath at his side. Macoco advanced slowly in the swamp boat, eyeing his target, harpoon raised. Tranh tried a break toward the shielding vines, but the Indian cut him off with a line of bullets, penning him in for the harpoon throw.

Tranh had a sudden grim picture of that catfish Billy had speared, and saw himself joining a few on this wild man's barbecue. He looked up and spotted an overhanging branch. Macoco wasn't 10 yards away when he let fly the seven-foot long harpoon. Tranh sprang into the air, clutched the branch, pulled himself up in a swift jerk. The harpoon stuck in the tree below. Macoco raised his rifle, coming forward, but Tranh swung down, kicking the rifle from the savage's hand, slamming him into water. Suddenly Tranh's branch broke, and he fell down into the slime. Alligators on both sides came barreling toward them. Both men swam for their lives. Tranh made the shore. Macoco, though stunned by Tranh's kick, was able to reach his boat, before the alligator reached *him*. He grabbed a second harpoon, had Le Tigre turn, and was after Tranh, who scrambled 10 yards into the thick growth, pulling his suit along after him, sliding it on the moss.

"*Yahoooooo*!" Macoco screamed as he sighted the suit. He slammed through the brush toward Tranh, the deadly harpoon glistening like the eyes of death.

When he was ten yards away, he let it fly. Tranh sprang like a cat as the missile whizzed by, slicing a deep gash across his right thigh. He winced in pain, but grabbed the harpoon planted in the tree and snapped the weapon out. He ran with it and dove into shallow water, slithering like an eel below the surface. When Macoco swam after him Tranh lashed out, brandishing the blunt steel. He thrust at the Indian, cutting a deep jagged slash across the giant's broad chest, covering the warrior with red. The giant swam away as Tranh took another jab.

Macoco reached his boat, and it roared away, with him hanging on the side.

Tranh, exhausted, crawled out of the muddy water. He sat panting, awaiting the Indian's return. But the killer didn't return. He could hear that the fighting had stopped in the distance, then the reassuring sound of Tri-bikes putting toward him. Sure enough, it was Roberto and Billy. Their visors were open. They apparently weren't expecting trouble. Their Tri-bikes moved low in the water from their weight, rocking in the swampy waves they churned up.

"You look like hell," Billy said as he sighted the exhausted Tranh.

The medics attended Tranh's wounds as Billy told him that Catsin had gotten back, and the C.A.D.S. Force had routed the swampers, destroying many of them, the others scattering far away into the swamps. Then Fenton came over and shaking his head in disbelief, told them the bad news.

"I'm afraid we've not been able to find Colonel Sturgis. No one's heard from him since he was run down by one of their fucking air-boats. I saw him run out of ammo, start back wading for the Rhino, when one of the swamper's biggest craft just knocked him over in the water. He could be their captive—if he isn't on the bottom somewhere."

"We've got to find him," Tranh exclaimed, jumping to his feet. He winced in pain as the stitches in his thigh stretched the skin out.

260

"You lie down," Frenton said, "*we'll* find him. *You* stay here. If we don't come back, or if — anything — you're in charge, Tranh."

Tranh watched Fenton, Billy, and Roberto splash off into the sodden undergrowth, following some mad hunch of Fenton's.

If those swampers had Sturgis, God help him. *God help him.*

CHAPTER NINETEEN

Waist deep in water, Sturgis had fought for his life with two swamp Indians. He was having just a little difficulty—the servo-mechanisms of his C.A.D.S. suit had blown a fuse, so he was hampered, not helped by his armor. Every movement was like lifting a hundred pound weight. Suddenly—flashing in his helmet—radar warnings—something coming from behind—fast, big, and closing on him like a shark. Too late! It slammed into him. He was falling, sinking under the water.

The C.A.D.S. commander awoke with a titanic headache, blurred vision, and an instant premonition that things weren't going too well. He was out of his C.A.D.S. suit, drenched with water. Panic grabbed at him; he was on his back, men's legs around him. Batting the water from them and focusing his eyes, Sturgis saw several of the war-painted Indians in a far corner of the clearing pulling at his armor, playing with it like children with an over-sized doll.

"We splash you a little to wake you up."

Sturgis followed the voice to its owner. The speaker was big, and strong, but starting to run to fat. His left eye was half shut, puffy from a recent wound. A scar crossed his chest, also recent, crusted with dried blood and dirt. Shaking a reddish-brown finger at the C.A.D.S. commander, the man said, "You dun know us, do you? You should! You came to play in our swamp, dun pay your respect, dun ask magnificent permission—what I do with you, soldier-snail?"

Sturgis tried to rise shakily to his feet, only to be knocked down by one of the feet attached to the bare legs around him. "Dun get up. You relax, you let Macoco think what we do with you."

Sturgis answered, "I'm an American . . ."

Sharp laughter erupted throughout the swamp dwellers. "*American*, huh? Wha's that? Where's 'a-mare-a-caaaa,' snail?"

The fat one who called himself Macoco waved his hand, signalling the others to stop laughing. Pointing at Sturgis, he snarled, "Let us tell you something— you be dead meat if I want. We drag you and your shell here; take long time to get you out of big shell— What you think?"

"I think," replied the C.A.D.S. commander, "that the smell of you and the rest of the pigs around me is enough to make me puke."

Macoco slapped at Sturgis, but even slowed by the pain in his head from his collision with the air boat, the C.A.D.S. fighter was fast enough to avoid the big man's hand. Grabbing Macoco's wrist while he was still off balance, Sturgis twisted his arm and then pushed, sending him sprawling into four of his men. While the group crashed to the ground, Sturgis jumped up, aware of a number of rifles pointed at him.

The swamp leader scrambled back to his feet and lurched across the distance between himself and Sturgis. Thumping the colonel's chest with his finger, he snarled, "You dun die now, snail! I think maybe you good for somethin'—I think maybe you teach Macoco to use toy suit—so I let you live. I let you take a taste of women at my table.

"You dun know a good thing when you see it. You ask me—you look for death too quick. Snail want to die—dat okay. Slow, long, awful—Macoco promise you that."

"Men," Macoco shouted, "Put down rifles. I handle snail."

Sturgis watched the bull of a man circling him. Keeping one eye on Macoco, he glanced around the camp, trying to take in any chances for escape. Things didn't look good. More of the swamp morons had gone over to play with his disassembled suit. Luckily, they couldn't turn on anything until all the pieces were connected with an operator inside. The C.A.D.S. commander actually hoped one of the drooling idiots would fit himself into the C.A.D.S. suit and try to operate it. Without giving the computer the newly installed entry sequence, anyone donning the armor would be juiced by the suit's electrical field—before it blew to pieces.

Then Sturgis spotted it—*the LWA*—lying on the soggy ground. One of the fools toying with his armor had picked it up, shaking it as if it were a birthday present, the contents of which he could identify by the rattle it made. Seeing the laser weapon gave the

C.A.D.S. commander renewed hope—if only he could get to it. Which wasn't going to be easy, considering the number of men and guns in his way. Sturgis counted 16 so far—and he knew there were more out of sight.

Turning in a slow circle, the C.A.D.S. commander kept his eyes constantly on Macoco, never letting the swamp man get behind him. As they moved around each other, Sturgis caught sight of something which knocked even him off guard: *Women*, dozens of them, squeezed into trapper's cages. He stopped and stared, realizing what the laughing man he was circling with had meant when he had said "taste of woman at swamp table." Macoco and his men were cannibals. Several female bodies, bled and dressed like slaughtered cattle, hung from the gates of the swamp stockade.

Sturgis only looked at the cages and the women crammed into them for an instant—but it was too long. With a screeching rush, Macoco was on him. Grabbing Sturgis around the neck, he squeezed hard, cutting off Sturgis' air as if he were in a machine clamp. The C.A.D.S. commander pulled at the swamp Indian's wrists, straining to break the bigger man's grip.

"Now—the bug eyes, they come. They pop out, then the cracking neck. Fun, dun you think?"

Weakly, hissing with his last oxygen, Sturgis answered, with actions, not words.

Letting go of Macoco's left wrist, the C.A.D.S. commander pulled back his fist and then slammed it forward, knocking down the painted savage with one punch. While Sturgis pulled in ragged breaths of air

266

through the burning lining of his throat, Macoco recovered. Wiping his bloodied nostrils, he rose unsteadily to his feet.

"Oh," growled the swamp man, "you one tough snail, huh? You tough for a soldier all right. So, maybe Macoco, maybe he better even the odds, eh?"

While Sturgis caught his breath, the swamp man held out his blood-covered hand, accepting a Marine combat knife from one of his men. His air-boat pilot, Le Tigre, stepped close, handing him a chain. Sturgis glanced around, hoping the way might be clear to the LWA. But more of the swamp men were in the way than ever. He had thought they might become engrossed in watching their boss fight, but such was not the case. In their own way, they were obviously a well-trained, battle-hardened bunch. They might not have any education, but they knew their job was to keep the C.A.D.S. commander covered and away from his suit. Sturgis knew that even if he did get a chance to make some kind of move, at least five men with rifles would be ready to pull their triggers in a flash.

Again, the circling Macoco set up a spinning wall of steel with his chain, snapping out at his enemy's face. Sturgis danced out of the chain's way each time, failing to rise to Macoco's bait. The C.A.D.S. commander knew the swamp man wanted him to grab for the chain. The least that would happen would be a few broken fingers for Sturgis. But if he did manage to grab it, it would take his full attention — the perfect time for Macoco to strike with his blade.

Baiting his foe, Sturgis shouted, "C'mon pig face. You're going to have to do better than that. You might fool brainless women with such tricks, but not a real man."

Sturgis could see the hate rising in Macoco's eyes. Good. Mistake time. The pair continued to circle in a ballet of death, lashing out continuously at each other. Suddenly, Macoco leapt forward and snapped the chain at Sturgis' eyes. The C.A.D.S. trooper side-stepped to the left, but it was what Macoco had expected. With startling speed, the swamp man pulled the chain back and swung it overhead, bringing it down on Sturgis' left shoulder. The pain lanced through his side like an electric shock, but Sturgis kept himself from crying out. Gritting his teeth for a moment, he swallowed and then laughed.

"Oh. Ouch. Right? That's what I say now—'ouch'. Right?"

The swamp man laughed back. "Good. Real good. You think Macoco is stupid. You dun know him too well."

"Yeah, right. Your mother was a virgin when the side of bacon you call 'daddy' vomited up her crotch to give birth to you."

Macoco's men laughed. Macoco didn't laugh with them. Eyeing the circle, the C.A.D.S. commander could see that the guards were as cautious as ever. He could also see, however, that he had begun to get through to Macoco with the insult. Staying out of reach of the deadly chain, Sturgis pressed his advantage.

"I hear your mom is here in camp, pig face. Too bad she couldn't be here to watch the fight, but then, she's got a busy schedule, flat on her back in the mess hall, calling for more—"

Macoco went wild, swinging the chain and slashing

with the Marine knife without any skill or pattern, chasing Sturgis like a mad dog. The C.A.D.S. commander stayed easily out of his way, stepping quickly backward, taunting him with an imitation of the swamp man's mother.

"Calling, *soouuueee* — here's pig, here's pig, c'mon, *soouuueeee* . . ."

"I kill you, shit bastard!" Macoco screamed, his face growing red as a pig at slaughter.

Macoco jumped at Sturgis, giving the C.A.D.S. commander his first good shot at the man. He jumped his attack radius, grabbing Macoco's knife hand. Jerking the swamp man's arm out, he ducked under another wild swing of the chain, and then caught the flopping end, slipping the middle of the chain around the blade of the knife. Macoco resisted, but Sturgis pulled hard, sliding the chain up around Macoco's wrist. As the Indian pulled one way, Sturgis jerked the chain the other, breaking three of Macoco's fingers within the grip of the Marine knife.

The swamp man howled, dropping the blade from his injured hand, that was all the advantage Sturgis needed. Swiftly jerking the chain back in the opposite direction, he broke the swamp fighter's wrist. Kicking the bleeding, howling man in the groin, Sturgis sent him flying backwards.

"Some leader you boys have," he screamed out to the worried tribe.

Le Tigre stepped forward. "You made Macoco look terrible bad soldier. Macoco can't even protect his own mother's name. He's old news."

Sturgis seized the moment, playing for time. "That make you the new boss?"

"That's right, soldier. But dun you look to break Le Tigre's claws—dey too sharp for you, mon."

"No way," agreed Sturgis. "I'm just looking to make a deal—something for you, something for me."

Le Tigre's eyes grew greedy. "Like what, mon?"

Sturgis had been forcing the fight over toward the LWA. He was within twenty feet of it—unfortunately a wall of rifles still in the way. Pointing at his LWA he said, "How about a radio for starters?"

"A radio, mon? What for we need that? Is dat wot de ting be?"

Sturgis walked past the gauntlet of weapons casually, as if there was no reason for them to worry about him getting to the other side. Le Tigre walked with him.

"Everyone wants music, man." Sturgis reached for the LWA, but Le Tigre snapped out his hand, reaching it first. Hefting it, he tried to take its measure through weight. Thank God it's so light, Sturgis thought. He might not think it's a radio, but he *doesn't* think it's a weapon.

"So," snapped the air-boat pilot, "how does dis ting work, mon?"

"You have to turn it on, friend."

"And how do I do dot, mon?"

Sturgis reached out, again slowly. He knew that Le Tigre was only waiting to discover the secrets of the C.A.D.S. suit and any other knowledge the C.A.D.S. commander might have before he killed him. Pretending that the air-boat pilot was not so transparent in his motives, Sturgis innocently wrong-way positioned the LWA in the man's hands, and said,

"To charge this thing? Why all you do is flip *this*

safety!"

Sturgis pulled the LWA's trigger, sending a beam of laser light on wide-discharge flashing into Le Tigre's face. The flesh melted like rancid butter, dripping down onto the wide chest with a sickening stench.

Seizing the momentary hesitation on the part of the swamp men, the C.A.D.S. commander grabbed the weapon out of the dead man's hands and turned it around, cutting down five of the crowd. The rest of the swamp men screamed out vengeance as rifles went off all around the camp. Running through the tangle of flopping, laser-burned bodies, Sturgis sprayed out the LWA's burning ray, criss-crossing the complex with its ruby-light destruction. Bodies fell like they were being mowed by a thresher. Eyes, retinas burned out in puffs of oily smoke. The swamp men tried to get a bead on the C.A.D.S. commander — but it was too late. Sturgis ran jagged-pattern laying down laser fire wherever he saw motion. In less than a minute, the entire encampment of swamp men had been subdued, twenty of them dead, many more severely wounded. Not waiting for the cannibals to regain their senses, Sturgis headed for the cages.

Ordering the terrified women to stay back, he cut away the locks on the small cramped cages with a narrow beam. From inside the animal-smelling cages stumbled dozens of women, their arms and legs numb from days, weeks, within the close quarters. Many of the captives couldn't even stand, the pain of returning circulation crippling them. To those who could however, Sturgis said, "Get their guns. Now."

Several of the heartier women moved haltingly out into the courtyard, grabbing up the rifles of their

271

former wardens. Paying no attention to the happenings behind him, Sturgis headed for his C.A.D.S. suit, mouthing curses for any of the swamp men who might have damaged his armor. Reaching the suit, he scanned the outside briefly—everything looked operational. Reaching down, he grabbed hold of the main torso section and pulled it upright, working his legs into it, feeling his way through each joint, looking for damage. Finding nothing out of place, he stepped into his boots, listening to the pressure seals clicking into place. Kneeling to slip into his sleeves and gauntlets, he tested the knee joints—they were locked. The servo-hydraulics system was out. Sturgis reached on the inside of the chest armor and found a popped fuse. He slammed in a replacement from his belt's maintenance pack and the servo lights flashed "go" on the visor readout.

Sliding one armored sleeve on and then the other, he shrugged them into their locked positions, turning this way and that, making sure each connection was perfect.

Through the mangroves he could hear the women rudely rounding up their former captors.

"Systems on," Sturgis said. All lights came on. He started forward, rattling off the twelve letter and number code that prevented the suit from self-destructing.

Macoco appeared suddenly at his feet, begging him, on bended knees, as Sturgis held the LWA over him.

"Please soldier. You kill me—okay? Dun let these wild bitches take Macoco. *Please*."

Sturgis looked down at the gutless swamp leader.

Backed by dozens of rifles, he had been a strutting king, ready to kill anyone on the slightest whim. Now he was nothing, a fact which made Sturgis laugh out loud. Ignoring the sniveling doomed man at his feet, the C.A.D.S. commander called out, on Amp-Mode. "Hey ladies! Don't forget this one."

He pointed down at Macoco, slipping down his visor with a clang.

Several of the women ran over in response to his call. The bleeding, whimpering form at his feet bleated, "Please, mon, don't let them! Please! Kill me! Dun let dem have Macoco. *Please!*"

"Kill you?" Sturgis replied in mock horror. "Why, I couldn't do anything so horrible. Surely you know how squeamish I am."

A tall, ragged clothed woman approached the pair, a wicked looking carving knife in hand. Several other women flanked her with rifles. Macoco had taken each of them to his shack repeatedly, but the tall one most often, abusing her in a different way each time. Now she stared at Macoco with flame in her eyes. "We'll handle things here now," she said. "Whoever you are, thanks."

"Do you need any help? I can help get you out of here," answered Sturgis.

"No thanks," the woman replied. "We'll be all right. We've got the weapons. We're in charge here now, right girls?"

There were shouts of vengeful assent.

"What are you going to do with this one?" Sturgis couldn't help but ask.

The woman kicked Macoco in the ribs. With a smile as tight as a razor, she said, "You see this knife,

273

mister? I'm going to take his skin off with it, one inch at a time. And I'm going to make a dress out of it, and wear it. And I'm going to keep him alive as long as I can—so he can keep growing back more skin. After all, a woman can never have too many clothes."

She sounded half mad. Sturgis knew she would carry out her promise. He gave the woman a crisp salute, and then, running at top speed headed for, and *through*, the wood-hewn front gate. Opening his com-link to its widest band, the C.A.D.S. commander broadcast a coded greeting, hoping one of his men might be close enough to hear him through the static-filled fog of the swamp. Moving in what he remembered to be a path toward their position, he sent the message over and over, praying for any response. Could they all be—dead?

He ran for ten minutes in the fortress-of-a-suit, searching frantically for anything that looked familiar. As he at last reached open water, he screamed, "Where the fuck are you guys?" into the helmet mike.

After a few seconds, a faint voice crackling with static answered, "Sturg? Is that you?"

"Tranh?"

And then, position-lights dimly lit on his helmet's R-screen, showing him the forward location of a three-man search party made up of Billy, Roberto, and the Vietnamese. Sturgis headed directly for their position.

"I'm coming to meet you. Hold your course."

News of his survival spread from search team to search team, a network of questions racing back to the C.A.D.S. commander via his com-link. Sturgis told them all to wait until they had returned. For a moment, he just wanted silence. Seeing all the women in their cages, seeing the dismembered, gutted torsos dripping blood into the mud below had started him thinking of Robin again, and what might have happened to her. He saw her in his mind's eye, caged, naked and helpless. Captive of the Russians, or of the likes of Pinky Ellis, or Macoco, or any of the other degenerate bastards they had the pleasure of meeting since the war had started.

But his grim thoughts were interrupted as the overjoyed C.A.D.S. team met up with him. Tranh, limping along in a dead trooper's C.A.D.S. suit, slapped him on the back as Roberto demanded to know how in hell Sturgis had escaped.

They walked back through the swamp to the other men. For a moment all was joyful.

CHAPTER TWENTY

The trooper who actually found the refuge-island was Robert Fuentes. He found it by running the front tire of his Tri-bike against its steep bank and almost toppling over. Despite the high rocks, he had not been able to see them through the shroud of fog. He called Sturgis over his com-link and told him what he had discovered.

Using various radar-modes Sturgis scanned the jungled island before them, thick with the clucks and caws of a thousand hidden birds. He hadn't thought such a land mass could exist in the Okefenokee. He sent Roberto and another man, Martino, onto the island, off in opposite directions on foot to reconnoiter their find. Both men stayed in constant radio contact, finally meeting nearly forty-five minutes later on the other side.

"It's solid the whole way 'round my side," Roberto reported back. Martino's findings were the same.

Sturgis asked if either had seen a way to get a Tri-bike onto the thing. Robert answered that he had passed a sandy area where they might be able to drive a bike up.

The C.A.D.S. commander told the men to head for the spot, see if they could get one of their Tris up. The C.A.D.S. troopers moved toward the advance party.

Minutes later, the troopers found their two companions, laboring to force one of their bikes up onto a lip of chewed earth. Both men were waist deep in the swirling, silt filled water, their armor covered with mud. They had obviously had to break away the edge of the hill, using their powerful suits to smash a runway to the top. Spotting the rest of the C.A.D.S. unit, Roberto hailed, "Colonel, we scouted up to the top. Flat and dry—well, dry compared to the rest of this place. This might be what you're lookin' for."

"Well," replied Sturgis, "we won't know that 'til we get up there with our equipment, will we?"

"No, sir."

"Then let's get up there. Meyers, Dixon—get over there and give them a hand."

Working together, the four C.A.D.S. troopers got the first Tri over the edge to the cheers of their compatriots. Once the bike had been raised, Roberto took the driver's seat and spun the back tires, using them to trim the remaining lip of earth down to water level. In another two minutes, all 78 surviving members of the C.A.D.S. unit were on top of the hidden island, stretching and relaxing. For the first time in

278

days, they got out of their suits.

Knowing his men were tired, and yet knowing that certain things would have to be determined before they could really rest, Sturgis walked in front of the prone ranks. "I know you're all hot, tired with all this miserable wandering around we've been doing in this stinkhole. But that doesn't change the basic facts. There are a number of things we need to know about *where* we are. I have to decide if we're going to camp here for a night or for some extended period. If there are any eager beavers who just can't bring themselves to do anything as commonplace as sleep or eat, sing out and make your colonel happy."

"Let the kids goof off," came Tranh's voice. "What do you need, Sturg?"

"Scout the far end, see if those trees offer any area we could do some bunker-building in."

"Roger."

Others slowly volunteered. Horner and Roberto set out to move the Tri-bikes into an orderly, and less space wasting, arrangement under a covering canopy of trees. Sturgis began to see endless possibilities — setting up a long term campsite here — from which they could fan out across the South and East wreaking destruction on the Reds.

His musings were interrupted by Tranh's urgent shout, "You'd better get over here, Colonel."

Rushing to the far end of the clearing Sturgis and some other troopers were stopped in their tracks by the sight Tranh had been so excited about. *Ruins*, looking to be hundreds of years old and covered with

279

heavy vines, were spread throughout the thick woods. Sturgis walked forward to inspect the crumbled structures. The buildings, no matter how old, showed considerable promise. Someone had dug deep and brought a lot of stone together. For a modern construction crew, armed with bulldozers and explosives, it was the work of weeks. The original builders had more primitive methods. Sturgis knew he was looking at the work of months, if not years.

Billy ran up to them, gasping, "Sir, you're not going to believe it."

"Try me."

"Someone must have done some planting here at one time. Rossiter and I found wild onions and beets, carrots and all kinds of stuff."

Rossiter interrupted, "I can't believe it, Sturg. We've found wild rice, watercress and even rum cherries. There's a big patch of wild sunflower, they have these potato things on their roots, and we've got catfish, and . . ."

"I take it," interrupted Sturgis, "that you've found the fixings for dinner; is that right, Rossiter?"

"Yes, sir," came the trooper's quick response.

"Then start making it," the C.A.D.S. commander ordered. "I'm starved."

After dinner, the C.A.D.S. troopers lay flat out, or propped against trees, satiated looks on their stubbly faces. After weeks of nothing but canned military rations, the taste of fresh vegetables and fish made them wolf down everything placed in front of them.

Relaxing with Fenton against the sidearmor of the

Rhino, Sturgis said, "Got a job for you."

"Don't you Yanks ever take a good lengthy tea break?" the Brit asked.

"Yeah, but now's not one of those times."

"Pity. What's the job then?"

"I know you're tired, but before you knock off for the night, I want you to start a sequenced re-charging program. We've been running around for days. A lot of our suits are at half power. Some almost down to none. The work we're going to be doing over the next days won't call for the suits — so this is the time to get every suit up to full power. Twenty-four hours a day. There's got to be a suit hooked up every minute. Okay?"

"Right." Looking around the Brit sighed, "O'Leary, you haven't had a volt for days. Get your suit and hook up."

As the trooper worked at hooking his armor to the atomic generator output of the Rhino in the ever-increasing darkness, Fenton set about lining up more men to take their turns after O'Leary. Once Fenton had the men set to get recharged, Sturgis called him inside the Rhino. He was busy working at the battle-wagon's computer-console. The C.A.D.S. commander pointed to one of the screens, drawing the Britisher's attention to a computer-generated map of the area they were in. Sturgis pointed to what appeared to be a railroad line some 20 miles to the north.

Turning to the C.A.D.S. commander, Fenton said, "I don't like to appear the class dunce, but why am I supposed to be doing the highland fling, sir?"

Bringing a close-up grid map of the railroad line into focus on the monitor Sturgis said, "*This* is what's worth dancing over."

Fenton read the data displayed on the cross-section Sturgis had called up. " 'Fieldbrook Railroad Yards'—yes?"

"Supplies," snapped the colonel. "A rail-yard, closed, but likely undamaged by nukes. It's bound to have a lot of things we're going to need—whole freight trains filled with parts, machinery—God knows what. Just waiting for us to come and take them out by the truckload. We can make east coast headquarters here—grow our own food—and be within miles of our own private supply depot. We can use this island of refuge as a forward east coast base."

That night with the men bedded down, Sturgis and Tranh walked slowly around the perimeter of the hastily thrown together camp. They had walked side by side this way in the old days—And now with just Airforce issue 9mm's belted on their waists they patrolled again.

"Billy figured something out," Sturgis said in the chattering darkness.

"Oh? What's that?" Tranh asked as they walked toward the ruins.

"Seems he remembered a story his grandfather told him about the swamp. The old man was a Civil War buff. Told Billy once that back when the 'Underground Railroad' was in operation, moving escaped slaves up north to freedom, a large group of escaped slaves decided that white man's civilization was a hell hole no matter where they were. They struck out for the swamp to build a new home for themselves. The story goes that they found an island, and they built themselves a small settlement. Then they farmed and lived happily-ever-after, and all that. Needless to say, they were never heard from again!"

"Do you think this is Billy's grandfather's fairy-tale paradise?" Tranh asked.

"Yes."

"Why?"

"Because," Sturgis said, "I found their graveyard." They stopped just in front of concentric circles of piled stones and weathered mounds. "There's a couple of slate slabs with some simple etchings." They walked about, looking at the markers in the spirit-heavy air of the graveyard.

Tranh seemed to become transfixed. Sturgis had never seen the Vietnamese act quite so strangely. After a few minutes Tranh said, "*I was here once* — in a former life. I suppose you don't believe in reincarnation, friend. But I know I was here . . . I'm buried *there*." Tranh pointed to a weather-beaten piece of slate. "My name was Cyrus. Just Cyrus. I was a runaway black slave. I died of swamp fever at the age of 27. — Do you believe me?"

"Well," answered Sturgis, "I don't remember any life except this one. But I don't doubt you, Tranh. If you say you were here . . ."

Tranh squeezed his shoulder. "Let us leave this place." The Oriental turned quickly away from the ancient graveyard. Sturgis followed.

Sturgis sat alone by the small campfire long after all the men, even Tranh, had gone to sleep. This was an odd lonely sanctuary. Vegetation and warm temperatures—what could anyone make of it? The swamp was only slightly radioactive; it was like some sort of haven sent by God himself for the C.A.D.S. unit to hide in and recuperate. He couldn't take credit for God's mercy; it wasn't earned.

But there was something else on his mind. Something that couldn't wait any longer. *Robin*. He had seen what Macoco did to his caged women captives; had heard what the Russian torturer/interrogator Turkov did to women. Was Robin safe? Or was she—right at this moment, while he sat by the fire—in mortal danger?

He sat staring at the red dying flames for a minute longer. Then he made his decision. Things would be quiet for awhile. Tranh would take charge of the unit. He was a good man—the best. It would take only a few days—a week at the most.

He awoke Tranh and quickly explained. Tranh agreed with him that there was no reason not to go. There were weeks of work consolidating the Okefenokee base ahead. And Tranh knew what Robin meant to Sturgis.

Sturgis walked to the Rhino for some supplies and

ammo. Then he unhitched his suit from the charging unit. Batteries read "3/4". It would have to do. He got into it, turned the multisystems on and headed to the Tri-bikes parked a hundred yards away. He rolled his bike to the edge of the island, then hopped onto the familiar worn seat. He started her up and roared away into the mists, heading due north. He had to find her.

Find Robin.

ASHES
by William W. Johnstone

OUT OF THE ASHES   (1137, $3.50)
Ben Raines hadn't looked forward to the War, but he knew it was coming. After the balloons went up, Ben was one of the survivors, fighting his way across the country, searching for his family, and leading a band of new pioneers attempting to bring America OUT OF THE ASHES.

FIRE IN THE ASHES   (1310, $3.50)
It's 1999 and the world as we know it no longer exists. Ben Raines, leader of the Resistance, must regroup his rebels and prep them for bloody guerilla war. But are they ready to face an even fiercer foe—the human mutants threatening to overpower the world!

ANARCHY IN THE ASHES   (1387, $3.50)
Out of the smoldering nuclear wreckage of World War III, Ben Raines has emerged as the strong leader the Resistance needs. When Sam Hartline, the mercenary, joins forces with an invading army of Russians, Ben and his people raise a bloody banner of defiance to defend earth's last bastion of freedom.

BLOOD IN THE ASHES   (1537, $3.50)
As Raines and his ragged band of followers search for land that has escaped radiation, the insidious group known as The Ninth Order rises up to destroy them. In a savage battle to the death, it is the fate of America itself that hangs in the balance!

THE SAIGON COMMANDOS SERIES
by Jonathan Cain